D1457586

SO CALLED TRAITORS

Lou Hobbs

SO CALLED TRAITORS

LOU HOBBS

NEW DEGREE PRESS

SO CALLED TRAITORS

ISBN   978-1-63676-886-1 *Paperback*
        978-1-63676-887-8 *Kindle Ebook*
        978-1-63676-888-5 *Ebook*

CONTENTS

———

AUTHOR'S NOTE

At the age of fifteen, this story came to life between three teenagers. My two best friends and I decided to write an adventure based on three women who were villains. After hours of discussion in my friend's parent's fifth wheel, we had morphed together a plot idea and characters. Each of us took a main character upon ourselves to write for. I chose Sirien, Amy chose Misty, who is now Amalie, and Julia chose Anabel, who has become Davina. Working together, we had a lot of fun mapping the events the sisters would experience and, even embarrassingly enough, "acting" it out in person.

Between writing, theatre, high school courses, and choir, our plates were overfilling. Finding little time during the week, we resorted to try and write on Friday nights and Saturdays. Of course, as teenagers, we were more interested in talking about life, playing cards, and having fun which distracted us from writing. We passed a three-ring binder between us throughout each week, tasked with writing a section in our perspective for the chapters. Failing to make time, we set the idea aside.

After a year, we decided it wouldn't work well and chose to discontinue the project together. We all had separate perspectives on what the characters and world should and shouldn't look like and disagreed on the time period and writing style. As time passed, I couldn't move forward on any other works I pursued without being drawn back to our manuscript. Through high school and part of college, it sat undeveloped until I finally reached out to Amy and Julia, asking if I could take the original idea and change it to continue our work. Giving me their okay and wishing not to be a part of it anymore, I hit the notebooks and dove further into each character, the world, and the driving force behind their decisions. Now here I am, eleven years since the concept came to light excited to share this adventure with you that's full of moral dilemma, pain, loss, fear, abuse, and personal growth.

Being at just the beginning of a great adventure, I look forward to sharing my character's highs and lows as they embark on the journey of their lives.

To Amy Pond and Julia Krohn, thank you for your help, your ideas, your friendship, and your willingness to allow me to expand further into this exciting creation. Without our friendship and minds collaborating together, this book wouldn't have been born.

Thank you.

ONE

———

Amber rays of light glimmer across the fields and rolling hills, illuminating the crops that grow late in the season. The air is cool and crisp, proving winter is nearly upon the people of Aldhorran. Once a city of peace, now clad in the blood of the innocent. It's still morning in the overcrowded city, which is a time of day Sirien takes advantage of. The guards are always present no matter the time, watchful for signs of the gifted or drifters coming and going much like herself. However, they never asked her for an explanation of why she was there or even bothered her, allowing her the peace she much needed among the wildflowers along the towering walls.

Often she simply sits and watches as figures litter the fields one by one with each new stream of light the sun shares. She prays for each person, nameless to her but nonetheless real. Gathering flowers is an excuse to be alone and watch the people of her old life in the fields, breathing in freedom in every second. The gift of sight is a heavy burden to carry in a city with laws against such things. As a descendant of the Nasinreth, her bloodline carries the possibility for such blessings: visions, healing, great wisdom, or tactical strength and insight. Each one is valued greatly among her people and at one time, in Omideon as well.

Why me? She asks herself silently.

It is a blessing and an honor, my child. Be proud, and do not fear. Our God has a purpose for you. Her mother's voice echoes in her consciousness, answering the question.

Before her birth, it was foretold of her gift as a visionary. She would be the last of her people. Now the visions, more regular in occurrence, have plagued her sleep and life. Confinement has lasted for weeks until suddenly the visions stopped, releasing her. Days have passed without the sight, freeing her from the walls of her small home.

A breeze gently combs her deep hazelnut hair, and she closes her eyes in response. Her fingertips tingle with the grip on her basket, and she sighs. Looking over the expanse of fields and rolling hills in the distance, she turns, walking back through the southern gate. The streets are nearly empty in the early morning hours, inhabited only by those preparing their shops or caring for livestock. Men stumble from establishments and pubs, and she averts her gaze as she walks past.

Suddenly, a numbness creeps into her hands, threatening her grip. "*No,*" she whispers, panic rising in her chest.

The distance from the gate to her home is short, but time is shorter. The visions come quickly, the warning signs often too late in advance to prepare. Her feet drag as her body begins to feel the weight of darkness. Images flash before her eyes in the streets—a woman, pale, marked, white hair, and silver eyes. Sirien stops, staring, chills taking over her body. A fear she had never felt before fills her gut as she watches her. The woman tilts her head, looking to Sirien's side. Moving her own gaze, she recognizes the home she's beside. Sirien shoves herself in the direction of the door, looking back to the woman absent from the street.

Shrugging off the unease, Sirien throws a fist at the door, pounding with all her might, breaking the skin in response. The door flies open, a woman in its way, with a baby on her hip and children running behind her. Her face softens at the awareness of Sirien's presence then turns to concern.

"Amadae, please." Sirien reaches forward, falling into Amadae's open arm, disappearing into the blackness.

"Mama, Mama watch!" Giggles float across the meadow. Sirien looks up to watch a boy bouncing up and down on the back of a large blonde horse. Davina, her youngest sister, smiling and laughing as she watches.

The day is beautiful. The sun fully shining upon the meadow adorned with wildflowers while a breeze whispers through the willows surrounding them. Sirien's head, heavy with sleep, falls back, drifting as the sun warms her skin. The hiss of clashing iron jerks her from rest, heart pounding. She leaps up. She tries to run to them, screaming, but she doesn't move or sound.

Davina, surrounded by the King's guard, is drug away into the shadows of the forest as the boy wrenched from his horse kicks and thrashes. The ground gives way, and she falls, watching a blade pierce through the small boy's heart. Sickened by the sight, her eyes close, a wish for it to stop, to wake.

"Sirien, wake up." Hesitating in fear, Sirien clenches her eyes tighter. "Sirien." Amalie, her sister, stands over her, hands on each shoulder, shaking her. Sirien opens her eyes, taking in her sister's face, young and beautiful. "It's time. Come."

Amalie walks away, crossing the room, motioning for Sirien to follow her direction before vanishing through the door. Sirien lays there in the bed of her family home. The fire burns hot, the usual kettle hanging above boiling water, the small box of coins on the table, and the chest of important possessions in the corner. The door remains wide open, and from it, she can hear the voices of her father and sisters.

Rising, she crosses the room to the doorway. The light is blinding as she moves over the threshold, finding herself in the meadow once again. Wanting to escape, she turns to return inside. The home is gone, and in its place, her father and younger sisters stand huddled together. No longer adults, the girl's faces are buried into their father's tunic, tears streaming down their cheeks, whimpering.

Moving around them, she searches for the object of their focus. She sees a pyre, unlit, holding a recent victim of death's call. Heather, overgrown around its base, mocks the deceased with its abundant life. Step by step, she begins to recognize her surroundings—a memory. Climbing the mound of logs, she sits at the top, staring at the figure before her.

Her mother, beautiful with long dark locks of hair, rich caramel skin, always smiling and laughing, now lays silent and somber, dressed in a gown mirroring the deep violet surrounding her. Looking back to her father, she sees the calm, emotionless look on his face.

He loved her deeply. I remember he cried—she thinks, confused.

Amalie's face buried in his thigh, and Davina, so small, arms wrapped around his neck, her red eyes peeking over her arm. Sirien and her father lock eyes, his chest rising and falling with every breath, eyes sad as they begin to lose their shine, his face graying. Startled, she looks back to her mother. She can't breathe as she sees the woman is gone, and in her place, a new body rests, hands placed, cradling her swollen belly, long dark locks of hair trail over her shoulders, and a face Sirien recognizes.

Sirien looks at the mirror of herself, lifeless before her. Terror seizes her as the eyes of the dead open wide, and together they whisper, "flee." The world envelops bright red splotches, and a shrill scream rings in the air.

"Darom, fetch Castor quickly. Do not speak to a soul, do you hear? Run!" Amadae speaks urgently to one of her boys.

The sound around Sirien is muddled as if underwater. She lays in darkness, numb and lifeless, alone in her thoughts. She never understands the vision's meaning or why they come, but this she can tell. One, Davina is in danger, and two, she will have a son, and he will die. For a long time, it seems she lay on the floor of Amadae's home, regaining control of her stiff body, pain lighting every nerve and muscle. Slowly, she feels heat as it runs in streams to her ears—tears.

Light brings freshness to the dark like a sunrise in the early hours, until the world is a blur of color and life. Small figures huddle in the corner of the firelit room, terrified at the sight of the woman they know on the floor. Little movements cause her pain, and she winces with every twitch.

Why does it have to hurt so much? Who would call this a blessing? She groans, thinking to herself.

"I came as quickly as I could. When did it happen?" Castor's voice is quiet and controlled. His touch is like lightning as he runs a hand over her brow. Sirien focuses on his face, still unable to speak, calmed by his presence.

"Not long ago. We had to be sure no one saw her come before sending Darom," Amadae replies, reassuring them both of safety and care.

Castor, taking Sirien's hand in his own, sits on a stool by her side. They look into each other's eyes as if communicating in silence, one mind. He nods to her in reply, and she grins, struggling to pull up the corners of her mouth before drifting into sleep.

* * *

Groaning as she stretches, Sirien wakes to the warmth and comfort of Amadae's home. Freshly baked loaves of bread sit on the windowsill, children play, and the fire crackles with delight. She sits slowly, head spinning from the excitement of the morning, searching the room for her friend or husband. Castor and Amadae sit under the window watching the children outside, each holding a newly carved cup filled with cider. They jump at the sight of her, rushing to her aid until she pushes them away.

"I need to see my father." Sirien tries to stand on wobbly legs, falling into Castor.

"I will send for him. You are too weak to ride." Castor forces her into a chair nearby.

"No. I just need to move a little, and I will be fine. Castor, I need to see my father." Her voice is dangerously serious. Castor looks around the room to the open windows and door before turning back to her.

"What did you see?" He braces himself for terrifying news, afraid of his father-in-law's death or one of her sisters.

"Davina. She is in trouble." Sirien closes her eyes, dragging the pain for her child deep inside. *I have to focus on now.* She thinks to herself, justifying the secret.

"Let me go. Stay with Amadae. I can warn him." Castor says, attempting reason with his wife.

"No. I am going." Sirien stands defiantly. Slowly and carefully, she walks around the room, gaining control with each step. "Get the horses. By the time you return, I will be well enough to ride." She closes the gap between them, touching his cheek with her fingertips. "Trust me," she whispers.

His jaw clenches tight, and without a word, leaves the house.

TWO

———

"Pick it up!" Amalie guides the blade of her sword underneath the one before her on the ground. Forcefully, she flings it across the open space between her sister and her. Jaw clenched, Davina stoops, picking it up out of the dust. Twirling it in her hand, she lunges for Amalie. In response, Amalie draws her own sword up, meeting Davina's blade.

The girls spar back and forth, metal clashing with every strike. Exhausted from her efforts, Davina falls back a few paces, catching her breath. Amalie smiles in victory, irritating Davina beyond her will to stop. Glancing to her side, Davina sees the small leather bag, torn and battered from overuse, filled with various weapons. The hilt of daggers and swords peak over the brim as well as arrows and a bow.

Running to it, she jerks a sword out, drawing it up and around just as Amalie reaches her. With both swords in her hand, she swings and jabs, pushing her sister back, her smile disappearing into full concentration. Pushing the sword side to side in an attempt to knock one's grip, Amalie searches for an opening in her sister's stance. Finally seeing an opportunity, she dives, barreling into Davina, knocking her to the ground. Amalie snickers at her fallen sister, dust puffed up around her.

"Again," Amalie says, turning her back.

As she takes a step, Davina swings her feet around, catching her sister by surprise. Falling to the ground, Davina takes advantage of Amalie being weakened by springing to her feet and running. Retrieving her swords, she faces Amalie, shaking the dirt from her clothes and a fire in her eyes. No one takes the advantage over Amalie, something Davina knows well. Yanking a dagger from her belt, Amalie brings her hand back, slicing the air as she moves it forward, releasing the blade.

Eyes wide with shock, Davina has no time to react as the sharp iron flies over her shoulder, leaving a breeze against her face before digging into the side of the stable behind her. Amalie walks with a heavy foot toward her, menacingly dangerous as she grips the hilt of her blade tightly. Davina watches every step and movement her body makes, anticipating her sister's full anger to unleash on her.

Bringing her blades before her in an X, Davina catches Amalie's jab. Pushing back, Davina breathes in deeply, shaking with nerves at her sister's force. Amalie swings and pushes Davina backward, hard and strong. Davina's heart races as she ducks and rolls under Amalie's arms but manages to find her footing. The blow takes her off guard as the hilt of the sword knocks against her jaw. Tears erupt from the sweltering pain as she stumbles. Without another thought, Davina swings one blade around, followed by the other.

Blood dripping down Amalie's left arm ends the battle. Davina looks at the gash. Her jaw clenched in shock yet unashamed.

She could have killed me with that dagger. She thought.

She walks to Amalie, sticking the blades straight into the earth. "I would heal you, but seeing as you just attempted to take my life, I will let you bleed." Without another word, Davina slides around her sister and walks away into the nearby field.

Amalie, annoyed with herself and irritated by Davina, pulls the swords from the ground. A few steps toward the stable, she deposits the three weapons into the tattered bag with the others. The dagger, deeply sunk into the wood of the stable wall, reminds her of her fury and loss of control.

Control yourself.

She pulls the dagger free with her blood-soaked hand. She looks at the mark, a deeply indented groove, blending into the large collection of similar marks she has made over the years. Anger, grief, and frustration are what drove each dagger into the splintered planks. She runs her hand over the rough surface, memories flashing through her mind.

"Amalie!" The voice jolts her from her trance as she searches for its origin.

Her father, Brien, moves swiftly across the yard, eyes trained on her. She watches as he takes her arm in his hands, working the long strip of linen he had carried with him around the wound. The tightness of its binding makes her wince against the stinging throbs.

"It isn't as bad as it looks," she tells him, pulling away. The dagger in her hand streaked and dripping from her seeping wound. Wiping it on her folded skirt, she tucks it back into its sheath before gathering the bag of weapons in her hands.

"I will take care of it. I need you to go check the snares. I haven't the time this morning," Brien says, sliding the bag from her arms.

"I can take care of this. The snares can wait a little longer," she replies, taking the bag back.

"I need you to go now, Amalie. I will saddle your horse a…"

"I will saddle my own horse. I'm injured, not dead, father." Fiercely she shoves the bag against his chest, turning and stomping away from him into the stable. She doesn't understand why she is so annoyed. It only takes a few minutes to prepare her horse before taking off from the stable, flying across the open space and over the first hill.

The small grove of trees is a short distance from their farm. Set against Aldhorran's boundary, it is the perfect place to hide and relax. The trees are her comfort; something Aldhorran has little of. Amalie slides from her horse's back, planting her feet in the soft grassy earth, breathing deeply to take in the woodsy scent, slinging her satchel over her shoulder. Tethering her horse to a fallen tree, she glides through the grass, her dress snagging the tall leaves as she passes.

Her fingers find the first snare just past the edge of the tiny forest's entrance—empty. Moving on, she winds around trees, ducking under limbs, her hands rubbing the rough bark before dipping to the ground at the next trap. A large rabbit is in this one, the light out of its eyes, limp and gone. Untying it, Amalie shoves it into the satchel at her side, resetting the thin twine before moving on. Five more snares and two rabbits later, she finds herself back where she started. The horse peers up for a moment, looking her over, then dips his head back into the grass, enjoying the fresh snack.

Amalie grins, turning her back to him and walking in the opposite direction. She finds the narrow creek that cuts the earth around the grove, following it to a modest pond. Two poles, stuck into the ground and supported by rocks, are wound with thin rope. Her fingers, cold and red, wrap the tough, prickly material, pulling it gently from the pond, as a net gradually appears at the surface, wielding a handful of fish in its grasp. Smiling, she reaches in and takes each fish one by one, cracking its side against a large rock nearby. The fish fall limp and lifeless.

She takes her time, pulling the blade from her belt, cleaning the fish, wrapping them in large leaves from a plant near the water's edge, and depositing them inside the satchel. Trees line the water on the opposite side of the pond, leaving little openings between them but enough to see more rolling hills beyond. She sits, staring out into the unknown, knees tucked up into her chest, thinking over every possibility of life beyond Aldhorran, without her family—alone.

I deserve to be alone.

* * *

The rider barrels fly down the road, flinging dust in a cloud behind him. Brien grits his teeth at the figure, watching him ride onto his property. The man, tall and broad-shouldered, sits high on his horse, looking down at him with a seriousness and hardness across his scarred face. Dismounting, Ascher hides away his horse in the stable, emerging to follow Brien into the house. Closing the door behind them, the men stand across from each other, comparing strengths and weaknesses.

"What is so important to need to speak with me, Ascher?" Brien, arms folded before him, coldly inquiring the young man's intentions.

"You know well why I am here, Brien," Ascher speaks without hesitation.

"You know the answer. Daventh will kill you, and I will not put my daughter in the hands of that man." Brien's voice is dangerously low, hinting at his anger and fear.

"Daventh is dead," Ascher emphasizes the final word crisply.

Shock crosses over Brien's face, quickly covered by glare as thoughts and questions saturate his mind. "I didn't kill him. You aren't the only one to question if I did, which is why I am here."

Brien stares, unsure of Ascher's honesty. He had every right to kill his father. Anyone would expect no less of an event. To many, it is a shock Ascher has survived as long as he has given the hell Daventh put him through. But he persevered.

"You had better explain and quickly. There's no telling how long the girls will be gone." He waves his hand toward the window where the hills and field are visible. Both men draw their gaze in the same direction before focusing back on each other.

"I am scheduled to make a supply run to the port east of here. I have papers. Let Amalie come with me. We can board a ship to Netheis or Divanthra, where we will be safe. I cannot stay here. You know this." Ascher speaks quickly, watching Brien closely as his expression changes with each word.

"And what would you do? Where would you go? My daughter will not live among *your* people." His voice is fierce, defensive as he steps forward, pulling his arms to his sides, fists clenched.

Ascher takes an instinctive step back, ready for a fight.

"I would never go there. Do you think I would submit myself or my wife to my people's savagery? Why would I go to a people I don't even know!" Ascher's voice raises, angry to even be associated with his bloodline.

Brien moves, pacing back and forth, rubbing the back of his neck with his hand. He always knew the time would come that Ascher would appear to court his daughter. The pain his father inflicted would never be enough to drive the two of them apart, nor would his heritage. Daventh knew Amalie was Nasinreth but kept silent. He knew she would be a danger to his son if they were to marry and would be the death of Ascher if he turned the family over to the guard. Brien had hoped the beating would work or would go wrong at one point and end his life and the charade the two played. The last thing he wanted was to allow his daughter to wed a Romathan, specifically an Aulik clansman.

Shaking his head, Brien stops, back turned to Ascher, sighing with his next words. "Against my better judgment, I will allow it." He turns, facing Ascher once again. He looks tired and worn as if the weight of the world sat on his shoulders. "If I said no, you would only find Amalie yourself, and the two of you would disappear. But I swear Ascher, by your God and mine, if you wrong her, I will find you in the depths of hell, where even the devil will fear me." Brien closes the gap between them, speaking menacingly with each step until Ascher can feel the heat radiating from his body.

Ascher nods, his eyes slit as he glares toward Brien. The two have always had a mutual hatred and understanding with one another. Unspoken and threatening. Stepping back, Ascher turns, finding the door, and leaves. A few moments later, hooves pound away at the dirt, and Brien watches him ride away in the direction Amalie rode earlier.

"Maeda, if only I could have your wisdom now," Brien whispers, upturning his face to the ceiling and closing his eyes, imagining his wife's long-lost presence in the absence around him.

THREE

———

The dew of the morning still hangs on the grass and shriveled petals of dying flowers. Davina walks, in search of plants that are edible and medicinal, with dampness clinging to her skirt. Her fingers shake as she plucks the stems of little flowers close to the earth, still hanging on to life. The golden buds are useful when steeped in water until the petals separate from their center, then drunk to ease the pain. Sirien used the fragrant tea often, plagued with what everyone thought to be a painful illness. Davina, exhausted and sore from the duel with her sister, sits hidden among the overgrown plant life around her.

Davina thinks over the fight, remembering every clash of metal, her sister's face, and the wound she had inflicted. She wasn't sorry. *Amalie deserves as much.* She thinks silently to herself, scowling at the dirt, a beetle waddling across its hard surface. The glimmering green and gold across its plump dark back sets it apart from most insects, its beauty breathtaking.

Leaning back into the grass, Davina watches the sky, clouds floating silently by in waves. *I wonder where they have been,* she thinks. Her mind wanders, imagining what the world may look like elsewhere. She has heard stories of the great lakes and oceans, thundering rivers and mountains with peaks piercing the Everworld. Would she ever see any of it? Would freedom ever come in her time? Love? Peace? She rolls onto her stomach, chin resting on her crossed arms before her. Davina watches ants crawl by in tiny lines weaving through the maze of grass in their path.

The crunch of earth and dead plants break Davina's concentration. Looking up, she is startled by the golden eyes staring at her. A white wolf, large and handsome, inches its way closer, a bundle hanging from its mouth. Her heart pounds with the thrill of danger, and she is frozen in place by curiosity. Gently, the wolf releases the tiny pup at her knees, and it rolls, lifeless against her. She looks at it, realizing it must be the mother. Their eyes lock, communicating as if she were human.

Reaching down, Davina's hand touches the fur of the pup, never breaking eye contact with the mother. It breathes, barely. The tips of her fingers tingle, and her body flushes with heat. With a deep breath, she can feel the energy surge through her, lighting her veins with painless fire—the pup wiggles and squirms free of her touch, running to its mother. Apparently pleased, the mother wolf leaves peacefully, stopping at the top of the small hill and looking back a moment before disappearing.

Davina looks down at her hands, lying in her lap. *She sensed me somehow and sought out my help.* The thought seemed absurd yet comforting. A grin breaks across her face, and she lays back in the grass once again, proud, holding no regret. She closes her eyes as the feeling of such power fades along with her drifting mind.

* * *

Fastening the straps of the satchel to the saddle, Amalie takes one last glance at the grove, wishing she didn't have to leave. Hair stands on the back of her neck, and she hears the hooves pounding the ground and the snorting of a horse heading her way. Grabbing the sword attached to her saddle, she draws it, moving around the back of her stallion. Instant recognition puts her at ease. Returning the sword, she meets Ascher on the damp soil beneath her feet. His smile is wide and eyes full of excitement as he comes to a halt, throwing himself down from his saddle and grabbing her arm. Throwing the reins over the tree, they run into the forest grove.

"Ascher, what is it?" Amalie says nervously.

Within the cover of the trees, he stops, taking her face in his hands, and kisses her. Shoving away, she punches him in the shoulder.

"Do not ignore me, Ascher! What are you doing here, and what is going on?" Her voice rises in irritation.

Rubbing his shoulder, he laughs in surprise rather than humor. "Your father has given his permission for us."

Amalie steps back, brows raised and a smile hinting at her lips. "How? Why?" Her voice is unbelieving yet hopeful.

"I went to him this morning. I have papers to travel. If you will have me, I can release us both from Omideon's prison. We can start a new life." Ascher's face becomes serious, shoulders relaxing.

"But Daventh. He will kill you this time." She looks furiously around them, peaking through the trees in search of his father's spies.

Ascher reaches out, taking Amalie by the hands, pulling

her into him. They look at each other, concern engraved across her face.

"Daventh is no more. I have to leave before being blamed for his death, and I want you to come. Please, Amalie."

Amalie relaxes into him at his words, seeing the possibility for their future for the first time in her life. The demon Ascher had once called father is dead, and now he is free. She pushes away from him, nodding, her hard resolve broken, resulting in a brilliant smile.

"When do we leave?" Amalie asks, excitement in her voice.

"It would be best this evening, travel through the night. I'm not sure how long Daventh can go unnoticed."

Amalie nods, thinking it all through. She steps away, slipping her arm into his, and they begin to walk back.

"Let's get back then. I need to tell my father goodbye and gather my things. The sooner we leave, the better." Amalie releases his arm and takes two quick steps ahead of him before throwing herself into a run calling back to him. "Race you!"

Taken by surprise again, he digs his heels into the ground, launching into a sprint chasing after her.

* * *

Sirien sits in the saddle uneasily and weak but persistent. Much to Castor's disapproval, she rode alone rather than with him, pulling her horse behind them. They pushed the horses in a gallop along the road leading to her family home. Worry fills her from her core, and her heart sits heavy in her chest. Her child she could live with losing. She had never wanted children, never wanted the chance at passing down the curses called blessings. But for her husband, such a loss would bore a hole in his very soul. She couldn't tell him, not yet.

Davina, however, couldn't lose. As much trouble as she had been growing up, she was still her sister, her mother's final child, the one her father loves most. The memory of her mother flashes through her mind. Similarities between her and Davina make it difficult to define them apart. Davina could be her mother in looks and spirit. Perhaps that is why their father loves her as he does. She keeps the memory alive.

Castor slows his pace, catching Sirien's attention. She continues up beside him until they stop together. Ahead, a man is running, nearly tripping over his own feet. At the sight of them, he stops, gasping for air. Sirien and Castor look at each other, preparing for bad news.

"Naethom. What has happened?" Castor leans down toward the man, searching his face for any indication of the severity of the problem.

"I, I saw her. A-a hea-healer," he gasps, pointing behind him, attempting to catch his breath. Sirien looks ahead, squinting but finding nothing. "A whole patch of Levith, full bloom." He doesn't wait any longer and takes off running again.

Sirien stares at Castor as he watches the man run away. *Levith is a spring flower and died many months past,* Sirien thinks, wondering who it could have been that he saw, and she froze.

Without warning, Sirien kicks her horse, bringing it to a full-out run down the road. Castor follows close behind her. Her father's farm comes into view, the air rushing past her face, leaving it kissed pink. In the middle of the yard, she stops, dismounting quickly, flinging her reigns up to Castor. She rushes across the yard, thrusting herself through the door.

"Father?" Sirien calls out before looking around. The house is empty. She looks out the windows in search of him until she hears his voice behind her say her name. She whips around to find him in the doorway. Dropping the tools in his hands, he rushes toward her, grabbing her arms. He knows the look when she has had a vision, and this one is no different.

"What have you seen, child?" Her fear radiates to him, and he grips harder.

"Is Davina a healer?" Castor appears in the doorway as she asks, eyes flitting between his wife and her father.

Brien doesn't answer. Instead, he loosens his grip, stepping back, tightening his jaw. Her eyes widen, and her heart drops further into the pit in her soul.

"She has been seen," she hisses through clenched teeth.

Brien moves suddenly, crashing his fist down on the table. His other hand rubs over his face, smoothing the lines indented permanently from hardship and age. Looking at Castor, he speaks steadily.

"Castor. Saddle the horses as quickly as possible."

Castor disappears out into the late morning light, leaving Sirien and Brien alone.

Sirien's father walks past her to the chest pushed up against the wall, not meeting her eyes. Lifting away the lid, he discards it to the floor with a loud crash. Sirien turns, watching him as he pulls out a large bundle wrapped in linen.

"Your grandfather foresaw your birth, your gift, and your strengths. I trained you as a child because I knew the day would come when I couldn't protect you all anymore." Unrolling the cloth, he lays each weapon out on the table: knives, two swords, a bow, and a quiver of fine leather full of arrows.

"You always showed the most skill with the bow. You can handle a sword, that I have seen, but your strength, like your grandfather said, is a bow. You are the heart of this family, Sirien. Without you, I would have failed as a father, and your sisters would have killed one another. If anything happens to me, protect them." He grips the bow and quiver in his hands, passing them over to Sirien. Her fingers brush over the fine wood and leather.

"Let go of me!" Davina's voice bellows in the yard just before she dives through the door, stumbling then turning on her heel.

Amalie flies through the door after Davina, shoving her against the wall, fist in her shoulder. Before Brien or Sirien can react, Ascher is inside, scooping Amalie up by the waist and, pinning her to his chest, drags her away. She kicks and flails like a fish out of water, face red with fury.

Tears stream down Davina's face, shaking in fear and pain. Rushing to her side, Sirien pulls her into an embrace, cupping a hand over one side of her head shoving the other onto her chest. Castor, once again, stands in the doorway, confused, eyes scanning every face, finding the threat.

"Enough!" His yell is deep, like a growl stopping everyone in their tracks.

Setting Amalie on the ground, Ascher keeps a tight hold, looking to Davina then Brien.

"Amalie, gather yourself. I know your sister has used her gift, but that gives you no excuse for such harshness. Davina. What were you thinking?" He looks to her, piled on the ground in Sirien's arms.

"I can't control it. I-I" Amalie tries to break free of Ascher's hold but stops at her father's glare.

"We don't have time for any of this. The guard will be searching for us soon, so we have to flee and pray we survive long enough to make it to the Ancient lands." Brien takes the daggers and a sword from the table, crossing to Amalie and placing them in her hands. "Control," he says to her, disappointment obvious in his voice.

Ascher releases his grip on Amalie. She stretches, rolling her shoulders, glaring in Davina's direction. Castor and Sirien's eyes meet, and he motions for her to leave them and help. She brushes Davina's hair back away from her face, helping her to stand, then looks to Amalie with sad eyes. Releasing her sister, she heads to the door, meeting Castor in the yard.

"If the two of you plan to leave, I would go now. Whether on your own or with us, I don't care. But if you are with us, we do this together." Brien looks at Ascher and Amalie.

Amalie storms out of the house with a sharp exhale, closely followed by Ascher, leaving Brien and Davina alone in silence.

Davina stands, face turned to the floor, ashamed. Brien reaches out, gripping her arm to pull her into an embrace. She breaks, crying into his shoulder.

"We haven't time, my child." Brien distances himself from Davina enough to see her face and wipe away her tears. She sniffles, moving away from him, wiping her face across her sleeve.

"When your mother told me she was with child again, I told her it wasn't possible. Her father had only seen two children." He moved about the room as he spoke, gathering various items of importance and placing them into the hunting satchel of Amalie's.

"She told me her father had seen her on a throne, crowned in a beautiful hall full of flowers. But it wasn't her. Her father had seen a younger woman than your mother, and she believed you were that woman in his vision. She told me we would have another daughter." He stops by the table, eyes glimmering with fresh tears at the story.

"She told me you would be special. You had a purpose beyond our understanding. I watched you grow into a beautiful young woman. Your mother was right, you are special, and I have been fortunate to see it."

Setting the satchel aside, Brien reaches toward the single sword on the table. Davina watches as it splits into two glorious thin blades before her eyes. He hands them to her, and she takes them, feeling their weight in her hands. Not too heavy, yet not light. Fitting them back together, they work together as one piece or separate as two, unique, special.

"Let's go!" Amalie's voice drifts in from the yard.

Brien, taking Davina by the shoulder, walks through the open door. Together, they reach their horses and are in the saddle, ready to go, following behind their family, racing into freedom.

FOUR

———

Rheyhas boots click along the corridor, echoing in its emptiness. He walks, eyes fixed on the door at the end of the long
hallway. Passing through an archway, he sees the young man
staring up at a large painting, one the entire castle knows
well and admires. Stopping before him, he bows.

"My Lord Prince Americ." Rheyhas stands tall, looking
the prince over—fiery red hair, gentle face, and pale skin.
His silver-blue eyes pierce through any man's soul, almost
as if he sees everything in its depths. Rheyhas looks away,
clearing his throat.

"If you are looking for my father, now is not the time.
He is with the Ambassador of Netheis, discussing the final
bits of the treaty. Did you know the heir to the throne is on
his way? Should reach our shores in a week's time." Americ
shakes his head, laughing lightly to himself.

"Sir, it is vital I speak with the King," Rheyhas says, voice
urgent in his request.

"Why? What has happened?" A voice like a songbird floats
in from the shadows.

Rheyhas stands, rigid at her presence. Americ searches
for her wildly. A young woman, similar in looks to Americ

appears. Her blonde hair and crystal blue eyes make her features shockingly beautiful. Her slim face, rich caramel skin, and full lips entice every man in her presence.

Americ looks at her dreading what she will do. Rheyhas stands still as if facing a venomous snake. She walks to him, running her fingers across his chest, circling him, robes dragging in a trail behind her.

"You stand before the Crown Prince, Rheyhas. One day it will be his duty to carry your burdens and bare your truths." She stands behind him, whispering in his ear, staring over his shoulder to Americ.

Chills run down Americ's spine, watching the control she held over every person in this castle. Rheyhas swallows a lump in his throat before speaking.

"A girl, healer of the Nasinreth has been found. She was spotted in a settlement along the Western region of the border. I sent men after her, and they couldn't find her or any sign of the residents there." Charlotte whirls around him, finding her place at Americ's side.

"Why are you not out searching? Surely they haven't gone far," Charlotte says to him, appalled by his lack of independence.

"I sent a group to the border of Divanthra. I would like to travel to the West and meet my men in Warridian. I feel this is different than most," Rheyhas says, looking to Americ. Charlotte sees this, stepping between the two men, addressing Rheyhas further.

"So why haven't you gone?" Charlotte sighs, frustrated.

"Leaving now would take many guardsmen away from the Castle. It will still be defensible, but with the arrival of Netheis Royals, I couldn't make the call without my King," Rheyhas speaks logically.

Charlotte glares, thoughts spinning in her mind.

"Americ?" Charlotte turns to him, smiling. "Since father is currently occupied, and you are the future of this kingdom, shouldn't the decision fall to you? You must step up at some point." Her smirk is challenging him. She knows any decision he makes will anger his father, and it is choosing between two evils. Americ stands silently staring at Charlotte, trying to read her face like he once had.

"Go. Search for the Nasinreth girl," Charlotte speaks over her shoulder at Rheyhas, waving a hand to rush him away. Taking the hint, he bows and turns to leave. "Wait." Turning once again, she stalks up to Rheyhas, looking him up and down before standing so close their noses nearly touch. "Do not fail. It could ruin our young heir." Rheyhas passes by her after another wave of her hand, hustling down the corridor out of sight.

"Why do you do that?" Americ asks.

"Why do you always stare at that painting?" Charlotte asks in reply. Annoyed, he turns his gaze to it, taking in the sight of his mother staring back at him.

"Do you miss her?" Americ's voice is barely a whisper when he speaks.

"No. And you shouldn't either. She's been gone a long while. Move on Americ. Don't be such a child." Charlotte's tone is angry as she speaks.

"Go find someone in the castle to waste your time Charlotte. I'm sure someone longs for your company."

Charlotte's expression changes quickly from anger, to shame, and to fury. Her arm swings before he sees it, palm meeting the side of his head with a loud pop. Off guard, the blow knocks him off balance, sending him stumbling against the wall. Looking up, he sees Charlotte gliding down the corridor. He knows he struck a chord, one he wished he hadn't. Regret balls up in his chest.

"My Lord Americ," a servant nearby speaks quietly, holding a book out to him. He takes it and sends her away before opening it, searching for a folded page. Finding it, he lays it flat, pulling the loose sheet out, reading the neatly scrawled letters.

"Midday, the upper terrace."

* * *

Climbing the narrow winding stairway, Americ passes servants traveling down from the top, and he wonders what in the world Castah wanted and is doing on the terrace. Stepping out into the sun's light, he feels its heat radiating down on his face. Adjusting to the brightness, he stumbles a moment past another servant into the wide-open space. Pillars stand tall in the center, supporting the overhead structure to save against the elements. Castah sits in the middle of the room, a brush in hand, its tip full of the brightly colored oils from Netheis. Before her, a dozen fragrant bouquets of brilliant pink and red flowers lay strategically across the table.

"The Nethian heir spoils you far too much already." Americ steps into the airy room, nodding to the nearest servant to approve of his leave. The servant bows, leaving the room like a ghost.

"He does, doesn't he?" Castah responds to him airily, continuing her painting.

Americ walks the edge of the space, looking at every little detail in the pillars, stones, and faces of those forced into service. The click of Castah's brush against the wood of the table draws all eyes to the center of the room. She wipes the oils from her hands, handing the rag away to the nearest person.

"You may go." Castah looks to all the servants, waving her hand illuminating her words with actions. Suddenly the two find themselves completely alone.

"The book trick. I haven't seen that since we were children." Americ chuckles at the memory, stepping into the center of the room beside his sister.

"You still are a child, my dear brother. Just because you are the age of adulthood does not mean you are one." Her hand touches his cheek gently, leaving a warm imprint on his skin for a moment's notice. She stands, ordering her oils and brushes in a straight line, placing the small wooden toppers over the jars.

"If not age itself, then what defines a man?" he asks, confusion crossing over his expression.

Castah giggles, shaking her head. "I asked you here because I wished to speak with you about my marriage to Talos." She looks at him, digesting his expressions of further confusion.

"Wouldn't this be something to ask another woman? I'm not so sure how I can help you."

Castah looks at him, annoyed but shrugs off his comment. "No, you idiot. I need to know you won't do anything irresponsible after I leave. I know how you hate it here, hate father. I need to know you will stay safe, follow orders, stay alive." Her voice carries a tone of fear.

"Take me with you, Castah." Americ's response is nearly inaudible, his gaze at his feet.

"You know I can't Americ, or I would. He would hunt you, destroying anything in his path, Americ." She reaches forward, placing a hand under his chin, forcing him to meet her eyes. "Promise me you will be better than him. Promise me no matter what he says and does to you, you will be different. You are so much stronger than he thinks you are." Her eyes are warm and wet with tears at the thought of leaving her brother behind.

"I will do my best. That's all I can promise you."

Castah nods her head, knowing it had to be enough. She pats his cheek again out of habit, then turns back to her canvas. Americ follows, peering over her shoulder at the flowers spread across the fabric. Her touch has always been light and gentle, and her mind kind and patient. It is something he knows he will miss dearly, so he stays and watches her paint.

FIVE

Amalie and Ascher watch as Brien follows an old man out of the house, crossing to the barn where they hide. They walk quickly, searching their surroundings as they go. The old man passes by them, leaving a strong odor of manure and sweat trailing behind him. They follow from a safe distance, watching him cross the barn, stopping at the farthest wall. Kicking with his boot, he strikes a chain. Bending down, he pulls at it, lifting a hatch from the floor that leads to a wide-open space below.

"You'll be safe here. In all the raids, it has never been discovered." He looks to Brien with confidence.

"Thank you, my old friend." Brien reaches out, taking the man by the forearm before turning to the others. "The guards won't expect us to stop. Most would run endlessly to the border. Do you trust me?"

Each member of the group looks to one another before turning back to him, nodding. One by one, they toss in their saddlebags before taking a step forward, leaping into the hole. Amalie stops beside Brien, waiting for him.

"You will find some food stored, blankets, and candles. We always keep it prepared for times as this. I pray you go from here safely and complete your journey." He looks at each person before motioning to the pit.

Together, Brien and Amalie jump down, landing on a hard stone that shoots stabbing pain through their feet. Raining down straw, the hatch closes—tiny slivers of light peak through the floorboards, allowing them to slightly see their surroundings.

Nervous eyes look to each other as they feel around the tight space for the candles the old man had spoken of. Fingers fumbling over others fingers, they finally find the large rounds of wax along the floor. Brien pulls his stones from his bag, piles a small bit of hay before him, and works to light a fire. After a few minutes, flames erupt. Taking a matchstick from his bag, he lights it, carefully moving it to each candle.

"Be sure to watch them closely and trim the wicks," Brien instructs, as he carefully hands a candle to Sirien, then Amalie before taking one himself. "I'm unsure how long we will stay, so rest now. This will be a long journey." He falls back against the wooden wall of the small room.

"Everyone should rest. I will keep watch," Ascher speaks quietly.

Brien nods at him, accepting his offer. Davina finds the stashed away wool blankets, handing two to Sirien, taking two for herself and her father. Amalie glares in her direction as she sits, wrapping it closely around her. Davina raises an eyebrow cautiously to Amalie before rolling onto her side on the floor.

Ascher watches their exchange nervously. Before Amalie can move, he jumps up and walks to the small store of items in the corner. He gathers blankets and rummages the jars of dried fruit and smoked meats. As he crouches, he notices everyone already or nearly asleep, except for Amalie.

Dipping back down to the ground next to her, he settles, laying the food between them and spreading the blankets out over them both.

"It will only get colder as the day dwindles," he whispers, tucking her into the warm, thick blanket.

"I'm not sleeping. If you are awake, so am I," she hisses back to him. "This isn't what I had in mind when we spoke this morning." She looks around at the drowsy bodies huddled together in the room.

"I know, but there is nothing we can do to change that now." Ascher sits, staring at the wall as the candlelight flickers across it.

"We just need to get everyone to Aldara. Then we will be free." Amalie stares at her father—his head fell back against the wall, chest rising and falling, his limbs slack.

"You still want to leave them? Where would we go?" Ascher finds her face fixed on her father. She nods slowly.

"I don't belong with them. I never have. Ascher, I am not like the Nasinreth. They will all fit in well in any of the surviving villages. I want to find my own place with you." She looks at him, reaching out, taking his hand in hers.

Together, they sit and eat, watching the candles burn slowly, the wick growing in a dark charred length. Hours pass by as they trim the candles, allowing rest for the others. Returning to their seats, they find each other again, sitting closely to conserve heat as the temperature drops. The light outside dims until disappearing completely. The wind rustles the hay across the floorboards above, and the structure creaks under pressure. Their bodies, cold and heavy with sleep, threaten their reliability to keep watch.

A loud crunch from above startles Amalie from Ascher's shoulder, where she had fallen asleep. She bolts upright, listening. Whispers alert her to others as the crunching of feet find their way around the building. She taps Ascher furiously on the shoulder, causing him to fling his head around violently, ready for a fight. She pushes a finger to her lips when he looks at her then points up. He listens, eyes wide, heart thumping hard in his chest.

Amalie licks her finger before pinching out the flame, cutting the burnt wick free from the fresh. Pointing to her father, she crawls quietly to Sirien while Ascher moves to Brien. Brien wakes calmly. Understanding quickly what is happening, he turns, waking Davina, hand clasped over her mouth, then silences the flame in his candle. Amalie succeeds in waking Sirien and Castor, extinguishing their light as well, leaving them in darkness.

Hardly breathing, they lay on the floor. Through the opening, soldiers trickle in, combing the area for any sign of human life. Hay and dirt fall between the cracks, showering the occupants below.

"Who goes there!" Light floods the room above. Heavy feet stand, planted over the cellar door. Hearts race as they pray they aren't caught. "Who are you?" The old man's voice rings through the night air.

"Commander Rheyhas of the Kings guard. We have stowaways from Aldhorran. Have you seen any new faces in the area?" The man's voice is loud and heavy in the frigid air.

"No. And if I had, I would have reported it. I have no qualm with the King. I serve loyally," he replies to the Commander coolly.

"Very well. I am sorry to disturb you at such a time." Steps race across the floor as they exit the barn. The light remains a short time longer before vanishing, leaving the group shaken and on guard, unable to rest longer.

* * *

Two days pass in a blur to them, huddled together in the dark, barely speaking between shifts of watch. The old man comes and goes throughout the second day, often a horse in tow behind him to be housed inside the barn. Late in the evening, the old man returns, opening the hatch to release his willing captives. Stretching with stiffness from confinement, they walk the room, adjusting their sight to the moonlit world around them. Brien slips off with the man, returning with cloaks for each of them.

Amalie searches the room, glancing over the horses inside, saddled and rearing to go. The old man had prepared for their leave throughout the entire day. Walking to her horse, she inspects him, a smile wide across her face. He had been groomed, hooves trimmed and shod.

"You will need to leave soon. Word has your hunters south of here. They will cut north near the serpent's tongue, I'm sure, which only gives you a few days." Amalie glances over her shoulder at her father and the old man exchanging words. Examining the room for Ascher, she spots him in the doorway of the barn.

"Are you sure you feel well enough to ride? I'm sure we could wait here a few more days," Castor speaks softly to Sirien over the saddle of her horse as he watches the others preparing for their ride.

"Stop worrying. I am well. We are well." Sirien flashes him a grin, tightening the saddle simultaneously.

"What do you think they are talking about?" Davina's hoarse voice breaks their moment as she comes into view beside them.

The three pairs of eyes look at Amalie and Ascher in the

doorway. Ascher leans heavily against the solid planks while Amalie stands arms crossed beside him. They are speaking energetically, their silhouettes moving with each word they mumble to each other.

"It doesn't matter. Let's focus solely on this journey and worry about them later," Sirien says, peeling her eyes from the couple, placing her focus back on her horse.

Brien's voice softly rings out as he calls for Amalie and Ascher, drawing them back into the group. Black covers the land, sprinkled with rays of the moon, lighting a dim path. Mounting their horses, they ride in a flurry from the barn into the darkness.

* * *

The Yvirin River flows steadily around the bend, cutting through the growth of trees and bushes overhanging it. Crouched at its edge, Sirien stares into the still pool of water, trapped by rocks and branches. The sun barely peaks over the horizon casting a warm glow over them. The safety of night had given them an advantage, covering a large expanse of ground before dawn.

Listening to the world around her wake with the rising sun, Sirien peers around the trees at the chirps and squawks of birds and the scuttling of squirrels and other rodents among the branches and fallen leaves around her. The clash of metal and grunts draw her attention. She watches her father and youngest sister spar, her new dual sword drawn, blade in each hand. Like a dangerous dance, they move, spin, and leap around each other.

Nearby, Amalie takes advantage of a large tree, dying from sickness. Each dagger flies from the tips of her fingers, rolling through the air before piercing the wood deeply with a thud. Ascher watches attentively, smiling with each stick.

The breeze gusts, brushing strands of hair across Sirien's face. A hand clasps her shoulder, and she jumps to find Castor standing behind her. Smiling, she pats the rock beside her, beckoning him closer. He sits, staring in the direction of the others for a moment, relaxing beside her.

"You should join them. You have a bow. I would like to see you shoot." His face turns to her, interested in the thought of his wife as a skilled fighter.

She shakes her head shyly. He slides his hand behind him, drawing out the bow and quiver of arrows. Sirien looks at them nervously. After some consideration, she takes an arrow from the quiver, inspecting the tip and tail, then grasps the bow.

Stepping up from her place on the stone, she turns, eyes scanning for a suitable target. A small tree not far away stands out to her. Setting her sights on it, she raises the bow, drawing the string back, nearly touching her lips. Breathing in, she steadies, at exhale, she releases, sending the arrow into its target.

The man stands, clutching the arrow bore into his chest. Screams erupt around them as men from all directions flood into the small clearing. The river roars, drowning out the cries of pain and disaster. Sirien scours the area, finding the faces of Amalie and Ascher, light leaving their eyes, bodies lifeless on the ground. Her father is nowhere to be seen, and Davina writhes in the arms of her captor across the way.

Iron rings as it is drawn from its sheath and echoes loudly in Sirien's mind. She whips her head around violently, searching for the threat. Her eyes, falling on two figures across the river, make her catch her breath. A woman stands over a man, sword drawn. His armor, new and untouched, finely made, sits perched on his knees, staring up at her. Her arm raises above her head. Body twisting with the weight of her force, she brings the sword down across the man's throat and chest. Sprayed with blood, she turns, meeting the eyes of her twin.

SIX

———

The musk of fall hovers densely in the air as they move along the river's edge. Amalie stares ahead of her, watching her sister's wilted body sit loosely before Castor. Her horse tethered to his saddle. With what she had seen, they had no time to wait for her to recover fully. The silence among them sits heavier than the air with the revelation of Sirien's secret. Amalie, full of anger, rides, her eyes clouded with betrayal and jaw set tight. Ascher next to her watches her cautiously, knowing her temper all too well.

He has seen her angry before but never like this. The sun crosses the sky slowly as they travel, Sirien gaining strength with every passing hour. The danger is too great to stop, they trudge on until the light barely peaks over the horizon. Trees grow thicker the further west they travel, and now covered by the forest's protection, they rest.

At the first sign of stopping, Amalie pushes forward, leaving the group to scan the perimeter. Ascher, not letting her out of sight, races after her. Weaving through the trees, they circle the camp, never speaking. Amalie stops on the tracks they have all trampled into the earth earlier, scouring at the evidence they left. Looking intensely in the direction they had come, she sits, watching the stillness.

"Amalie," Ascher breaks the silence hesitantly.

"Go away, Ascher," her voice is cold.

"I can tell what you're thinking. You can't fight them all. The best thing you can do now is work with them till we reach Aldara. I know…"

She jerks the reins, spinning the horse around to face him.

"You know what, Ascher? You know the feeling of betrayal? You know how it feels not to be trusted? I see now why father was so protective of her, training me to keep her safe. Sirien and Davina are gifted Ascher. They are worth something!" Her voice rises in a fury with every word, hands clenching the reins so tight her knuckles are white.

In one swift motion, Ascher throws himself from his horse, stalking toward Amalie. Before she can react, he jerks her from her horse to the ground. He holds her by the arms, tight enough to leave bruises, his face filled with frustration. Her heart throbs as it pumps strongly in her chest.

"You have more worth than them combined. You fight, hunt, and have a fire deep inside you carry, driving your every emotion and feeling. Your compassion is deep and furious, strength unyielding and downright terrifying to anyone who crosses you. You have worth to me." He speaks the final words through gritted teeth.

Amalie stares wide-eyed at him, considering all he said as emotions well up in her soul. Shoving them away, she nods, biting the inside of her lower lip. His grasp loosens on her arms, and he steps back.

"We should go back. The perimeter is clear for now, but someone will need to keep watch," Amalie says, stepping back to her horse.

She mounts and takes off, leaving Ascher where he stands alone.

* * *

Sirien lays exhausted across the hard, cold ground, regaining her strength from another vision in the night. She stares at the sky, lightening in the early morning, waking the heavy sleepers around her. Davina, still in danger, sleeps by her father, huddled in her cloak and his. Sirien silently plans the next steps they must make. Another day's journey will bring them to the Mhoridian Forest edge, where they must split up to better their chances.

Unsure if the others will accept such an idea, she thinks over all the possible advantages and problems this could bring, preparing for the backlash. Feeling in her limbs has returned, but she stays still anyway, not ready to face the day. Castor's deep, sleepy breaths come and go beside her. She smiles at the comforting sound of his closeness to her. She feels safe.

Crunching leaves and cracking twigs prick at Sirien's ears, so she slits her eyes open. Amalie, moving slowly away from the group, heads to Ascher, who is sitting on the edge of the thin tree line. Sirien opens her eyes completely, watching the two with interest. Amalie places her hands on his shoulders, leans down, and kisses him. Feeling like an intruder, Sirien rolls onto her side, facing Castor, back turned to her sister.

Castor's face is peaceful, lips parted barely, brows relaxed, hair ruffled around his face. Restlessly she rolls back, facing her sister again to find Ascher is gone, and Amalie now sits alone. Mustering the strength and will to move, Sirien inhales strongly before pushing herself up. Sitting, then standing, she waits to catch her balance before taking a step. She walks hesitantly to Amalie, gathering her skirts in a clenched fist to her side, preventing them from dragging.

"Amalie." Sirien's voice is quiet yet demanding.

"What do you want, Sirien?" she speaks coldly, keeping her back turned to Sirien.

"I need to speak with you." Before she can say anything else, Amalie turns to face her.

"If you have come to tell me of your life of deception, I am not interested." Amalie stares, arms folded across her chest.

"I had another vision last night. We need to split up. We are too vulnerable together." Sirien's face is somber, eyes piercing as she speaks frankly to Amalie.

"Normally, I would say together we are stronger, but in this case, I believe you are right. It is the best strategic way to handle this. Look." Amalie turns, tossing her head in the direction from which they have traveled.

A light pillar of smoke rises up into the sky in the distance. With a village miles away in each direction, it can only mean by coincidence there are other travelers or hunters nearby, or the guards are on their trail. Sirien breathes past a lump in her chest.

"It's time we wake the others and leave. I hope you are ready." Amalie looks at Sirien before turning to walk back to the others.

"Amalie." Sirien reaches out, taking her by the arm. "Your future holds many adventures and greatness. You will lead people, not your own, fight many battles and conquer. This I have foreseen and have known since we were children. You were born for greatness, this I know."

Meeting her eyes, Amalie's face betrays her for once, showing confusion and shock. Pulling away, Amalie composes herself, storming away to arouse the others from their slumber. Sirien looks out at the pillar of smoke, praying she is right and this sacrifice she secretly bound herself to is worth it.

* * *

The wood, gripped tightly in his left hand, holds steady as he draws the nocked arrow back, aiming for the target across from him. Americ breathes in, releasing the arrow with his breath. It flies, cutting the air sharply before meeting the target. It sinks into the lower right of the center mark he had hoped to hit. Cursing himself under his breath, he reaches for another arrow, but to his surprise, his hand meets flesh. Whirling around, he is startled, finding Castah grinning ear to ear, an arrow in hand.

"What in the blazes, Castah?" He throws his free hand over his chest, feeling the rapid thump.

She laughs, reaching for the bow, releasing it from his grasp. She knocks the arrow, aiming and releasing. The arrow plunges into the center of the mark. Angrily, Americ rips the bow from her hand, throwing it into the large quiver perched against a stone.

"Women shouldn't handle a man's weapon." He shoots a glare in her direction.

"I'm no average woman Americ. We are descendants of Drumidia. Their women fight," she remarks.

He clenches his jaw, running a frozen hand over his face.

"What are you doing out here? You know father wouldn't be happy if he saw you." Americ looks around warily in search of any bystanders.

"He won't be missing me because he is searching for you. Negotiations are over, and he heard about Rheyhas. Charlotte has gotten you into a load of trouble again, I fear." She grimaces, taking a turn to glance around.

The blood drains from Americ's face, cold taking over every remaining place in his body that had held heat. It's never good when his twin is involved in their father's fury. She is just like him and knows how to boil his blood. He begins thinking over the conversation nearly a week prior with the commander. Charlotte, putting the fear of his life's end in her hands, did her bidding, leaving to hunt the runners assuming they were Nasinreth.

Has she dropped the blame and choices in my hands?

Furious, Americ pulls the quiver from the ground, stomping his way across the dying grass and up the slope of the hill. Castah runs after him, attempting to catch up to his long stride. She calls out to him, and finally within reach, grabs the sleeve of his tunic, jerking him to a halt.

"What are you doing?" She hisses, looking around feverishly.

"Getting this over with. His wrath has to fall on my head at some point. I may as well have it on my own time." He rips his sleeve free, turns on his heels, and stalks away. Looking around once more, Castah glides back down and follows the path from which she had come.

Atop the small hill, Americ reaches the gates to the northern courtyard. Welcomed by the soldiers posted there, he passes through, feet clicking across the cobblestone. One of the men rushes to his side, taking the quiver from Americ. Entering into the first corridor of the castle, he walks directly to the first stairwell in sight. The servants had been alerted of the King's unhappiness, that much Americ could see as he watches them disperse as he passes suddenly. They know to avoid the King and any who were in his Majesty's path of ruin.

Heat rises, flushing Americ's face, his heart races like a million young stallions, and his hand's quiver with nerves as he draws closer to the library on the second floor. Whenever his father had a bone to pick, he was always in the library. No one really knew why that was, but it is never good if he summons you there.

Americ stops, looking down a long corridor, seeing all doorways sealed except for one. Light flickers out from the opening into the dim space. The air is dense, full of smoke, and stifling hot—the fire inside crackles loudly, but it's the sharp ruffle of pages that catches his attention. Preparing himself, he stands tall, smoothing the front of his tunic, and walks the final stretch of the corridor. Turning into the room with confidence, he finds his father, sitting in a large armchair near the fire, reading.

His eyes shift up away from the material before him, jaw hard and eyes dead of all emotion. Americ stands before him, silently awaiting his punishment. Panic begins to rise as he stands there, and his father sits silently, looking at him.

What is he waiting for? Americ thinks, trying to stay calm.

"So you chose to play King rather than seek my advisors, I hear." It wasn't a question, an edge of irritation barely noticeable. The two look at one another long and hard in silence.

"Castah is to be wed in less than a fortnight, and over half of my guard is on a manhunt. One I did not approve." The edge is stronger this time.

"Father, I…" The King lifts his hand, silencing Americ immediately. He sets aside the book and stands, stepping to Americ menacingly.

"You allowed your sister to get into your head. I thought by breaking your bond, you would learn to rely only on yourself, yet you still listen to her. What do I have to do to make you into a man worthy of this throne? Charlotte is ruined. Listen to her, follow her, and it will destroy your future rule." His voice drops to a threatening whisper. "Women are not meant to rule, nor are the weak. Kings are made, not born. Remember that."

Stepping back, he peers into Americ's eyes then walks back to his seat, picking up the book and returning to his previous activity. Knowing the conversation has ended, Americ shakily leaves.

"When I find her…" He growls, heading in the direction of his private chamber.

SEVEN

———

The dust stirs in wispy clouds around them as they continue west. In pairs, they follow in a line through the dense grass, swaying to the playfulness of the breeze. The woods around them grow thicker, and the rush of the river grows stronger as the banks open wider the further upstream they travel. The day drags as they move forward, the mountains growing in height the closer they get.

Amalie sits uneasily in the saddle. Taking up the rear, her and Ascher fervently search the timber and overgrown plant life for any sign of human life. The soldiers wouldn't be too far behind them if the pillar of smoke was who Amalie assumed was the cause. The pair ride together quietly, reading one another's body language. Amalie glances at him, tall in his saddle, muscles tense and rigid as he twists his head in all directions.

He was right. I thought about leaving, but not without him. Never.

Her mind races with their conversation the night before, his expression and how he had dragged her from her horse's back. Shuddering, she blinks away the memory. Looking to the sky, she consults the sun for the time of day. Midafternoon she assumes, soaking in the rays beating down on her face. There would be very few warm days left with autumn drawing to its end.

Gently, she rocks back and forth, swaying to the steps of her horse and taking comfort in it. Glancing at Ascher again, she sees he hasn't changed. Guilt builds in her chest, and she considers reaching out to him, consoling him with apologetic words, but her thoughts are interrupted. Looking ahead, she sees Sirien rushing back to them. Her father stopped ahead with Davina and Castor.

"What is it?" Amalie calls out over the wind.

"This is the place. We separate here. Remember, soldiers will be in the meadow just over the hill. Stay south, and please be careful." Sirien's horse stamps, stopping just before Amalie and Ascher. Snorting in impatience, Sirien pats the large neck of the beast.

"You and Castor continue west, and father takes Davina northern into the forest. Are you sure they can make it to Divanthra this way? Would it not be better for them to go south instead?" Amalie questions Sirien, uneasy with the plan.

"No. You need to go south. Stay with the plan, and we will reunite in time," Sirien commands.

Pulling the reigns, Sirien turns, trotting away to Castor. She stops next to Brien, exchanges a few words, and continues forward. Shaking Brien's hand, Castor says his final farewell before following Sirien. Ascher and Amalie make their way to Brien and Davina, nodding to each other before departing ways in opposite directions. Making their way to the top of the hill, they watch as the conifers begin to thin until the bareness of the meadow unfolds before them. Amalie searches in the edge of the woodlands, meeting Sirien's gaze in the distance.

"I hope this works," Amalie mumbles to Ascher as she watches Sirien and Castor dart from the cover of the towering timber.

* * *

The wind sweeps across their faces as they ride hard across the meadow. Sirien's hair floats loosely like a veil behind her. Castor follows closely behind. Hoping the plan works, they focus on their path, glancing momentarily to the south to see two more riders riding furiously across the horizon. Just as Sirien had foreseen, soldiers appear from both the north and the south. Two small groups, yelling in their direction, hooves thundering in no rhythm. The forest before them grows larger with each pounding step, the guard hot on their heels. The world falls silent around Sirien, focus trained on her target, confident in her decision.

Suddenly, with great force, she finds herself weightless, gliding through the air. Smacking hard to the ground on her back, she gasps, unable to fill her lungs. Rolling onto her stomach, she gropes the ground, pulling herself up to her hands and knees, drawing in the damp, cool air. Her horse whinnies and thrashes in the wet soil, arrows protruding from its hindquarters.

The soldier flies across earth toward Sirien. She stumbles and slips, pushing up from the ground, running to her fallen horse. Wrenching her weapons from the saddle, she takes an arrow, sending it airborne into the closest soldier. Catching him in the neck, he topples to the side, falling out of sight in the tall grass. Castor, riding up to her side, extends a hand sharply. Taking it, he swings her up behind him, kicking the horse harshly to encourage speed.

Sirien grasps Castor's waist tightly with one arm while holding her bow and quiver of arrows tightly in the other. They race against time as the forest closes in around them. Maneuvering between trees, ducking below branches, and guiding the horse on the smoothest path possible, Castor concentrates, tense beneath Sirien's grasp.

"Hold onto me," she loudly whispers in his ear.

Loosening his grip with one hand, he swings his arm behind him, taking her waist the best he can, and gathers her dress in his fist. She pulls the quiver over her shoulder, securing it across her body. Twisting, she looks behind her as she pulls an arrow free of its keeping place. Securing it to the bowstring, she outstretches her left hand. Pushing against her palm, the wood of the bow is sturdy and fits perfectly in her grasp. Pulling the bowstring tightly, she releases an arrow.

Returning forward, she peers behind her to see the arrow in the front shoulder of the lead horse. It trips, throwing the rider into the forest, slowing the others trailing behind. Pleased, she finds her hold on Castor again so he can take full control of the reins.

"That should buy us time!" she yells again in his ear.

His only reply is a nod as he continues flying through the forest, weaving in and out of trees. Glancing behind her regularly, she sees the guards steadily losing ground until they are out of sight and earshot.

"I think we lost them," Sirien tells Castor.

"We need a bit more distance. The horse can't carry us much longer at this pace. Do you trust me?" he calls back to her, looking over his shoulder, the wind throwing back his hair in her face.

She nods, and they continue racing through the forest, growing thicker with every step. Soon, however, the horse noticeably slows, tired from the exertion and two riders on its mighty back. Castor's head whips back and forth, searching the forest until his gaze rests on a large thicket ahead.

"Untie the weapons and hand them to me," he calls back to Sirien.

The swords and satchel come free as she unties the leather straps binding them to the saddle, passing them along with her bow and quiver around her to him. Sirien looks back again, finding an empty path. Castor pulls the reins hard, and the horse skids to a halt, nearly sending Sirien flying. Their weapons fly off to the left, landing in bushes out of sight. Jerking her off the horse with him, Castor throws a hand hard across the horse's rump, sending it away in a blur. Grabbing Sirien by the arm, he runs, diving low into the thicket, dragging Sirien with him. Arms wrapped tightly around her. They lay on the ground, branches, and thorns poking them in every direction.

The earth rumbles below them as a flurry of horses and riders dash past them. Silently, they lay together, listening to the abnormal sounds around them. The woods sing as the wind dances through them, birds chirp high in the branches of fragrant pines and spruce. Decomposing leaves make a bed around them, their muskiness even welcoming. They lay there for ages it seems, before Castor feels it safe enough to emerge above.

Brushing leaves and dirt from her hair, Sirien can't help but take in the sight of the forest around her. The grove on the outskirts of Aldhorran is thinner and dreamier than this. This is mystical and vibrant with life.

"Here," Castor hisses, bending down to retrieve the weapons he had thrown.

Sirien races over to him, taking her bow and looking it over. Her fingers trace its curve, checking the tightness of the string before moving to the arrows. Inspecting each one, she finds them in one piece, smiling to herself in relief.

"What now?" she asks Castor, looking over the satchel and its contents.

Sirien waits for his reply, only to receive a low groan instead. Looking up, she sees his face, pale, brows raised, and lips parted. His hand clutches his ribs as he falls to his knees before landing on his side. An arrow protrudes from his back, just below the rib cage. Without hesitation, Sirien takes her bow and an arrow, searching the woods for any sign of movement. A glint of light catches her line of sight as it moves across rays sneaking into the crowded woodland. Drawing, she finds her targeted area, releasing it blindly, hoping by luck it strikes her enemy.

She leans by Castor, checking the location of the wound, then takes his sword, stalking away into the dense trees. Searching, she finds signs of life and a trail of bright red droplets over leaves and rocks. Following it, she tracks her prey until she has him in her sights. A soldier, dragging a leg, makes his way to a horse, tethered to a fallen tree. Sirien draws her bow again, sending another arrow in his direction, meeting his shoulder and dropping him to the ground.

He groans with the pain, pushing himself up, attempting to crawl the final distance. Charging him, Sirien stiffens the blade at her side. Grabbing the arrow in his shoulder, she rips it away, causing blood to gush down his back. With a shake, he falls, rolling onto his back to search her face. His eyes widen to see her, standing over him with a face of stone and eyes black with rage. Reaching down, she takes him by the front of his tunic, wrenching him up to his knees. A tear escapes the corner of his eye as she draws the sword above her, bringing it down across his neck.

Sirien's heart pounds as she listens to him gurgle, watching as the blood seeps from his throat, slowing from a harsh gush to a tender trickle. Satisfied, Sirien leaves him, taking the now riderless horse, winding back over the unmarked path to Castor, where she hopes to find him still alive.

EIGHT

———

"There are only three of them, Ascher! We can end this here and now!" Amalie yells over the roaring wind in their faces, horses gliding over the stony ground, muscles protruding across their shoulders and necks.

"No! We can't risk anything. Keep pushing forward!" Ascher calls back, focused on the terrain ahead.

Amalie growls at his answer, following his command. Sloping upward, the horses slow slightly against gravity's pull, just enough for the soldiers behind to gain ground. Frustrated, Amalie takes action, turning away from Ascher's guidance and back down to the river. Yelling after her, Ascher changes course, whipping his horse to give him all its power. Next to the river, Amalie dismounts, drawing her sword and a dagger from her saddle.

"What are you thinking?" Ascher throws himself from his saddle, drawing his weapon as well.

The soldiers fly like speeding bullets at them, swords drawn and waving in the air. Amalie throws a dagger, thrusting it from her extended arm into the closest soldier's gut. Dropping his sword, he grips at his waist, riding aimlessly past them. Ascher leaps forward as the next rider comes into reach, slicking his blade across the large muscle of the horse's leg. It squeals, dropping its shoulder, heaving the soldier from his back. The third rider comes close behind him, and before either Amalie or Ascher can react, he barrels into Ascher, trampling over him, and heads for Amalie.

Enraged, Amalie throws another dagger from her saddlebag, skinning the man's arm before diving out of his way. Rolling across the forest floor, she regains her footing, looking at Ascher lying on the ground before turning back to the soldiers. The man on the ground brushes away the dirt before charging her, blade drawn. Their swords meet as they spar back and forth, the third rider returning to help finish the job.

With all her force, Amalie slashes at the guard's sword pushing him back enough for a short reprieve. Slipping an arm behind her back, she yanks the dagger from her belt, sending it through the air at the unsuspecting guard riding toward Ascher's limp body. By chance, it hits him in the neck, leaving the single man before her to fight.

Stepping forward, Amalie blocks his swing, carving the air. Hurdling to the side, she avoids his jab. They move in coordinated steps in a circle around one another, sword clashes ringing through the air. Losing sight of everything except for the man before her, she forgets about Ascher until he appears suddenly opposite her, injecting himself into the fight. Taken by surprise, the man takes a slash across the shoulder by Ascher as Amalie disarms him. Looking at both faces for a second, he runs, escaping his near death.

"Let him go," Ascher grunts, pushing himself up from the ground as Amalie tries to pursue the injured soldier.

"What if he reaches his company? He knows our faces and where we are going!" She hesitates, tossing between pursuit and duty.

"I know." He looks out to the man running away, barely visible in the trees. "I know where we can go for a few days. If they come back looking, we won't be here, and they will leave empty-handed." He meets her eyes as he stands, face contorted with pain.

Amalie stamps her foot as she replaces her weapons into safety. Hustling to Ascher, she takes one arm over her shoulders, helping him to his unsettled gelding.

"Where could we possibly go so they won't find us?" Amalie stands confused, watching his expression.

"I have a relative nearby. She lives in a village called Dune just off the coast. It is not well known or a desired place," he says, slumping slightly in his saddle.

Amalie follows him hesitantly, knowing he is hiding something from her, yet she chooses to let it go for now. Taking the horses by the reins, Ascher begins walking them to the river, allowing a few more moments of rest. Clicking his teeth together in thought, he watches the river ripple and foam over and around stones, smoothing their surfaces. He cringes at the thought of his grandmother and what she will say to find her son dead and grandson at her door asking for help. But even worse is the thought of Brien and the threat he had made in his home the day they fled Aldhorran.

He will kill me.

* * *

The light begins to fade as Ascher and Amalie look out over the village of Dune from the mountainside. Torches glow, illuminating the perimeter of the high walls built around the people it secures. The ocean sits rosy in response to the sky above far in the distance. Ascher takes the slight slope in stride, Amalie trailing behind him until they reach the flat ground and walk their horses steadily side by side. Ascher sits rigidly, looking ahead and silent.

"What is it you haven't told me, Ascher?" Amalie inquires.

"Dune is a village of Romathan settlers. They came here during the war that split Eporiae in two."

Amalie pulls on the reins coming to a stop. She stares at Ascher, turning to look at her.

"Romathans?" Amalie asks, shocked.

"I told you, they aren't well known to be here or bothered. They will know me, so you have nothing to fear," he states, turning forward again and nudging his horse onward. Amalie follows behind in a trot, pulling up into his side.

"How will they know you? You have always been in Aldhorran." Confusion fills her mind, and she searches her memories for his absence from something other than injuries.

"Just trust me, Amalie. I will explain once we are in the gates and secured."

Before she can speak again, a voice rings out through the dark.

"Who goes there?"

They stop, watching as a man appears enough for them to make out a figure on horseback. His wild eyes cut the darkness as he grows closer, causing chills to sliver up Amalie's spine with unease. She watches Ascher and the man closely, looking at one another while waiting for someone to speak.

"I am Ascher Tamlik, son of Daventh Tamlik, who is the only son of Elra Tamlik. I have come to see your Chieftess," Ascher speaks with authority.

"I know the name, but not your face. Your intentions and honesty are unknown to me," he answers gruffly, swinging the horse around to leave.

"Stau Haulo I'm Sempt." The rider stops immediately, turning in his saddle at Ascher's words. "Ado Naie." Ascher nods, and the other rider repeats the phrase back.

The man motions them to follow. Amalie watches as Ascher falls in step behind the man and wonders what they had said to each other. She knew Eporiae once shared an ancient language, but it was lost long ago, or so she thought.

The walls surrounding the village of Dune grow with every step closer they take, and she can see it's made of large, round trees, stripped of their bark and runes carved into the weathered wood. The symbols are unrecognizable to Amalie, but to Ascher, they stand out familiar and daunting.

The large wooden gates creak behind them as it closes, ending in a loud thud. Inside, the streets sit abandoned, seams of windows and doors shine from the light within, housing their occupants from the cold air. A large stable sits nestled against the inner stretch of the wall, noisy with the restlessness of animals inside. Appearing in the doorway, another man steps out.

"Yrin." He nods to the man leading Amalie and Ascher in.

"We have visitors. The Tamlik have come home. Care for their horses."

The man's eyes are light, looking them over before eagerly taking the reins from them. Hopping down, Yrin, Ascher, and Amalie step away from the beasts and continue on, walking deeper into the village. Torches blaze along the path as silence crowds in around them. Amalie looks around her cautiously at the gloomy surroundings.

The homes are built of wood, quite unlike those of Aldhorran, which are built of stone. Weaving through the rutted dirt roads, they finally come to a stop before a large wooden home, golden light glowing from the foot of the door. Yrin nods to Ascher, swiftly turning away and leaving.

"Whatever happens, Amalie, you must let me handle it. I know these people." His look is cross, voice concerning.

Could we be in danger here?

Amalie's mind swirls with worry and questions. Knocking sharply on the door, Ascher stands, his back straight and feet planted solidly before it. A loud click from the other side stands in the air as the door opens slightly, sending rays of light into the street as a young woman's face appears.

"The Chieftess wishes not to be disturbed this evening." She snaps the door shut, and the light disappears.

Shaking his head, Ascher steps forward, this time pounding on the door. Moments pass before it opens a second time, but rather than the girl, a woman flies out, gray braids bouncing down her back, small in stature and aged yet spry. She barrels into Ascher, forcing him against the wall of a neighboring home, a long-bladed knife pushed up against his throat.

"Who are you to demand of my presence in this hour?" she hisses in his face.

"Hello, Grandmother," Ascher chuckles.

Her eyes close to slits, looking him over before stepping away and lowering the weapon.

"Ascher?" Confusion crosses her voice for a moment.

Her eyes drop to Ascher's chest, and in one swift motion, he loosens the ties shoving it, so a mark is seen over his chest. Pursing her lips, she turns silently into the house, leaving the door wide open behind her. Running a hand over his throat, Ascher wipes away the feeling of iron against his skin. With a toss of his head, Amalie follows him as he crosses the threshold into warmer air. The room is small in width but long, a table sitting empty in the shadows to the right while a few chairs sit before the raging fire to the left. A stairway disappears behind the stone hearth, unfolding into the unknown.

"Who do I owe the honor to for your presence in my home, dear child?" Elra says, sitting in the chair closest to the fire. The arms and back are covered in various pelts and woven blankets.

"The King and his men."

She freezes, curious of his meaning.

"What have you done?" She looks at Ascher, noticing Amalie for the first time, pondering her appearance in Elra's home.

"We are running from the guard. It is quite a thrilling chase for them, I am sure, but now we need sanctuary. For only a short time," Ascher says, moving toward Elra, finding the seat across from her.

"Again, I ask, what have you done?" Elra glares at Ascher.

"Amalie and her family descend from the Nasinreth. Her eldest sister is a visionary, and her younger is a healer. Davina, the healer, was seen and reported. To save her and each other, we fled." He motions to Amalie, watching Elra's expression change from irritation to amusement.

"Have you condemned your father by leaving, or will the guard pass him by?" Amalie's gaze flashes from Elra to Ascher and back to Elra, skin crawling with nerves.

"He's dead. Every person, including the guard, will assume I killed him. I had planned to leave quietly and unnoticed, but oh well. Here I am." He shrugs coolly.

Elra stiffens at the revelation, hands clenched on the arms of the chair. Her eyes gouge Ascher's face, searching for any sign of dishonesty or evil. Instead, she sees the scars spread over the side of his face, wondering how many are hidden across his body and how he had survived her son.

"Adyra!" Elra calls out to the darkness behind Amalie, where the young woman appears through a doorway. "Prepare the room upstairs immediately. We have guests, and please take her with you." She points to Amalie, brows raised, shooing her away.

Adyra moves quickly, gripping Amalie below the shoulders to guide her away up the dark, narrow stairway. The hall above is dimly lit by candles dispersed along the walls. Three doors line the hall, and she follows Adyra to the second one. Taking the candle down by the doorway, Adyra walks into the room and goes directly to the empty hearth. Setting the candle beside her on the ground, she pulls sticks of wood from a large barrel, stacking them carefully.

The small room is chilly, a draft floating in from the window across the room from the large bed budded up against the wall. A large trunk sits at its foot, embellished in elaborate carvings and silver clasps. Light unfolds up the walls and over items in the room as the fire comes to life, gently radiating heat. Adyra moves to the trunk, retrieving woven blankets and pelts from its depths to place over the bed.

Nodding with a grin, she leaves Amalie alone in the quiet.

NINE

———

The sight of Sirien, Castor, Ascher, and Amalie flying across the wide-open space to draw the soldier's attention away from Brien and her festered in her mind as guilt ground deeper into her soul. Davina tosses and turns on the cabin floor, absorbing the heat from the fire into her chilled bones. Davina and Brien sat watching as Sirien flew from her horse, helpless to any of them below, and once the area cleared, the two took to the north, traveling the entire day concealed in the forest.

Stumbling across an abandoned cabin, Brien took immediately to securing the little run down home, building a fire, and releasing the horses into the weathered paddock behind a fallen outbuilding. Now he slept, leaving Davina alone to her thoughts. Clouds cover the wide sky, blocking the moon and stars from view, holding the cold tightly enclosed on the world's surface. Her mind turns, bringing Amalie and Sirien's faces to the surface, recounting every detail from memory.

The log in the fire crackles, throwing sparks into the air. Closing her eyes, Davina brings a hand to her face, feeling every crook, bump, and smooth section of her features.

Translating her touch, she conjures an image older than herself and slightly different. Her mother and her share the same striking features from jaw to crown. They could be identical if she still lived. The face smiles at her, and a warmth comes over her as if her mother stood before her, embracing her tightly.

The fire spits again, crackling and fizzing ravenously. The brittle walls surrounding them sway, moaning against the wind, and the leaves rustle with the movement of feet outside. Davina jolts, sitting up and looking around her feverishly. Leaning to Brien, she shakes him awake. Her finger pressed over pursed lips. Brien crawls gently to the nearest window, peering out the cracks a moment before returning to Davina. Gripping her around the shoulders, he pulls her in close to him and rests his cheek against hers.

"You need to run. Don't stop. You were born for greatness. Now go," he whispers to her.

Brien clutches her sword in his hand, shoving them into her chest. He stands, pulling her up from the ground, and propels her to the window furthest from the door. She whirls around, tears in her eyes, clawing at his arms.

"I can't," she squeaks.

"You can, and you must. Our God has a future for you. Your mother knew that." He clutches her face in his hands, wiping away the tears. "My child, you have been the light in my life. I can't bear to watch it go out." He kisses her forehead, then, stepping away, mutters the word "go" again.

Before she can stop him, he turns, throwing himself through the door into the night. She hoists herself through the window and runs, leaving the yells of fighting behind her. Her skirt snags, shredding the hem, but she doesn't stop. The fighting has quieted, but the rustle behind Davina tells her she is being pursued, and though her lungs burn and shoulders ache from clenching her weapon in one fist tightly, she continues fleeing.

Stubbing her foot on a root, Davina heaves herself up out of the dense earth as twigs, and thorny bushes scrape at her body. Pain shoots through her body, but she doesn't stop. Forcing herself to her feet, Davina lunges forward, thoughts of her father driving her forward. Ahead, she sets her sights on the grandfather of all trees with a trunk as wide as she is tall. Diving around it, Davina hits head-on with a figure on the other side, then bouncing back from the impact. She falls, catching herself on her elbows and losing hold of her sword.

The soldier, clad in chain armor and a thick leather tunic plate, stands over her, laughing. His eyes skirt the woods around them before reaching for her. Snagging her ankle with a monstrous hand, he drags her closer, ruffling her skirt up to her hips. He looks at her hungrily. Davina claws at the earth, rolling away in an attempt to escape. He grips her around the waist, wrenching her from the ground and knocking the wind from her as he slams her against the tree. Gasping for air, she watches as he fumbles with his belt and clasps.

"Baldur!" The harsh yell rings across the forest, bouncing from tree to tree.

A dim light seeps through the treetops, glittering down on the tangled floor of branches, foliage, and root systems. A horse and rider appear, glaring down at the man he called Baldur.

"Commander." Baldur's voice is gruff as he reclasps his belt.

"Rejoin the others." The commander slips from the back of his horse, height identical to Baldur.

Baldur snarls, looking at Davina angrily before storming away. The commander watches him go, and Davina searches quietly for her sword. Catching a glint from the rising sun on the blade peaking from the hilt, she finds a sliver of hope. But before she can dive for it, the Commander sees her gaze and follows it to the weapon, retrieving it immediately.

"I will not hurt you, but I cannot allow you to injure any of my men." He turns to his horse, attaching the sword to the saddle.

Pulling a water pouch from the horse's side, he hands it to her gently. She takes it, gulping down the fresh spring water no more than a day old. Once finished, Davina hands it back, and he drinks from it as well before placing it back in its spot.

"Now, if you would please." He holds a hand out, inviting Davina forward.

She hesitates a moment, thinking over the idea of surrender versus fighting. She takes his hand, drawn to surrender under his safety, and he helps her up into the saddle before sliding behind, setting off back through the forest to the East.

* * *

Amalie groans as she stretches under the warmth of the thick wool blanket. The room is stuffy, with heat radiating from both the fire and sunlight pounding in the window. She rolls her head to the side, looking to the floor across the room where a pile of blankets and pelt lay in a heaped mess.

Had Ascher slipped away in the early hours, or maybe he never slept?

The thought crosses her mind, and she wonders what had been discussed late into the night with Elra. He arrived at the room late, wordless, only to nestle himself in the spot on the floor, leaving her the bed to rest. Slipping from the comfort of the bed, she hops to the hearthstones, finding its stinging warmth satisfactory. The fire crackles and embers twinkle in reds and oranges as little blue flames flicker almost unseen. In the daylight, the room is larger than she realized the night before, and she marvels at the skulls hung along the walls and pelts draped over furniture or spread over the floor.

Beams cross above the ceiling, holding the roof securely in place with wood stacked upon one another, sitting tightly and leaving no space between them. The only window sits large, pelts folded back to allow light and air into the room. A chest sits under it. Its battered display shows the age and adventures it has gone through its lifetime.

Taking in every inch of the space, Amalie's eyes finally rest on the similar trunk before her at the end of the bed. Clothing lays folded and draped over its face, and she moves to inspect it—two plain dresses, one covering the other and a shift over them both. Slipping the shift, then the deep brown dress over her head, she laces it up the front then turns to her hair. Untangling it from the leather tie she had placed the day before, her hair falls in waves of rich dark curls over her shoulders.

Feeling presentable, Amalie makes her way from the room to search for Ascher, and as she descends the stairs, she instantly recognizes his agitated voice and stops in her tracks.

"I will not! I swore to her father I would never bring her anywhere near my people and now this? He will kill me!" Ascher's whisper is an angry hiss.

"You have faced death your entire life. Why would this concern you?" Elra comments back, annoyed.

"That was different. I had no choice," he claims through gritted teeth.

"It is your birthright, Ascher. Daventh refused, and now it lays on your shoulders."

"No." He cuts her off fiercely.

Silence falls between them. Amalie slips carefully up a few steps before coming down, stomping over the final few. Upon her entrance, she sees Ascher, arms folded over his chest, staring intensely at Elra, who looks in the direction of the stairs with hands clenched over the back of the chair before her. The tension is like shackles in the room. Turning her gaze back to Ascher, she raises her brows.

"You will not leave here without committing to the oath." Pushing herself from the chair's back, she stalks to the door, swinging her cloak over her shoulders and heading out into the brisk morning air.

Amalie looks at Ascher bewildered. Like an enraged bear, he reaches out, slamming his fist across the small table near one of the armchairs. Candles, a mug, and books sail across the room, crashing against the wall. Adyra, the keeper of the house, rushes in, seeing the disorder.

She sighs, looking at Ascher then to Amalie.

"My apologies." Ascher storms out of the house, leaving the women and disaster behind him.

Shaken, Amalie moves to the broken and battered items, fixing the disarray. Adyra walks past her then falls to her side, thin fingers stopping her reaching hands. Looking up, Amalie meets her eyes, a beautiful golden honey-colored, paired with rich auburn hair braided back. She sees a cloak in Adyra's fist, stretched out before her. Taking it, she understands the action and wrapping it over her shoulders as she leaves the house.

The cold air hits, heightening her senses to the world around her. The streets flow with people talking and laughing among themselves. Carts roll in the ruts down the muddy street, and children laugh and scream as mothers shoo them away. She finds her way through the town until she comes to the destination she seeks. The wall surrounding the city and its people sits tall and strong, with men and women standing guard and conversing with passersby at ease.

Coming to the steps built, climbing the inner side, Amalie moves her way up to the top of it, peering out over the edge at the expanse of land around her. The mountains to her north and west sit immaculately veiled in fog. The sea rolls to her south against the island of Solost, far off in the distance, and as she faces east, she sees open land.

How far we've come, she thinks, walking the top of the wall until she reaches the bend facing north to the forest *and how much farther we must go.*

TEN

Sirien sits beside Castor, his cold, stiff hand resting in hers. Her eyes sting, red and dry, and are unable to shed further tears, her dirty face streaked with rivers from the last of them. She can't bring herself to move or leave him, even though all that remains is flesh. His soul will be making its way to the Everworld, where their God will welcome his faithful servant. Yet, even in this idea, she can't help but feel lost and hopeless, accepting her joy as all but dead as well.

The sun, now high in the sky, pushes her thoughts ahead. Sirien knows she must continue on, so she lets go, Castor's arm falling heavily against the stone of the cave. Gasping for air, she jolts to her feet and runs to the mouth of the cave, heaving into a bush on its edge. She wipes her mouth with the back of her hand and falls to the ground, leaning her head back against stone. Closing her eyes, she imagines her family together, happy and free.

He needs a proper ceremony.

Sirien forces herself up, setting her sights to the forest, hunting its nearest depths for anything that will burn—pile after pile, Sirien travels to and from the cave, surrounding Castor's body with wood, leaves, bark, and dried grass. With the firestone in hand, she constantly strikes until a spark catches, filling the hole in the rock with smoke. Retreating into the fresh air, Sirien turns and watches the darkness come alive with fire.

* * *

"I am not!" Amalie chases after Ascher up the narrow stairs to the upper level of the house.

"Yes, you are, Amalie. Elra's only interest is in me. She will let you go." He shoves through the door of their quarters and heads directly to the trunk.

"I couldn't care less what she wants. I am not leaving you." Amalie slams the door behind her.

"Do not argue with me. If Brien comes looking and finds you here, I am as good as dead." He spits the words at her in agitation. "I'd rather take my chances with her than him."

"I am not leaving." Amalie's voice is dangerously low like the growl of an angry mountain lion.

Chills run down Ascher's spine. He stands with teeth clenched and looks at her. Amalie's face is windswept, with rosy cheeks and nose, her dark hair falling loose from her braid in long waves. Catching his breath, he shakes his head, turning back to the trunk, pulling the necessary supplies out for her journey. Angrily, she stomps to him, hitting items from his hands and flinging everything else through the air to hit the floor with a crash. He jolts upright, towering over her. Searching Amalie's face, he sees nothing but her stubborn nature relentless against his own.

"You can't stay. You don't understand," Ascher whispers anxiously.

"I won't leave regardless. That's something you should know," she replies adamantly.

Ascher huffs, stepping away from her. Searching for anything to take his attention, he finds the fire beginning to smolder in a heap of coals. Amalie watches, arms crossed over her chest, confused by his sudden change. She watches as he stokes the hot coals before laying another log over the simmering bed. Her mind turns to the conversation she overheard earlier, recalling the mention of an oath he needed to take.

"What is the oath?" she asks without hesitation.

He stiffens at the question, pausing for a moment before turning to her, glaring.

"How much did you hear?"

"Enough to know we are in a bind," Amalie shrugs.

Ascher sighs harshly. Standing, he presses his palms against the warm stones above the fireplace.

"Elra follows the old laws and traditions. One in particular." Ascher's face scrunches as he clenches his jaw, debating whether to continue or not. "She will not allow us to leave here together unless we marry."

Amalie stifles a giggle with a sigh of relief.

"We are already betrothed. What can a marriage here harm?" Amalie says, attempting to keep her amusement from her voice.

"It is not a simple ceremony Amalie." He pushes away from the stones, stepping close to her and taking her by the wrists. "It is binding, an oath of a life to another's, an unbreakable contract. If I die, so do you. If not by your own hand, by another Romathan's, leaving everything and everyone behind."

He releases her, gritting his teeth and walking back to the stones of the hearth. Amalie stares at him, taken aback. She knew the clans of Romathe were harsh, but she didn't expect this. The idea of binding her own life to his is terrifying yet invigorating. Amalie steps forward, running her hands over his arm and shoulder, drawing Ascher to her.

"I would have it no other way. My life is already bound to yours," Amalie speaks gently and genuinely.

Looking into the fire, Ascher leans his head to the side, resting it on Amalie's forehead. Together they stand, arms linked before the fire for some time. Their breathing becomes harmonious, standing like statues. A light tapping at the door startles them, shoving away from each other just before Adyra opens the door.

"I'm sorry to disturb you. Elra wishes to speak with you." She nods to Ascher.

Ascher replies with his own nod excusing Adyra from their presence. Once the door shuts behind her, Ascher reaches for Amalie, pulling her into him. He kisses her briefly before releasing her from his grasp and leaves. The door closes with a light thud behind him. Amalie stands in the middle of the empty space, breathless and stunned.

* * *

Davina stares out of the window at the cobbled street, watching the soldiers come and go from the tavern below. Rheyhas paid for the small quarters, placing a guard outside the door with strict orders not to let her out of sight. The tavern keeper's wife and Rheyhas are the only people allowed to enter, and neither had visited since the morning. Three soldiers sit alongside each other, perched against the side of a wooden building, laughing and drinking. Davina watches curiously as the men startle. They jump to their feet, spilling their steins over one another as Rheyhas appears in her line of sight through the window. She watches, giggling at the clumsiness of them until she sees Rheyhas hand, one man, a letter.

Davina's heart sinks with the thought of the dispatch reaching the King's hands. Her head falls back against the frame of the window, wishing she had run faster or fought harder for her father's sake. A tear slips from the corner of her eye as his face flashes through her mind. Shaking her head, she straightens up, hardening her resolve to continue her focus on escaping. Rheyhas' men surrounded the tavern and Warridian. The city sits too close to the border to not be on guard.

If I could escape, I would have a clear shot.

She considers every option, including begging Abala, the tavern owner's wife, to help her.

But if she were to be loyal to the Crown. No, too risky.

Thoughts racing, she stands and paces the quaint and plain chamber. A bed in the corner and a small table with a single chair sat in the center. Dust covers every surface, and the floorboards creak with every step. She concentrates on her return to freedom, keeping her mind busy, ignoring her father's sacrifice. Brien crosses her mind again, and she begins to tremble but gulps, forcing herself to hold her composure.

I could fight the guard outside without a problem, but getting past the others would be too risky. I could go out the window and travel across the rooftops, but it had to be at night.

Her mind springs from escape as a commotion rises outside. Rushing to the window, she sees a man, clad in the Royal Guard armor, stumbling, supported by another guard frantically calling out for a healer. Davina's fingers throb at the sight of pain, seeing the blood crusted over the man's tunic.

Rheyhas appears again, gripping the man's face in his hands. Voices thunder around him as they watch the exchange. Unable to hear their words, she unclasps the hook of the window, shoving it open wide. Peeking out over the edge, she listens, straining to hear the two small voices in the crowd.

"The others, they, they're dead." The injured soldier breathes heavily, choking on the words. "She killed them," he sputtered before falling limp.

"Alfuir!" Rheyhas yells, pointing in the direction of the men he had interrupted earlier.

Alfuir runs to Rheyhas. The crowd around him quickly dissipates as they help carry away the wounded soldier. Alfuir nods to Rheyhas, standing before him tall and ready to take orders.

"Take two men and head back to the forest. There are two in the southern section. Stay away from the coast. We do not need a fight," Rheyhas speaks quickly, sending Alfuir away, then disappears once again into the tavern below.

So they met the wrath of my sister. Davina smiles to herself, glad to hear Amalie and Ascher are safely away.

Footsteps outside her door jolt her to awareness and she closes the window quickly, jumping to her feet just as Rheyhas enters.

"I have sent a rider back to the King informing him of your capture. He will decide where you will be taken. How many others traveled with you?" Rheyhas' stern eyes meet her gaze, sending chills down her spine.

"My father and I were alone. There was no one else," Davina replies without hesitation.

"Lies!" Rheyhas slams a fist down on the small table.

Davina jumps at the loud crack it makes under the force of his fist.

"I have two men dead by a woman's hand. Who was it?"

Davina stares, trying to think of anything to tell him other than the truth. When she says nothing, though, Rheyhas growls, turning his back to her and leaving in a fury.

With a sigh of relief, Davina glides to the bed, collapsing into it. Forcing her father from her mind again, this time, she turns to a new face, one she never thought she would be so happy to think about. Amalie drifts across her mind's space, thankful to hear of her sister's safety.

ELEVEN

Boots click rapidly across the newly glossed floor as a soldier makes his way down the corridor. He passes by Americ sitting in the window across from the portrait of his mother. Seeing the soldiers haste, Americ springs to his feet, chasing after him. Together, they walk into the throne room in search of the King. The soldier's eyes fall on him in the far corner of the large room, speaking with his advisor. Americ walks past the soldier as he stamps firmly into the ground, waiting to be acknowledged.

"Has Rheyhas sent word of his efforts, or have you brought me something with more importance?" Agnai's voice grumbles through the air to the soldier.

"Your Majesty, we have captured the Nasinreth we pursued," the soldier replies, eyes focused ahead of him.

Agnai's head shoots up, looking in his direction. Seeing his son, he commands Americ to bring the dispatch to him. The room falls silent as Agnai reads the correspondence carefully. His face lights with the information, thrilled by the chase and capture of his newest game. Americ stands, hands folded behind him, the overwhelming curiosity building as he waits.

"Tell Rheyhas to transfer to Balaoug and remain there. The rest of the company may return here. I will be sending my son to Balaoug as the interrogator. No one is to touch or harm this one until he has completed his task." Agnai speaks quickly and without hesitation, glancing briefly at Americ's pale face. Dismissing the soldier, Agnai returns his attention to his advisor.

"Father." Americ's voice is barely a whisper.

Agnai stops, drawing his attention to Americ.

"You will go. Castah is to be married in three days' time. You will leave the next day. By the time you reach Balaoug, so will they, and you will take care of this." Agnai says harshly, turning back to his advisor, and they begin to walk away.

"I don't understand," Americ says loudly. "The other day, you were angry they were sent out, but today, you want to send me to interrogate a prisoner holding valuable information? Why?" His voice quivers with anger, remembering the threat his father had made.

"Because you will be King someday, and with that, you have hard decisions to make. Bring me the information I need to know. Show me you are ready for the undertaking. Being King is not for the faint of heart, and I expect you to drive the information from this traitor, no matter the cost. Only then will I know you have what it takes." Agnai whirls around, shoving his index finger into Americ's chest.

"So a king can only rule with blood on his hands? You think me weak? Why do you hate me?" Americ yells with all the anger built up over the years, finally pouring out.

"You are nothing until you prove yourself!" Agnai's voice thunders as he grips the front of Americ's tunic, pulling him so close his father's breath hits him in the face like a stone. "Your sister Charlotte put you up to this, and you accepted it without a thought. A king must make his own commands, not listen to a whiny, sniveling partner. Women are not made to rule. You strike them down until they are silent." Shoving Americ away with great force, Agnai rolls his shoulders, fixing his own clothing before walking away, the advisor close behind.

So that is what Charlotte had told him. The captain asked me for guidance, and I turned to Charlotte instead of being a man.

Americ watches him march away, leaving him alone in the large room. Anger courses through his veins, and he breathes deeply, taking his own heavy steps out of the room in the opposite direction. Ignoring the servant's stares as he passes, Americ dives down the corridor, headed for the courtyard, but before he can escape, he sees her.

Charlotte's blonde hair streaks through the shadows toward the barracks. Her dress flows around her as if she floats. Without another thought, Americ follows her, intent on setting her in her place once and for all. His step is silent compared to her heels, clicking fervently over the stones. Doors line the dark corridor leading into the rooms that house the guard. A man's head peaks out at her, smiling and commenting in an attempt to grab her notice. She stops, speaking in a small voice to him, folds of her dress clenched in her fist at her chest. Obvious disappointment spreads across his face as he shakes his head, ducking back in when he sees Americ lurking in the distance.

"Charlotte, you conniving little vixen!" Americ calls, darting after her.

Americ takes Charlotte's arm as she spins on her heels, facing him, a look of shock spread over her face. Charlotte can feel his anger in the piercing of his strong fingers. She whimpers in pain as he drags her back up the hallway.

"Do you know what the King has done because of you?

Because you sent Rheyhas and the others out?" Americ forces Charlotte ahead of him.

She stumbles, falling into the wall to her left. The grip on her dress loosens, and one shoulder of it slithers down her arm. Americ sees the bruises crawling brightly over her fair skin. Americ reaches for her hair, moving it aside to inspect her neck and back further. The bruises, deep and rich in color spread up her neck and down her back.

"Charlotte." Americ's voice is soft and full of shame. Jerking away, Charlotte pulls the dress tightly around her, concealing the marks. "Who did this?"

"What does it matter?" She peers over her shoulder at him, her face like stone.

"It matters to *me*. No man should treat you in this way." Americ's heart sinks as he thinks over what he had just done.

"It matters to no one. Especially not you. Leave me Americ. You will only make things worse." Charlotte chokes back the tears forming, gulping down her emotions.

"Charlotte, I..."

"No." Charlotte silences him. "I know father is sending you away. It is for the better. Perhaps you should leave now and never look back." Glancing around, she walks away, ignoring Americ's calling after her until she is out of sight.

* * *

Mulling over Charlotte's words, Americ wanders the castle until he finds himself stumbling before Castah's chamber doors. Considering the idea one last time, he knocks, waiting for one of her lady's maids to answer. To his surprise, it is Castah's bright, cheery face who answers him, immediately welcoming him inside.

Ladies sit strewn around the room, laughing and drinking. At the sight of Americ, they all sit up, acting proper as taught to be around any man. Castah smiles at them, leading her brother through a pair of doors that separate two rooms. Closing the doors behind her, she turns to Americ, embracing him childishly.

"Oh brother, how I have missed you." She smiles widely, looking him over as if they have been apart for years rather than days.

"As have I." Americ smiles weakly in response.

"What has happened?" Castah asks, surveying his face.

"Charlotte has been beaten, and she refuses to tell me by whom," Americ says, regret from his actions still stinging in his chest.

"You know there is nothing that can be done. Americ, you must leave this alone. Remember what happened the last time you stepped in?" Castah speaks with sadness.

"It is a day I will never forget, Castah. Nor will she." Americ swings his body away from her, swaying as he walks to the oversized window, filling the room with bright, natural light.

"Father is sending me away to Balaoug. Rheyhas and his men have captured one of the Nasinreth runners, and I am in charge of his interrogation. I will ask for his blessing to leave tomorrow." Americ faces her again.

Unsettled, Castah moves to the nearest chair, plopping down into it.

"I agree. Father will find this pleasing, Tialen!" she yells behind herself at the door, startling Americ.

The door swings open, and a woman comes rushing in, bowing low before them.

"Find Joanquil and bring her to me immediately. Also, send word to my father Americ, Prince of Omideon, wishes to speak with his Majesty in the Council Chamber. Immediately." Castah sends away her lady, then, turning to Americ, smiles.

Shaking his head, Americ crosses the room to her, bending to kiss her on the forehead. "Thank you," he whispers. "Farewell, dear sister. May we meet again someday."

Rising to his full height, Americ walks from the room, refusing to look back at his sister, the one who took the place of his mother and his final ally.

* * *

Americ studies the massive room, overflowing with scrolls and books over one wall, while maps of the Kingdom lay sprawled across tables. A wooden throne stands at the front of the room before a long table, encompassed by twenty council member seats. He walks to the broad chair, eyes fixed on the detailed carvings, fingers tracing each slash and curl.

"Perhaps one day, it will be yours."

Startled, Americ looks anxiously around for his father, finding him in the doorway, looking cross.

"I would like approval to leave for Balaoug at dawn. I know it is customary for the Crown Prince to be present in royal ceremonies, but your rule and this kingdom has far more importance to me than witnessing Castah's marriage," Americ speaks quickly.

Entering the room, Agnai slowly begins circling the table, touching the back of every chair. He speaks after a moment, his voice cool and calm.

"Fear is a powerful force that can drive any person into a senseless nature." Agnai slips past Americ, sitting upon his throne. "You may have use to me yet. Bring me the information I seek, Americ. Do not fail me." Americ bows, turning away from Agnai to leave. "And Americ."

Americ stops, cringing.

"As your sister has learned, fear doesn't stand alone. Pain is its greatest conductor."

Americ nearly runs from the room at his father's words. He recalls the marks and bruises on Charlotte and feels sick at the thought of his father placing them there. He weaves through the people in the corridor and down flights of stairs until he reaches his chambers. Joanquil, steadily at work, greets him and with delight, he enters, relaxed in her presence.

TWELVE

—

"Our women fight," Mungar says, leading the way down the path, away from the settlement.

Amalie glances at Ascher, walking closely beside her. His lips form an obnoxious smile, keeping his eyes forward, focused on Mungar's head. The sea glimmers ahead in the distance, waves riddle its surface, giving it a life of its own. Dropping into lower ground, the three of them walk into a flat area. Wooden pallets stand, encircling the tight area, and a large trunk sits in the center.

"A sword and shield are common among our people. However, a few of our women prefer the bow or ax. You may take your pick among these." Mungar bends, cracking away the lid from the trunk, setting it aside, and stepping away with a few items in tow, giving Amalie and Ascher a wide berth.

Amalie inspects the treasures inside, running her fingers over blades and hilts. Pulling from the plethora of weaponry, she takes a sword, daggers, and an ax. Mungar watches with amusement at her choices, unaware of her true skill. Ascher finds an ax as well as a sword, walking from the box to where Mungar stands.

"Now, I see you have a few dirks and an ax. The ax you can use much like a sword, but the dirks are only for use if you are dangerously close to the enemy. They are a final defense…" Mungar stutters before stopping his lecture.

Amalie flings each dagger seamlessly from the tips of her fingers. Rolling through the air, one after the other, they find their marks near the center of the distant pallet. The hiss of steel behind her sends a current of energy through her body. She rolls away as a sword comes down over where she stood. Looking, she finds Ascher wielding it and smiles, reaching for her own sword. She stands ready. He dives at her, and she meets his blade. Flickering around each other, they spar.

Focused on themselves, neither take notice of Mungar, allowing him to retrieve his own sword and charge Ascher. From the corner of her eye, Amalie sees him. Squatting low, she swings her leg out, hitting Ascher hard in the shin, knocking him to the ground. Pulling her blade up and cutting the air, she smacks Mungar's weapon, slicing down at Ascher. Pushing it to the side, she finds an opening, tackling Mungar to the ground. She rolls over the top of him, finding her footing quickly flying back to him sprawled over the hard earth.

Before he can catch his breath, Amalie straddles his chest, landing a foot over the wrist of his sword hand. Unsheathing the hidden dagger at her back, she pushes it to his throat. Her eyes, black with adrenaline, pierces Mungar's, and for a moment, his heart races with fear. A hand finds her shoulder, and she relaxes, releasing her stance from Mungar's body and moving away from him.

"You could have mentioned she could fight Ascher," Mungar grumbles as he slowly sits, taking Ascher's outstretched hand for help to stand.

"You could have asked," Ascher says, jerking him from the ground.

"We're done here. Elra will be satisfied." Mungar nods, looking at Amalie.

Amalie grins at him. Stooping to retrieve fallen weapons, Mungar tosses them back into the crate with the others. They watch as he replaces the lid and begins climbing up the trail back to Dune. The Sun hangs low over the horizon, illuminating with water in the distance with golds and oranges. Amalie stands still, looking out over it, entranced with its beauty until Ascher calls out, dragging her attention to him. Taking a final glance out into the serene view, she follows them, nervous for the next adventure.

* * *

The grinding of the pestle etches into the background as Amalie sits before Adyra, her long strands of hair intricately woven into thin plaits. Adyra's light touch and gentle strokes are soothing as she pulls each bit tightly into its form. Amalie's hair lays in two braids to the front of her left side, then loose at her back and left shoulder in waves, while the right side is braided around her ear in three tiny trails. One single braid wraps the crown of her head from the left, interweaving with one on her right, trailing strongly down the center of her shoulders.

Another woman appears from behind, placing the mortar full of finely ground charcoal before Amalie, then leaves the room. Pouring a small stream of water from the pitcher on the table, Adyra finishes the process, stirring the mixture with a fine sliver of alder. Taking the blunt strip of wood, she orders Amalie to close her eyes.

Scraping over one lid, Adyra covers it in the black mixture. Dotting along Amalie's eyebrow in three spots, she now moves underneath, placing three more dots along the eye bone. Mimicking this on the other side, she orders her to open and look at her. Covering the lid under her eye, Amalie looks at Adyra and watches the intensity of her face grow with each stroke. Adyra moves to Amalie's forehead, poking the blunt end of the wood against her skin with another three spots and finally ends, slashing down over the center of her full lips, trailed by three pokes over her chin. Nodding with approval, Adyra sets aside the mortar.

"Come." Adyra lays her hands open before Amalie.

Taking Adyra's hands, Amalie stands. Robed only in her shift, Amalie shy's from Adyra's gaze. A rich burgundy dress lays out across the bed, drawing both of their attention. Adyra reaches for it, her skin like snow against its rich color. Bringing it to Amalie, she slips it over her head. The thick warm wood falls loosely around her. Unlike Adyra, the red compliments Amalie's stunning caramel skin tone. Slipping her arms into the sleeves, Amalie begins to fully realize what she is about to do.

Adyra moves behind her, pulling the thin leather string tightly, wrapping the dress snugly around Amalie's curves. Heart racing, Amalie takes deep breaths, focusing on her current position rather than what is waiting outside. She listens to the soft patter of rain on the roof, feels the warmth of the room around her, and thinks of Ascher, putting herself at ease. Moving back into Amalie's vision, Adyra fastens the leather ties of her sleeves to hug her forearms tightly. Looking over Amalie again, Adyra nods in approval.

"Are you ready?"

Amalie replies to her with a silent nod.

Moving from the room to the main one downstairs, they stop before the door, fastening their cloaks tightly around them. Amalie's cloak is new and as black as night with no moon. Adyra pulls the hood up over Amalie's head before heading out into the storm. Together, they walk the empty dreary streets, following the dim light at the end. In the village center sits a large lodge where the people can all gather under one roof. It is lit, glowing ferociously against the shadows, but they don't go there. Instead, Adyra turns away, heading to the large open courtyard before it.

Drums begin to beat steadily, the sound throbs as it resonates in her chest. Around the corner, she sees them, the entirety of the people overflowing the space. Large fires line the walk, creating a dim yet intense light over the sea of dark cloaks. A guttural chant sets the eeriness as her sights fall over a tall, hooded figure before a woman clad in white, face painted white and black, her hair flowing loosely about her. Amalie's heart drops into her stomach as she walks along the path, heat licking her skin painfully.

Eyes peer out at her, blackened with the same dark mixture she had across her own face. Amalie moves until she reaches the front of the group, finding her place next to the other hooded figure. Elra, the woman in white, stands before them soberly, a stone table before her. A copper basin and dagger lay upon it. Raising her hands, she takes Amalie's left arm and places it over the figures, connecting their palms faceup, side by side. Flitting her eyes to the side, Amalie sees his face poking out from the hood and feels peace come over her at Ascher's nearness.

The chanting behind her overtakes all other sounds as she watches as Elra takes the dagger and moves it, gashing across their open hands in a solid connecting line. Moving the basin below, she pushes Amalie's and Ascher's hands together, allowing their fingers to entwine as blood pools beneath their gushing hands. Once satisfied, she tears two strips of cloth from her garment. Tying the bandages around each of their injured hands, they watch as Elra places her fingertips into the bowl. The world falls silent, and a chill climbs Amalie's spine.

"Segitt aii deluai, Grundiha vetil," she says, flicking the blood in Aamalie's face, turning to Ascher, repeating herself.

"Bondun higard," she yells out, lifting the bowl high before her in the direction of the people before tipping it and pouring the contents over her head. Blood streaks down her face, staining the white clothing around her. The crowd hisses simultaneously as Ascher and Amalie turn, releasing their grip from each other and move to the path in the crowd. Hands reach out, tearing the cloaks from their heads and shoulders, leaving them in their rich burgundy clothing. Together, they walk to the lodge in the center of the settlement, followed by a new hum and chant.

* * *

"Will it ever stop?" Amalie asks, listening to the chaos of celebration outside.

"Not until dawn," Ascher chuckles.

Amalie lays in the bed, back huddled up to Ascher, his arms wound tightly around her. She traces the edge of the bandage wrapped over her palm, thoughts slowly moving through her mind. The fire crackles quietly in the hearth, and the room is still around them.

"What did it mean? What Elra spoke during the oath?" Amalie's voice is gentle and curious.

"Segitt aii deluai, Grundiha vetil. Bondun higard. Secured by blood. Grounded as one. Bonded everlasting." Ascher's fingers run up and down her arm as he speaks.

"And what about the other one? You said it to Yrin when we first arrived." Amalie rolls, facing him.

"It is what the Aulik live by. Stau haulo im sempt, ado naie. Steady heart and soul, for honor." Ascher speaks the phrase with a genuine appreciation for the words.

The two fall silent, listening to the world and feeling each of their presence. Amalie thinks of her father and sisters, wondering where they could be now and if they are safe. She imagines how they will react when she sees them next and find her a married woman. She hopes they approve.

Feeling foolish, she presses her ear against Ascher's chest, listening to the beat of his heart, steady and strong. She can see the white ridges across his chest and ribs, remnants of his father laid into his flesh as scars. The largest one sits at Amalie's fingertips below the ribs, still pink in healing. He almost died from this one, and she nearly killed Daventh for it. Tearing her eyes away, she looks to the window and watches as the morning light begins to peek in through the window.

Ascher's breathing becomes long and deep as he is overcome by sleep, Dune following his example, settles into a village of silent rest.

THIRTEEN

———

Snow spits and floats across the sky in every direction.

Aldara lies in the Northwestern corner of Omideon, in the thick forests along the coast. Sirien sits on the village edge, watching the busy lives of the people. Men work on the small huts, women haul baskets of food through the narrow paths to the store, and children run aimlessly, screeching and laughing.

This is freedom, Sirien thinks, seeing joy spread across the faces of the Nasinreth.

Sirien's eyes droop from exhaustion. Grief consumes her every waking hour and haunts each dream. A child runs giggling down the path, a man following closely behind, scooping him up in his arms and walking back the way they came. Exuberant cries of glee come from the little being. Heart-wrenching to witness, Sirien struggles to her feet and turns to the forest behind her.

Tears burn Sirien's cheeks as she faces the cold forest, blending into it as she wanders deeper. The little boy and his father sit, imprinted into her mind as she walks, trailing around trees and bare foliage. Clutching at her abdomen, she weeps, collapsing to her knees in a ball of hysteria.

"Why would you give me this child? Why must you torture me with his future that doesn't exist!" she gasps, crying out to the emptiness around her. She weeps, thinking of her mother's words as a child. What purpose would she have to her God being so broken and alone, questioning if he even cares for her existence? How could her God be so cruel?

Sirien sits on her knees, folded into her cold, numb body, wishing she had taken the arrow and Castor had lived. His face, smiling at her, flashes across her memory, and she screams with anger—her heat flutters when she hears the crack of a branch to her left. Unafraid of the possible dangers around her, she turns her face in the sound's direction. Through blurry eyes, she sees a figure she recognizes.

Her face is clear. Davina smiles at Sirien, and her tears flow freely in overwhelming joy to see Davina safe. Davina stretches out her hands before her in Sirien's direction. Standing, Sirien steps forward to take them, only to stumble aside as a man walks past her, enveloping Davina in his grasp and kissing her sweetly. From the corner of her vision, Sirien sees a dark figure, sword drawn high, ready to attack them.

Screaming, Sirien rushes toward them, taking the blow across the chest. Pain erupts across her body, blood pools, and the world begins to fade into darkness. Unable to breathe, she rolls her heavy head to the side to see a crown at her fingertips, lying in the crimson pool. A humming in the air grows louder until the words spoken are clear enough to understand.

"The first heir will fail the kingdom, the second will unite it, and the third will rise to glory." The voice echoes into silence as death takes her.

* * *

Viala stands in the small, warm room, watching Sirien awaken from her vision. Brewing a herbal concoction, she waits and silently works until Sirien moves from the bed with ease, finding a seat across from her.

"How did I?" Sirien begins to ask, searching the cozy hut.

"Hunters found you and brought you to me," Viala says, pushing the carved cup in Sirien's direction.

"So you are a healer?" Sirien takes the brew, wrinkling her nose at its pungent smell.

"No. My sister was. She wrote everything down in case we were at a loss of one for a period of time. She was very wise in that way." Viala nods to the cup.

Sirien takes a hesitant gulp of the floral liquid. Immediately it eases her pain and tension, and she looks at Viala. A smile spreads across her face, putting Sirien at ease.

"You look much like your mother, but I also see your father's face. A beautiful blend." Sirien chokes as Viala speaks.

Coughing vigorously, Sirien sets aside the cup, still staring at Viala.

She knew my mother? As if she could read her mind, Viala laughs nodding before speaking again.

"Maeda and I were very close as children. I was sad to see her leave the village, but when the visions come, you follow." Viala stops, watching Sirien's expressions change erratically.

"What?" Sirien chokes out the only word she thinks of before freezing in her thoughts.

"Your father was a trader. He brought us goods from the city when Omideon was free. After time, he caught Maeda's eye and asked her to go with him. You come from a long line of visionaries, and your grandfather was one of the greats.

He foresaw their union and children with great purpose in their futures. Your father was skeptical but accepted the vision to marry your mother. Once Agnai took the throne, we didn't see your mother again and were sad to learn of her death." Viala's tender voice rings in the heavy heat as Sirien listens.

A thousand questions rise in a flurry to Sirien's mind. Silence falls between them as she searches through her thoughts, looking for the right words and questions to ask. *Could I have living family here? Are there other visionaries? What was she like as a child?* Question after question rises unspoken and unanswered in her mind.

Viala reaches behind her and slides a large basket away from the wall. Pulling out a needle, she begins nalbinding mindlessly as they sit. Finally, Sirien speaks, asking the only question that nags her daily.

"Am I truly the last visionary? What did my grandfather see?"

Viala stops, setting the needle and her work on the table, nodding. Silence becomes stillness as Sirien freezes, afraid of the next answer.

"What exactly he saw was not spoken to any but her. What she told me is all I know. He foresaw two daughters. One would be the final visionary, and the other would be unlike any Nasinreth, unparalleled to any strength or wisdom held by our ancestors…" She stops, allowing Sirien to grasp what she said before continuing.

"But there was another sight before they left the village. He saw Maeda, young and beautiful, with a crown of golden roses before the people. It was with this he knew Maeda would bear the children who would fulfill the prophecy of the heirs."

A knot forms in Sirien's stomach. *Could this be why her visions have come so often of late?*

"Dear child. What is it you have seen? What has brought you to us?" Viala stretches her hand across the table, gripping Sirien's hand.

Viala's eyes are dark brown, nearly black. Her silver hair trails down her back in long straight strands, but her face denies her the look of age. Her cheeks are flushed, and her features are full of youth and energy. Recounting the visions infesting her life over the recent weeks, Sirien pours out her heart.

"You were right to leave. Davina is in danger, but she also has a great destiny that is unclear. As for Amalie, she is seen to be great, just as your grandfather had said. As for you, um," Viala inhales deeply, averting her eyes and releasing her grip from Sirien, "our child will not survive, but this, you already know. But neither will you. It is not clear, but your life is in fate's hand, waiting to be cut." Glancing at Sirien, Viala's face appears shadowed with sadness.

"It's as well. My desire for life was lost in my husband's final breath."

* * *

The leather straps of the saddle are soft in Amalie's hand. Still tender from the oath, she winces as she cinches it around the beast's belly. Ascher stands across the yard, speaking with Mungar and Yrin seriously. She smiles at the men, sadness pulling at her heart to leave Dune and its people. For once, she felt at home and like the people around her.

"My dear."

Amalie turns to see Elra crossing the yard. Her large, heavy cloak sweeps the ground.

Embracing Elra, Amalie wraps her fingers into the fiery red and orange pelt wrapped around her shoulders. The heat of the fur is overwhelming in the chill of the air and comforting. Releasing the grip they shared, Elra steps back, eyeing Amalie up and down. Dressed in a long tunic, pants, boots, and a vest she looked Aulik bred, which fills Elra with pride.

"You are a strong woman, and your ferocity serves my grandson well. Watch over him as he does for you. He is my only remaining blood, and I cannot bear to lose him or you." She smiles, allowing brief vulnerability to surface.

"I will bring him home, Elra, I swear it." Touching Elra's shoulder, Amalie conveys her intentions clearly in an unspoken secret.

Stepping back, Elra unclasps her cloak and slips it from her shoulders. Swinging it around Amalie, she settles it over her, clasping it once again and nodding.

"The Fire Lion is a revered animal, but also dangerous. I killed this one before leaving the homeland. Now it is yours, as is tradition. You are Aulik. May the Nylehre watch over you and favor you as they have me."

Amalie smiles at her, still confused by their customs and language but grateful for their hospitality and acceptance. Before she can question Elra over the Nylehre, Ascher appears beside her. Ascher wraps an arm around Amalie's waist, pulling her close to him.

"Now now. You must make your way to Minik, which is a two-day ride from here. There is no time for procreation in the coming hours." Elra says mischievously.

Amalie slides away from Ascher, face hot with embarrassment as Ascher rubs his neck with his now free hand. Laughing, Elra turns from them and walks away. Together they go to their horses, and without meeting eyes, they take off from the large stable and dash out the gates, heading north to the forest-covered mountains.

Riding together, they climb the steep inclines, further up toward Nasinreth territory. They take to the river, following it upstream, knowing it will lead to the village of Minik. Hours pass as they travel, one behind the other unspeaking. Birds sing in the swaying conifers around them while the sun hides behind clouds full of moisture. The forest illuminates the world with the essence of peace, and Amalie loves it, taking it in deeply with every bat of an eye and deep breath. The fresh scent of pine electrifies her senses, and for once in her life, she truly feels happy.

Well into midday, they find a slow pool among the rushing river to rest and attempt their hand at fishing. Amalie on one end of the slow water, sits with some thin twine and hook, dipping it in the water to entice any passerby. Ascher stands on a boulder at the other end, watching through the crystal surface in wait for the perfect chance to release an arrow. After a few failed attempts, they achieve their goals.

After skewing the cleaned carcasses, the fish are placed on a rock to cook. The fire Ascher built surrounds the large stone, heating it with its glimmering red coals. Amalie watches him as he works the hot stone, turning the fish often and feeding the fire with pine cones, the needles and bark fill the sky with a cloud of smoke.

"How far is Minik?" Amalie asks, breaking the silence.

"About a day's ride," he replies, shoving more needles over the coals. A new plume of smoke emerges, sending Ascher back, coughing it out of his lungs.

"Can I ask you something?" Amalie ventures, her voice crossing over the cooking meal.

"Anything. You never need to ask." He smiles, not taking his eyes off the fire.

"Before we left, Elra mentioned something called the nealray?"

Ascher chuckles, looking up to her. "The Nylehre. They are the messengers. There are five, and each serves The Great One in different ways. Forunna oversees our souls and spirits. Ilisac is the bringer of safety and our futures, while Cadiome determines love and family. Sigina takes our praises and gratitude, and Gu¨nth reprimands us for our immorality." Ascher pokes the fire, turning the fish over on their other scaly side.

"So they are Gods?" Amalie watches his ceremonious actions.

"No. They serve the overseer, The Great One. They are messengers to us and from us too." Ascher looks up, raising his open hands slightly to the sky above.

Smiling at her, Ascher removes the fish from the stone, and walking around it, he crouches beside Amalie, planting a kiss on her forehead before handing her the skewed meat. They eat their meal quickly then quench the fire with piles of dirt. Leaving behind their quiet resting place, they move forward, the thoughts of the Nylehre on Amalie's mind.

FOURTEEN

Warm under the fire fox pelt, Amalie lays in a dreamy state under the trees canopy. Feeling Ascher's body close to hers, she sinks her body and soul against him, relaxing with ease. Suddenly, a hand clasps over her mouth. Her eyes jolt open, and she squeaks in surprise.

"Shhh," a voice whispers softly, blending in with the wind. Amalie immediately recognizes it as Ascher's.

Releasing her tension, Amalie lays like a statue, listening. After a moment, she hears what Ascher had, and the tension returns, making her body rigid. Hooves crunch the frosted earth, and their snorts echo in the mist. Words form across Ascher's breath into her ear, barely understandable.

"Stay put. Ilisac will keep you." He rolls away, crawling to the nearest horse.

Upon its bareback, Ascher takes off. Cries of eager surprise fill the air before a stampede of pounding erupts, moving away from her. Amalie stays in place, wrapped in a cocoon of warmth until the quiet rests into stillness. Adrenaline surging through her veins, she moves to her feet, saddling her horse and gathering supplies left behind. She hadn't heard Ascher take his weapon and is pleased to see he had grabbed it. Waiting, she scans the forest for shadows and the sounds of his return.

Finally, ears prick, alerting her of another presence in the distance. Mounting her horse, she watches as a figure materializes, silhouetting a man on a horse. Without needing to see his face, she knows this is not Ascher and promptly flies away.

With haste, the figure follows her, and a thrilling chase begins. Unable to see very far ahead, Amalie takes caution as she veers right and left over a difficult path. The sun beats down through the canopy of branches above, and the mist glimmers like a thousand cloudy diamonds. Suddenly, the white breaks into wide-open space. Frost covers like a blanket over grass, branches, and bushes, leaving a scene of white before her.

Chasing her across the icy grass now, they drop down into a valley and race its length. Drawing her sword, she jerks the reins, pulling her horse into a circle. Caught off guard, the soldier dives off his long-legged steed to avoid the blade. Cutting back the way she had come, Amalie takes to the left. Pushing her horse hard, she clears herself of any danger. Panic begins to take hold of her as she watches for signs of Ascher or other soldiers.

The return of the fog clouds her vision, so she begins to climb again, hoping to break the barrier for a better view. Unable to see her path, Amalie soon finds herself rolling through the underbrush as the large, saddled stallion cries and screams. Gathering her wits, she jumps to her feet, running to the injured animal.

Amalie finds he has stepped on a large, loose rock, rolling his hoof between two, slicing into its flesh. Toppling to the side, the leg remains stuck, breaking the bone with immense pressure. Her heart flutters, and her stomach churns at the sight and guilt. Drawing her sword once again, she moves over the animal and swings down hard to sever the throat and release it from the torture of pain. Struggling for only a moment longer, the horse succumbs to his injuries, laying limp and heavy across the ground.

Unable to carry their supplies, Amalie unties the straps with the spare daggers attached and fastens them to her belt. Taking a final look at the chestnut stallion, she moves forward, shoving herself over the rough terrain in search of anything that could guide her in the right direction.

* * *

Coming across a body of water, Ascher stops, stooping from his horse to drink the fresh liquid. Losing his trail, he sits there, tired yet guarded. Hours have passed, and the only thing he can think about is Amalie and if she is safe. Making his way back to their camp would likely prove pointless because she would have left by now. Cupping his hands, he fills them with the water, taking long gulps, depleting the store.

Thirst quenched, he sits back, taking a knee in his chest as he combs the forest around him. The small den in the mountainside is beautiful. The lake sags into the earth, leaving a craggy wall of rock rising up to a landing where the river rushes over its side. Two streams flow from the glasslike pool below in opposite directions. Ascher lays back, closing his eyes to listen to his surroundings. He finds the calm roar of water raining down, the wind's whistle, and birdsong peaceful.

If Amalie could see this.

As if she sensed his thought, her voice echoes over the sounds of nature. Throwing himself up, he follows the sound of her voice, finding her in the most precarious of situations.

She stands, back turned to him within a slit in the rock above the lake, three soldiers before her. Heart thumping, he turns to retrieve his bow from the saddle, finding only coarse hair where the tough leather should be. He glances back to see her running toward him.

As if time nearly stops, Ascher watches as Amalie throws herself from the edge of the rock. Heart-stopping as he watches her fall, hitting the water with a force that sends shallow waves to the edge, he dives headfirst into the freezing water to retrieve his wife. Shivering erratically, he takes her in his arms, pulling them both back to the edge onto dry ground. The soldiers, gone from sight, send Ascher's nerves into hysterics. He hauls her onto his horse before hopping up behind her. Like never before, he rides, pushing the beast as hard as it can go in search of safety.

* * *

Davina stands along the treeline, looking into the forest where her sisters disappeared over a week prior. The trees stand as a barrier between her old life and future, merely a step away from where she may escape. Yet, she feels pulled in an undesirable direction as if being called to an untold fate, foreign to any reality. The fire crackles behind her as she stares, thoughts on her sisters, Castor and Ascher.

Do they still live?

One last look into the darkness of the trees sends chills down Davina's back, and she turns away from the monsters lurking in its depths. Warming at the edge of the flames, she sits silently, avoiding Rheyhas gaze.

"We camp here for the night. We should be in Balaoug by tomorrow's eve," Rheyhas speaks mechanically.

Davina nods in reply, pulling her cloak tighter around her shoulders against the biting cold. Darkness slowly overtakes the land as the sun falls behind the mountains. Offering food, Rheyhas looks kindly to Davina, only to be dismissed as she curls up on the ground to sleep. Laying still for a time, Davina listens as Rheyhas becomes restless and paces their small camp. The firelight flickers in the darkness as night falls on them, and Davina begins to flit in and out of consciousness until a new voice startles her.

"Sir. What a chance to find you here," the husky voice says lowly, as not to wake the prisoner.

"I am transporting our captive to Balaoug," Rheyhas says. "Did you find any trace of the others?"

"We found a body burned to ash in a cave to the north, and we traced two others coming up from the south, heading over the mountain," the husky voice says.

"We tracked them and chased them both. The man escaped and the woman, well…" a new voice, higher in tone, speaks.

"If she survived the jump, she will be dead by the morrow. The mountain waters are very cold. I couldn't believe she jumped from the cliff side," the husky voice returned, still in shock.

"Very well. Head back to Aldhorran at first light. If they survive, they will be beyond our reach by then," Rheyhas tells them, and tromping across the grass, they find a place to rest.

Eyes pressed tightly closed, Davina lays on the ground coming to terms with the new information.

Someone has died, but who? Not Amalie. She's the only one who would throw herself off of a cliff. Could Sirien have lost her life, or is it Castor? Or an unfortunate soul who happens to be there?

Thoughts rapidly fly through her mind as she concludes she truly is the angel of death for all but herself. As the men settle, she begins to hear their deep breaths become snores as they drift to sleep.

Opening her eyes, she rolls over in search of Rheyhas, who is absent from the fire. Seeing a single blade of grass, she touches it with the tip of her finger, turning it a rich deep shade of green. Tingling runs through her hand at the simple touch, full of energy and life. But then, something changes. She thinks of her father and sisters, the tingling turns to chills, icy through her veins and the blade of grass shrivels into a brown stalk, curling in on itself.

Shocked, Davina rolls back over, confused by what had just happened. A new feeling surges throughout her body, and it scares her. Shutting her eyes again, she forces the images of every face she knows from her mind, trying to sleep. However, the drowsiness fails her, and she sees that single blade of grass continuously until exhaustion consumes her, overruling all else.

Screaming startles Davina from her sleep. Bolting upright, she searches the dark for the terrifying cry. A pair of golden eyes glow, floating toward her. Adjusting to the darkness, she watches them come nearer until the pale fur breaks the blackness of night. Familiarity catches at her stomach to see the female, white wolf from Aldhorran. Their eyes meet, connecting as though conversing without words.

Davina, outstretching her hand, invitingly waits for the female's reply. Gently, the snowy wolf brings her head to Davina's hand, caressing it softly, drawing her face up. Red drips from the slit of her mouth, and Davina stops breathing. Stepping away from her, the wolf breaks contact, running into the void. A torch finally lights, shining a light out upon the shaken faces. Before her, one of the soldiers lay sprawled across the ground, the bed of grass shriveled and brown.

How?

Looking at her palms, she sees they are streaked in blood, and with horror, she screams.

FIFTEEN

———

Moisture seeps into the stitches of fabric throughout the room. Americ struggles as he shoves his arm into the sleeve that clings to every inch of bare skin. Smoke fills the room as it floats aimlessly from the fireplace to the open window across from it. Waves thunder loudly outside, and the wind howls, bringing in a storm with its fury. He saunters across the room, peering out into the darkness glazed with the sun's final rays. The prisoner has arrived, and by his order, sent to a cell in the upper levels. Heart pounding in his chest, he watches the last light leave the crashing waves before turning for the door.

The quarters he occupies sits at the very peak of the prison, dug deeply into the cliff side. Outside of the window, he sees the jagged rock piercing the sky along the mountain as water rolls up its side. The upper levels are the safest, farthest from the salty sea, whereas the lower levels flood with each slap of water. Americ shivers at the thought of prisoners sentenced to that hell, waiting as their lives inch closer to their end.

Outside of the room, a narrow landing sits leading down to a winding stair. Being the only one way up and down, it fills him with the feeling of imprisonment, far worse than the castle itself. The stone is slick underfoot as the moisture from above collects and drips, echoing around him. Carefully, Americ steps through the darkness into a lit corridor below. Heavy with the stink of death's rot, bodily waste, salt, and sweat, his stomach aches in repulsion.

The stone walls are stained darkly from time and moisture, while orange patches riddle them, spreading infectiously. Slowly, Americ makes his way down the unoccupied stretch, passing torch after torch until he sees a guard standing before a closed iron door. As he approaches, he recognizes him to be Rheyhas and stops before him, surveying his bruised and bloodied face.

"You are not to address me in any way other than by the name, Meric. The last thing I want is the prisoner to know who I am," Americ speaks before Rheyhas can, as he stares at the latched door.

Nodding in reply, Rheyhas turns to open the door, wincing as he grips the handle, knuckles bruised and wounds crusted over. Heaving in a deep breath, Americ steps across the threshold into a dimly lit cell. The door squeals as it closes behind him, clicking loudly. A steady drip sounds in the corner, and he listens to his surroundings as his eyes adjust to the light. Searching, he finds a small fire in the corner, barely burning, and a figure huddled on the ground beside it. Gathering the courage he needs, he squares his shoulders before speaking across the cold room.

"Why did you flee Aldhorran?"

The small head looks up, her hair falling over her shoulder. He freezes, astonished at the sight of a woman instead of a man. She doesn't answer. Instead, she tucks her head back into her folded arms. Regathering his composure, he speaks again with much less authority than before.

"Who are you?" Looking up once more, she glares at him.

"Kill me now and end this." Davina's tone is hard and cold.

"No. I have questions that need answers." Shaken, he turns, pounding on the door.

Rushing out as soon as it opens, he turns on Rheyhas angrily, watching him close the door.

"Did you tell my father the prisoner was a woman?" Americ whispers furiously.

"It was in the dispatch I sent, yes," Rheyhas replies, following Americ as he walks away.

Stopping a few feet from the cell, Americ looks at Rheyhas, face purple with frustration, his eyes silver as a precious metal.

"You will know her best. I need to know everything about the girl to know how to go about this situation." Americ grits his teeth, containing his aggravation.

"I can't tell you much other than she is smart. She seems to have a gentle spirit, yet I have seen her angry. There is a fire in her, and she quenches it. Be wary of her. She is powerful." With a slight glance at the door, Rheyhas sighs, turning back to Americ, and bows slightly before returning to his post.

"Cadison," Americ begins, and Rheyhas looks over his shoulder at him, surprised to hear his given name spoken aloud. "Did she do this to you?"

"One of the other guards. I found him—harassing her, and I put an end to it. He is in much worse condition, I assure you." He grins, returning to his place at her door.

Leaving, Americ turns, trailing up the steps to his room, where he latches the door behind him, breathing a sigh of relief to be alone.

* * *

"*Maeda, stop speaking such ridiculous notions. We cannot leave here. This is our home!*" Brien raises his voice in agitation.

"*We must! This child will be a visionary, and we must keep her safe! The King is out for blood Brien,*" Maeda howls back.

"*Your father could have been wrong. We can't know for sure,*" Brien replies.

"*I know. I believe.*" She lowers her voice, the depth rumbling in her chest.

"*If we leave now, we will never make it. Wait until the child is born. We can leave then.*" Brien's voice is cool, soothing as he relaxes his temper, moving to her.

She places a hand over her swollen belly, rubbing it in circles.

"*She will be the last visionary, the one to set all right. Somehow, she is the key. No one knows why or how, but she is,*" Maeda whispers, looking at her belly as it ripples and rolls to the side.

Brien gasps for air, water running down his face as it emerges from its depths.

"Answer me, old man. How many of you traveled together?" A large man jerks back Brien's head by his hair, sneering in his face.

Brien simply looks at the man, noting the missing teeth, distortion caused by scars across his face, missing eye, and waits. He stays silent, irritating the questioner beyond his ability to control. The questioner shoves Brien's face back down into the water, rising from the incoming tide.

"*I told you she would be a seer, and you didn't listen, Brien,*" Maeda paces across the floor nervously.

"What do we do now?" Brien stands hunched over, palms flat over the table surface. His face pales in the firelight.

"The visions won't happen often, I'm sure. We will tell those who call on us she is frail. She will never be able to have a normal life. Not even Amalie can know the truth," Maeda says, looking at her feet.

"If Amalie ever finds out, we will have turned sister against sister," Brien speaks blandly.

"But it will be for the better. Amalie cannot know."

Brien resurfaces, light blinding as black splotches cover his vision. Falling to his knees, they knock against the ground, weak at his captor's feet.

"You are useless, old man." The questioner looks up at the soldiers standing guard nearby. He waves them forward, stepping back away and motioning to Brien, who is lying across the stone floor. The two men walk to either side, taking an arm and dragging him away, and slips between reality and unconsciousness.

"She had another spell?" Brien looks at Maeda, seeing the tears in her eyes.

"I had hoped it would change, hoped I had interpreted it wrong, but I…" Maeda averts her gaze, refusing to meet his eyes.

"She has seen this before? What is it? What are you not telling me?" Brien reacts with impatience, grasping Maeda by the arms.

"We will have another child, a girl, and she will be the answer to the old prophecy." Maeda cowers in Brien's grasp.

"Your father saw only two daughters, not three, Maeda." His grip loosens slightly.

"No. He saw me on the throne, younger than I am now, which only means one thing. Sirien and Amalie look more like

you, and Sirien has seen it, and I know it, for I am with child," Maeda announces strongly.

Brien stumbles back, shocked at the revelation, his eyes searching for his daughters. The children not within sight allow him the opportunity to speak freely.

"We cannot afford another mouth to feed. Would Ingra know of anything to stop this?" Brien whispers, ashamed to even ask.

"How dare you! I will have this child, and she will one day sit on the throne of Omideon. I will not be here to see that day, but you will, and by our God, you will be sure she succeeds. It is my dying wish!" Her words sting like a hot brand, and he stares at her questioningly.

"This child will be the death of me, but the freedom for so many. My life for hers, a sacrifice I am willing to accept. You do not have to agree with me, or like my decision. You just have to live with it. I am entrusting you with our children's futures. I beg you, do not fail my children."

* * *

The fire pops and crackles in the hearth, flickering light over the shadowed room. Unable to sleep, Americ slumps in the large chair before its heat, thumbing rapidly through a book packed away into his trunk. A book brought from Drumidia along with his mother stayed hidden in his chambers, and the only one who knew of its presence there: Castah.

Searching through its pages like he did as a child, Americ looks for a hidden note, their way to communicate privately. Surely enough, it is there, written between the lines of their favorite story as children, telling how Gü̈nth punished the people for their selfish nature.

My dearest brother,

I hope you find my letter before it is too late. I know father has asked Rheyhas to remain as your personal guard. I beg you to invite him into your confidence and ask him of the history of our Grandfather's rule and his service to The Crown. Americ, there is so much more father hasn't told you, and you must know.

Dear brother, I know you have had questions you have never found answers to. I have hope Rheyhas may help you to see the light and find what you are looking for. Netheis will always be a place of refuge if you so choose or ever are in need. I love you and wish you safety, your beloved sister, Castah

SIXTEEN

———

Light filters softly into the room, glowing red through Amalie's eyelids. A sweet hum of a chanting voice draws her gently from sleep. Amalie's eyes open into slits, and she looks out into the brightly lit room, confused at first but settles at the sight of Ascher. His dark hair falls loosely, barely brushing the tops of his shoulders as he kneels before the window, head bowed. The hoof-shaped bruises across his back are lightly colored now, but the scars from his past remain prominent across his skin. Amalie stares at him, focusing on the large, strong muscles that lay under his olive skin.

She listens to Ascher, barely making out a word or two she doesn't recognize, other than the name.

"Forunn, alisan skoel, mii akask. Moern dai`n."

Feeling as though she is intruding, she rolls to her side, groaning with pain and stiffness.

Ascher flies to his feet and rushes to Amalie. With no words, he feels her head and looks her in the eyes, anxiety flowing from his.

"I have prayed for days for you to open your eyes," he whispers.

"Days?" Amalie's voice is hoarse.

Amalie pushes herself up, frantic with the thought of the time they lost. Pushing against her shoulders, Ascher sits on the bed next to her, resting her against him.

"Where are we?" Her voice is raspy in his ear as she feels the weakness rush over her.

"Minik. We never stopped, and when we did, I couldn't tell you what happened because I don't know," Ascher says, his words quieting, eventually falling to silence.

The rays of the sun stretch across the room, shifting until stretched across their outstretched bodies. Ascher twirls strands of hair in his fingers, gently brushing it away from her face.

"What were you saying in the window? I heard you as I woke." Amalie turns into him, laying her head over his chest.

"It was just a prayer. We should get you something to eat. The sooner you gather your strength, the sooner we move on to Aldara." Ascher moves abruptly away from Amalie, scooping his shirt from the end of the bed and heading for the door.

Alone, she slumps down, balling into herself, and promises to be well soon to travel.

* * *

The sharp knock at the door startles Americ, exhausted from the sleepless night and questions pounding in his mind. Jumping to his feet, he crosses the small room, swinging it open to find Rheyhas standing before him. He is a tall and slender man, his strength a surprise to any who challenges him. His dark hair is peppered with strands of silver, and his eyes are a rich amber. Bowing his head in respect to Americ, Rheyhas waits for an invitation to enter the chamber.

Americ steps aside, allowing him inside. Bolting the door closed, Americ motions to two armchairs before the stone hearth enclosing a rolling fire that heat radiates powerfully. They sit together, observing the demeanor each holds themselves in before speaking.

Unable to bear the silence any longer, Americ shifts in his seat before saying, "I have asked you here because I need your honesty. I would like you to read this and perhaps explain exactly why it was written."

Americ leans, slipping the book from the floor beside him and opening it before placing it into Rheyhas hands. Pointing out the page, Rheyhas sees the scrawled note between lines and reads it hastily multiple times. Each pass, his face drains of more color until his eyes stop, frozen in place over the page.

"I… uh, I am not really sure what you want to know, your highness." His words stumble as Rheyhas addresses Americ.

"Only the truth. Cadison, I have no quarrel with you. I am not my father, and what you say in my confidence will remain there." Americ attempts to speak soothingly but instead seems annoyed.

"Very well." Rheyhas hands the book back to Americ, sitting tall in his seat. "What is it you'd like to know?"

"Why does my father hate the Nasinreth people? I know we aren't to trust them, and they are dangerous, but why?" Feeling like a child asking for a story before bed, Americ sits forward with his arms folded across his knees.

"Americ, your father, was in an impossible situation, and he chose the less honorable path. If I tell you, it may change your perception of your entire bloodline, not just him. You must be sure this is what you want." Rheyhas leans back into the armchair, slumping into his age and exhaustion.

"Tell me." Americ replies without hesitation.

"You grew up knowing the Nasinreth were an important part of the kingdom during the reigns of the three Kings before your Grandfather and also during his rule. You know the Nasinreth betrayed your Grandfather, but it's not the truth. As the only boy of your Grandfathers, Agnai knew his future would be the honor of King until the prophecy threatened that. One of the Visionaries serving your Grandfather foretold the first heir would be the kingdom's downfall, but the second heir would unite the people, and the third brings it to glory.

So the King, Daenus, your grandfather, prayed for another son. He had many children with many wives. Agnai's mother, the first wife, died from the plague. Daenus' second wife gave him two daughters and a stillborn son, dying with the lad in childbirth. His third wife killed herself after her son of two years died suddenly from an unknown cause. It is speculated your father killed him to regain his birthright as heir. Daenus had poor luck when it came to having sons, but daughters he had an abundance of. Never marrying again, he chose to find your father a wife who could maybe control his wickedness."

"My mother," Americ whispers.

Rheyhas nods in reply. "In those days, Romathe and Drumidia were one, unified countries. The Chieftains of the superior clans were distant cousins and had promised each other continued unity as long as a first son and daughter between them were to be married. Devenus reached out to the Chief of Drumidia, Haictor, and asked for an alliance between countries through marriage. Haictor betrayed his fellow, Chieftain of Romathe, and sent his daughter across the Sea of Kings, bringing the country into war and eventually splitting into separate nations. Your mother and father loved each other for a time, but greed and fear of not having a heir destroyed them. He began hunting any who could be connected to the Nasinreth, gifts or not and slaughtered them. The people lived in fear, and your mother was angry.

Once you were born, Amesah was relieved, hoping your father would come to his senses and return to the man she had once loved. But he never relented. He wanted, as he would say, to rid the kingdom of the vermin for his son to easily rule. Amesah, afraid of what he would make you into, came to me one night and asked for help. She feared her husband and wanted to keep you all safe, so she asked me to arrange an escape for her during the next hunt. She planned to sail home to Drumidia from the Uutithean coasts. The day she planned to leave was the day she disappeared. No one could find her, and after months, your father ended all searching. Many think her to have left for her homeland, and others believe her to be dead by the King's own hand."

"Do you know if it was his doing?" Americ asks, eyes wide in childish wanting.

"No. But I surmise it could be. I was there when your father killed his own brother and have been kept silent." Rheyhas straightens at this, energized by the memory.

Americ's face drains of color at the revelation of murder. Thoughts begin to fester in his mind, looking over the demented memories that make him sick. Thoughts turn to the beatings and punishments he received as a child, and his sister Charlotte comes clearly into view.

"Does Castah know this? Is this why she wrote me?" Americ asks, staring at the floor.

"Castah has been in my confidence for some time. She and Prince Tallak believe your father to be a threat to Netheis. They plan to remove him from the throne so he cannot do any more harm. It is time he pays for his crime, even if it costs my own life and war stems from her betrayal." Rheyhas becomes confident again.

"And Charlotte? What will become of her?" Americ looks at Rheyhas, sadness overwhelming him.

"Charlotte, I believe, is beyond repair. Castah and I both see her to be a danger to everyone in her path, including herself." Americ's heart drops at Rheyhas words.

"So you will imprison her." It wasn't a question, and Rheyhas knew it.

"It will depend on the fight she brings. Your sister has her claws in many men and controls much more than even your father sees. She is devious, and imprisonment may not be enough," Rheyhas speaks carefully, watching Americ flinch at the thought.

Nodding, Americ sinks into the chair, leaning his head back in submission to his misery. He never thought it would go as far as to end the lives of his family, nor did he imagine the brokenness of the family would cause such extreme actions. As if a stone were resting on his chest, he breathes heavily, the pain of the future overwhelming him as he knows it is a necessary evil.

* * *

Davina sits in the corner of the dark, cold room, knees pulled into her chest, holding in as much heat as possible while her body aches from dormancy. With no fire for heat and light, she shrinks into the darkness near the entrance, plotting her next move for freedom. Hours have gone by with no sound besides the ocean waves slashing the cliff side and constant drip from the ceiling above. In a trance, she loses herself in the blankness of her mind until keys jingle nearby.

"Leave us," the mildly strong voice commands outside.

Stiffening, Davina waits, the door wailing as it opens and closes with a thud. Glancing with one eye she can see the figure, searching the stillness of her lair for life. As he turns his back, her body comes alive again. Springing to her feet, she dives, wrapping her arms tightly around the unsuspecting soul. Landing with a breathy huff, the man rolls, but before he can escape, she latches her fingers around his arm. Pulling herself over him, she manages to shove a knee into a wrist, and he winces.

"I will begin breaking bones if you do not tell me who you are and what you want," Davina's voice growls deeply, sending gooseflesh in a ripple down Americ's back.

"My name is Meric, and I was sent by the King. I'm not here to hurt you," Americ says, panicked.

"Liar. If the King sent you, you are here to silence me," Davina menacingly hisses as she grips one of Americ's fingers in her own.

"I swear it! He sent me, but I have other intentions for being here, and you are not one of them." Americ gasps as she twists slightly, shooting pain up his already throbbing arm.

"What intentions?" Davina loosens her grip on his finger, eyes narrowed at him.

"Escape. I want to disappear and find freedom," Americ answers hastily.

Staring for a moment, Davina lays a hand on his chest, feeling his heart pulse rapidly beneath it, gauging his honesty. Full of fear, she senses the adrenaline rushing through his body in response and decides to release him cautiously.

"Why would you want to escape? You are obviously in the King's favor." Davina slips away, moving across the room to the dead fire.

"Quite the opposite. This is his way of punishing intolerable behavior only his eyes see," Americ absentmindedly speaks while he rubs his wrist, aching from the attack.

"What do you want from me?" Davina curiously asks as he steps closer, and she can see him; his deep fiery red hair, silver eyes, broad stature, and crisp features.

"Your honesty and trust. I won't leave a girl in this prison to die. I want to free you." Americ says, his voice barely audible.

Davina glares, unsure whether to believe him or not. Without warning, she slaps her arm against the rock wall, splitting open the top of her hand. Seeping blood, it begins pooling and running down her fingers, hitting the ground one droplet at a time. Flinging her hand at him, Davina sprays his face with her blood, and as she screams, he is rattled to the core by the shrill and horrifying sound. Pausing a moment, she reaches beside her, taking a large rock in her hands.

Americ shakes, his body lit with terror and the overwhelming need to run. He can barely breathe as she screams again, flinging the rock hard against the wall. As the crash echoes in the room, her cries stop, and they follow the reverberating sound until silence finally falls.

"Prove it, and I will help you," she whispers, stepping close enough to him to wipe her bloody hand across his chest and down his sleeves.

With nothing to say, Americ stumbles to the door, tripping over his own feet. He can hear the guards outside pacing before the door and jumping to his aid as he pounds on it fiercely.

Eyes wide, the guards take in his new appearance and shrink away from him. Americ rushes away, glowering at everything he passes until he reaches his chamber and is safely locked inside. There, he collapses to the floor, shaking as memories infiltrate his mind, full of the traumas of his past and that same scream seared in his mind a few years before.

SEVENTEEN

The door screeches open, and the echo of boots cross the small cavern Davina occupies. Colder than she ever had been before, she doesn't try to move. Instead, she ignores her visitor, hoping he will be unimpressed and leave. However, to her surprise, the familiar snap of the flint stone draws her gaze up from her crossed arms to the eyes of Rheyhas, kneeling before her. Sparks fly over the small pieces of wood he had silently laid out, and she watches as it lights. Flames climb the slivers of wood and engulf the dried leaves and grass sprinkled generously over its top. Growing with intensity, he adds more wood, then, without a sound, crosses the room again, leaving out the open door.

Davina sits, dazed by his sudden appearance but thankful as she relishes the growing fire. The heat put out is a blessing, and she scoots so close it nearly burns her.

I could burn on a pyre for all I care, as long as I am warm.

Rheyhas reappears as a shadow in the dimly lit door, a large bundle in his arms, followed by another man with a similar load. Dropping both loads on the ground, Davina sees it is more wood for the fire. The man she doesn't recognize leaves immediately, and Rheyhas lingers, stacking the pile neatly.

"Why?" Davina asks bluntly.

"Because it is cold, and Meric ordered it," Rheyhas replies, continuing his work.

"He is a fool and weak. I know this game, and you will not win at it," Davina defiantly speaks as if he is testing her.

Stiffening, Rheyhas turns to her and approaches, sinking to his knees, so his face is at the same level as hers. She looks into his amber eyes and sees something in them she wanted so badly to ignore. Kindness. She wanted to hate this man because he served the King, yet, there was something about him. It wasn't just in his eyes, but also in his manners and the way he spoke, as if he didn't serve out of choice, but rather necessity.

"Meric is true of heart and well-intended. Just as I am," he whispers to Davina, knowing she sees his own goodness of heart.

Davina gulps, intimidated by Rheyhas and his sincerity, questioning whether she is being played or if this man is truly good, but in a horrible position. Standing straight, Rheyhas moves away and leaves the room. She thinks over their encounter in the evening, remembering what he had said.

"Escape. I want to disappear and find freedom."

If he has spoken the truth, could he be my ally? Could Rheyhas be on his side and be working to free me together as well as themselves? Surely not, or he would have let me go in the forest. Or am I the bargaining chip?

Confusion arrests her mind as she tosses thoughts and questions back and forth while soaking in the glorious heat of the fire. Feeling alive again, she begins rubbing her hands together, tracing the broken skin on her palms, raw and tender. Her joints ache with inactivity, and her desire to run through the open space and air overwhelms her.

Davina's father crosses her mind like it always does throughout her time, and she brightens at the perspective of the freedom he had died to give her. If the two men were tricking her, however, the consequences of her foolishness in trusting them will be grave, and it would be a fight to the death for her freedom.

Watching the flames lick at the air around her, she contemplates compliance with Meric, considering all avenues of betrayal or the even more unlikely aspect of honesty. She may not trust him, but he would be her best chance of survival and escape. They could flee to the forest where she can slip away from him and make her way to Divanthra for her best chance at survival. Or should they drop to the sea, and she stows away on a boat to wherever it goes?

So many options and possibilities flit through her thoughts she barely notices the door swing open again where the young man appears. Keeping his distance, he stands across the room, watching Davina closely. With a crash, the prison door closes, and the room falls dark and quiet, with only the fire to be heard and seen. They stare at each other for a long while, absorbing their appearances and moods.

Americ waits, eyes slits and head ablaze with his fiery hair unruly upon his head. He watches Davina remaining still as a stone, her vision piercing the guard he thought he put up before entering. His knees shake slightly at the thought of her the night prior, and his stomach knots with nerves.

"Are you going to lurk in the cold or join me by the fire?" Davina asks, her voice strong and fearless.

Taking a forced step forward, he moves into the flickering light, feeling the heat seeping through the dense, salty air. Like an owl, Davina's eyes follow him, head turning slightly until he stops across the fire from her. Sitting, they share the awkward space between them, tense and questionable.

"Ha… Have you thought about what I said yesterday?" Americ's voice breaks at his first words, flushing his cheeks with embarrassment.

"Yes. I will help you only because I like Rheyhas and feel he is trustworthy. He seems to think you are too," Davina speaks with cautious optimism toward the thought of uplifting Americ's spirit.

"Good. I don't need to know where you intend to go or truly care for that matter, as long as I get away from this place," Americ says confidently.

Surprised by this, Davina relaxes a tad, searching his words and actions for anything suspicious.

"I'm sorry this happened to you." Americ is quiet, his voice low and gaze fallen to the ground.

"I need my weapons. Rheyhas took them from me, and I want them back. Be sure I get them when we leave, and I will allow you to go your separate way." Davina shoves aside his apology, not allowing herself to fall vulnerable.

If there is anything she learned from Amalie, she knows vulnerability is a weakness that leads to imprisonment and death.

I refuse to die.

Davina looks at him as he stares at her, his silver eyes piercing the mask she created to hide herself from any onlooker. Heat rises inside her from a place the fire cannot reach, and it startles her how she finds herself at ease in his presence.

"You were sent to interrogate me, correct?" She shakes away the feeling, returning herself to distrusting the stranger.

He nods slowly, tensing at the memory of their last encounter.

"I traveled with my father and two sisters. They should be long gone by now to safety so the knowledge now known cannot hinder their progress," Davina casually speaks, freely giving Americ the information.

"Very well. I will keep that in mind, in case I am asked." Standing, Americ places another log on the fire before turning his back to Davina.

Davina looks closely at him, his clothes finely made and expensive. She watches as he straightens his tunic and walks to the door. Before leaving, he turns, taking a final glance her way, and their eyes meet briefly, sending chills down their spines.

* * *

"Swear it." Maeda's face trickles with sweat. Her body pales against the bed in their small home.

Her grip, weak yet solid in Brien's hand, only proves the inevitable. The small child in her one arm becomes unsettled, wiggling in search of tender care and nourishment. Seeing this, Brien scoops the baby up, and his heart drops heavily in his chest as he sways to soothe the little human. Tala slinks in beside him, scooping up the wiggly girl from Brien's arm.

"I need you to promise me, Brien." Maeda's voice is weak as she pleads with him.

"I would give my life for them. You know this." Aggravation fills Brien's words, covering the pain.

"Promise," Maeda whispers.

"I promise." Brien's voice quivers as he watches her sink back, relaxing into her perspective of death.

Slowly, she fades before Brien, the light leaving her eyes all at once with her final breath. Brien knew his promise to

Maeda would be a difficult one, or maybe even impossible, but now he had to try. Her father saw her leading the country, standing before the throne of Omideon, and now that vision will fall to their youngest child's shoulders.

The cries of the new infant are a burden to his angry and hollow heart. How he had wished she would never have been conceived, never been foreseen, or maybe not even survived. She would be a mouth to feed, replacing the most important one in his life. At this moment, he hated the Nasinreth and their "blessings," hated he had married one, and regretted loving her so deeply.

But in his pain, Brien knew the feelings would pass, and as he turned coldly away from the still-warm body, he vowed to himself till his dying breath, he would try. Sirien would be the tool he would need to know when the time would come to run from danger, and Amalie would be his left hand in the fight. Caring for them would be simple as he has always done, but to love would be a whole new aspect of life recently lost to him.

The main room of the house was stifling hot as he made his way to the rocking chair along the wall. Tala, rocking softly with the small bundle in her arms, cooing to her as she slept. Brien, looking down at the sweet newborn, instantly seeing what he did not want to. The sweet child's face perfectly resembled her mother, melting his hardness away to love her.

If she was the only person he could truly love for the rest of his days, he would. Taking her from Tala, Brien snuggled the tiny baby to his chest, cradling her in the most fatherly fashion. Pacing the room, he stared, heart afloat of emotion.

"Davina. My Beloved."

EIGHTEEN

"Leave me be, Amalie." Sirien stamps into the room, Amalie hot on her heels.

Since their arrival to Aldara, Amalie has been relentless in planning a search for Davina and Brien. Sirien, tired of listening to her sister's schemes, chose to leave, finding refuge in the home her mother grew up in, finding peace short-lived. Amalie and Ascher followed her, taking up a room to themselves and continuing their plans to find Davina and their father.

"How can you just sit here so content? They are out there somewhere, Sirien! We need to find them!" Amalie raises her voice in sheer frustration.

"We can't!" Sirien whirls around, stopping before Amalie. The two collide, stumbling back. "It is too risky to leave here. There aren't enough of us, especially with Ascher ill. We knew the risk of running and accepted that. It's time to move on, Amalie." Sirien looks defeated as she speaks, distraught with the idea of their losses weighing on her shoulders along with Castor's.

"Unlike you, I am not afraid of the fight, Sirien. To hell with anyone who gets in my way." Amalie slashes her hands through the air, speaking vibrantly.

"And you along with them! Amalie, think sensibly. Your rashness will get you killed, and you will be of no use if they are alive!" Sirien bellows, frustration peaking.

"Think sensibly? If you had been honest with any of us, we could have avoided this altogether! Sensibility is not logical. Now we need action!" Amalie steps toward Sirien threateningly.

"You will never care to understand. I stayed silent to protect you all. Knowledge of this could have only led you to your deaths. It was best…" Sirien tries to keep her voice even as she explains herself, only to be suddenly cut off.

"You had no right to make that call. You don't know what is best. You aren't my mother and could never replace her." Amalie's anger is unsteady, quavering the tone of her words slightly.

"Yet, I did," Sirien speaks through clenched teeth. "I am the one who loved you in all your faults and greatest achievements. I praised you when it was due, have been your voice of reason when necessary, comforted you in sickness and sadness, and have always been there when you needed a shoulder to cry over. I was the mother none of us had and received nothing in return. Where was my love, comfort, and place to rest my head or wipe my tears? I have two shoulders, so I cared for myself, choosing the dryer one so I could move on.

"I have been a means to an end, Amalie. You may not have been loved by anyone other than me, but you have always been needed and valued. I made my choices under the circumstances I was given, and I stand by them every day." Tears stream down Sirien's face as she delivers her speech with a vengeance.

Shocked by her bluntness, Amalie stands speechless, watching the fury slowly dissipate from Sirien. Slumping her shoulders, Sirien looks defeated and tired. Too often, Amalie wakes in the night to hear her sister moving like a ghost through the house or crying out in her sleep. Sensitivity eluding her, Amalie pushes it aside for a later time, wishing Davina were here to be the caring one.

Shaking her head, Amalie turns from the room, exiting the home into the frozen world. She heads straight for the forest. Like in the grove of trees outside Aldhorran, Amalie set course along the line of snares laid out just days after their arrival. Jack rabbits were the most common catch of her little traps, but occasionally she would find a cubba or a turkey would stumble their way over the thin wire.

Uplifting her spirits, the first snare holds a wild turkey. The huge feathery animal flaps and clucks, jerking its leg in an attempt to free itself from the wire. Amalie removes the dagger at her back and slips cautiously closer to the glamorous feast before her. Taking the snare wire in hand, she drags the bird to her, fighting its enormous strength. Once close enough, Amalie throws herself over the turkey, fighting to grab hold of its head to slit its neck. Finally, after a tousle, she wins, blood squirting from the severed artery as the bird fights with its final bits of life.

Cleaning her knife, she waits for it to still, then, taking it by its clawed feet, moves forward to the next snare. Though the other snares were empty, her spirits brightened with the feeling of worth. She may not save Davina and her father, but she could feed them and keep the others safe. Amalie knows Sirien has a point but hates to admit it.

Seeing a boulder at the base of a tree, Amalie plops down, dropping the bird at her feet. Her breath fluffs into mist in the air, and little crystals of frozen moisture riddle the leaves and earth beneath her feet. So often, she sits and sees the world around her, allowing it to tell her the story of its being and the adventure that crosses through the trees. A twirling flake floats across the outer edge of her vision then another a few feet before her. Looking up to the sky, that little piece of happiness held in her heart vanishes.

The clouds, a dense gray, move slowly above her, spitting tiny frozen drops from them. If her father and Davina were alive, they couldn't make it before the snow without help. Closing her eyes, she finally accepts the fact she may never see them again and leaves her last hope on Elra and the letter she wrote asking for her help.

* * *

Shaking his head, Ascher waits outside until the screaming and yelling end. Returning to the wood stack he had just left, he begins splitting the logs strewn across the ground. The crash of the front door stops him, and he watches as Amalie darts across the small open space then disappears into the forest.

She will want to be alone.

It takes all his strength to pull his attention away from her and leave her be. Taking up the stack of wood recently split, he marches to the door with hopes of Sirien still being there to give him insight into the situation. Happily, Ascher finds her perched before the window across the room from the door. Unflinching, she stands still, looking out over the mountains. Gently, Ascher moves to the hearth, placing the large bundle of wood to its right and stoking the fire.

Through the corner of his eye, he watches her, never acknowledging his presence or caring about the disruption he brings. Leaning back into his squat, he plops to the floor, resting his arms over his folded knees, and pauses before the flickering coals. Knowing the family all too well, he rests there, knowing she will be the first to speak and he need only listen. Sure enough, after a moment, Sirien mumbles with a shaky voice to him.

"She will get killed trying to save people who are likely dead."

"Unless she finds it to be true, you know she will not stop looking," Ascher replies, keeping his focus on the fire.

"Is it my fault? Keeping secrets and being absent from them these last years?" Sirien's voice is so low and full of despair he can barely hear her.

"You have done the best you could have. Their fates were written long ago, as is ours. The fault is not yours," Ascher speaks with soothing confidence as if Sirien were nothing but a small child.

"It may be best if you leave Ascher. Take Amalie anywhere but here, where you may flourish together." Sirien turns, facing him, her eyes puffy and red and face pale as the whitest silk.

"Where would we go? Why would we leave now?" Ascher looks at her, strongly confused by the suggestion.

"Anywhere. She should not have to bear any more loss than she has now. She needs to find her place and purpose, which I have seen to be great." Sirien moves to a chair near the hearth, sinking into it slowly.

"When will it happen?" Ascher straightens, tense with anxiety over her pending answer.

"I'm unsure. There is no telling when, but it will happen in the near future. I have seen my fall many times, and I welcome it." Her eyes find Ascher's. "Amalie is not to know. She cannot prevent such things, so she needn't try." The severity of her tone surprises Ascher, and he nods immediately in agreement.

"Ascher," Sirien utters, and he looks up to her, afraid for an unknown reason. "Amalie was born to lead. I don't know why or how, but I have seen her future clearly, always connected to you before our people. Stand by her, and you will live your lives in greatness."

With this final statement, Sirien rises, gliding across the room to the stairs, and leaves to retire to her room. Ascher doesn't know what to think about their conversation. Sirien seems as if her spirit was dead, and she lives only to prepare the way for others.

And perhaps that's precisely what she is doing. Could our future be with the Aulik? Is that the reason Brien hated him so?

A sudden realization of his life and relationship overwhelms him. The draw between Amalie and Ascher went far beyond mutual need and respect. It was fated for reasons expanding far beyond his own comprehension. But if Amalie never knew of his place in the Aulik, would their purpose change? What would become of them?

Ascher's hand instinctively moves up to his shoulder, fingers tracing the scars through his tunic, placed there by his own father. The thought is sobering as it terrifies him. Inhaling deeply, he moves from his place on the hearth, tossing another log into the fire before leaving the house in search of distraction from duty.

* * *

Sirien sulks in the shadows of her room, fireless, the chill bites at her skin but she doesn't care. Running a hand over her slightly swollen belly, she stares at the distant wall, imagining an unrealistic life with Castor and her unborn child. Memories flicker through her mind of the times Davina was only an infant and how she hated it. Not because of the crying, dirty clothes, endless feedings, or constant need for attention, but rather the fact she couldn't trust herself. Her visions would come and go as they please, leaving her helpless in a second's notice and the child without a caregiver.

Remembering Davina wailing, red in the face, and kicking free of her swaddle haunted Sirien. She couldn't move or speak after her vision or see the world around her. Sirien didn't know if Davina was unharmed, and she feared she wasn't and would hate herself for it. After a time, Sirien was able to release an arm from her affliction and slowly outstretch it, finding the tiny human body on the floor. Instant recognition warmed Sirien's heart as Davina clamped her little fingers around her eldest sister's hand and ceased crying immediately.

Since that moment, Sirien knew the fear of being a mother but also saw the joys. She knew she could be the mother her sisters lacked but never wished motherhood of her own children. To curse a child with the blessings would be unforgivable, and all she wished in this life would be to let it die with her. Now, she contemplates the fact she carries the very thing she swore she never would and feels the love for it that was so unwanted. A piece of Castor survives within her, and it makes her sad and angry because she has only one question she'll never receive an answer to.

Will I get to hear your first cry, or will you go alongside me to the Everworld?

NINETEEN

The shackles weigh heavily on Davina's wrists as she marches closely behind Rheyhas. She searches the dim corridor for any other signs of life or an idea of where she could be going, but there are no other faces, just the groans of men whose souls abandoned them long ago. She doesn't dare speak in fear she could cause Rheyhas trouble, so she follows silently behind him. She likes Rheyhas because he is kind to her, and she believes they could be friends in a different life.

Stopping before a tall winding stairway, Rheyhas turns, motioning Davina upward before him. The steps are narrow and slick under foot which she finds uncomfortable against her bare feet. Grimacing with each sharp or slimy step, she moves forward until the path comes to an end. Reaching past her, Rheyhas knocks on the door then steps back to wait.

Light and heat flood from the doorway as it swings wide open. Americ, solemn as ever, greets them and invites them in. The room is drowning in quilts and furs, well-made armchairs, a table, and a small bed with an ornate chest tucked up against one end. So entranced by the elaborate room, Davina barely hears the door close behind Rheyhas, and when Americ finally speaks, it startles her.

Steering her toward the fire and into a chair, he retrieves a small platter of food seemingly untouched and unwanted, handing it to her. Americ smiles then leaves her to fetch something from the trunk. Meats and cheese are piled on the dish, giving sharp and savory scents, making her mouth water. Davina cannot ignore the temptation and begins eating, vigilant of the man she knew as Meric and his intentions for her to go to him rather than him come to her.

Other than the fire's crackle, the room is quiet and peaceful, far surpassing the comforts of Davina's lair below. She watches the man rummage through his things, curious about him rather than reluctant about his character. His visits were often and amicable, full of stories and intentions of escape. As much as Davina wished to hate him, she couldn't and instead looked forward to his visit every day.

There is just something about him.

Finally finding what he had been searching for, Americ closes the chest and happily walks to the chair opposite Davina.

"I read this as a child very often. It fascinates me." Excitedly, Americ hands Davina the book in his hands.

"You asked me here to read a book?" Davina asks.

"No. I asked you here because the men were questioning my methods to interrogate you. Rheyhas suggests I change things and allow the men to think what they must." Americ chuckles with an air of vexation.

"I see." Davina's face flushes, and she scolds herself silently for such foolishness.

He is an enemy, not a friend. Mind yourself.

"This book holds stories and legends of the clans of Eporiae before it split. It was my mothers." Taking the book back, his fingers move over the spine and cover, worn to near shreds. "My favorite story is of the first clan leaders. I won't bore you with all the details, but one man took the Chieftain seat, and because of greed and lust, the man standing as his confidant killed him, taking his wife and becoming Chieftain. A slew of murders between houses happened to take the place of a spouse or even reach as high as Chieftain. The Great One saw, and angry with such immorality, sent his messengers down upon them and punished them. A new law was created that in every marriage, an oath would be taken that blood could only be paid in blood. If a union is broken by death, it ends in death, meaning if the husband dies, so must the wife and so forth. Nothing can change that. It stopped the murders and allowed the clans to finally flourish." Americ smiles at a memory crossing his mind as he summarizes the legend.

"How could that work? If one dies, so must the other. How have the clans survived?" Davina glares at Americ, slightly annoyed by their logic.

"After many years, the messengers answered the peoples' cries and relented. The only people who take the oath are those within the line of the Chieftain seat. If an outsider steps in by claiming victory in battle, he must perform the oath to take his place." Americ shrugs, entertained by his retelling of the story.

Davina sits, staring at him with irritation. The story, however interesting, is unimportant to her and confusing. Her own people are not savage like the people of Drumidia or Romathe. The Nasinreth are gentle, kind and will not fight unless highly provoked, and somehow, she feels as if he is trying to tell her something. Tilting her head to the side, she looks him over, hoping to see something she hasn't before during his visits but finds nothing.

"What are you thinking?" His eyes are on her, focusing intently on her face.

"The story is very odd. I cannot imagine such chaos in people," she answers, hiding her true thoughts deep inside.

"Your people are much different?" His tone suggests true questioning, something Davina hadn't seen coming.

"The Nasinreth aren't fighters. They live to serve," Davina speaks, holding back her frustration.

"Then why do people fear you so?" Like a small child, his eyes glisten with the thirst for knowledge that melts Davina's heart.

"I truly don't know. There was a prophecy spoken when the King was a child that his father disliked. The story of the heirs." Davina ponders over the stories told to her as a child.

"I see," Americ's voice drops to a barely audible tone.

He sits, folded over, supporting his arms on his knees. Davina, feeling nervous, shifts in her seat, and when he looks up at her, she freezes. His eyes, an icy blue, represent the clans of Drumidia as well as his deep red locks of hair. Hearing of the clans and seeing them in person was always a rare moment as they fled at the Queen's disappearance.

Feeling uncomfortable, Americ stands too quickly and, losing his balance, catches himself against the hearth stones. A whoosh of air inhaled before the strangled grunt escapes his lungs. Americ jumps wildly, whipping his hand through the air in severe pain.

Rushing to his aid, Davina loses all sense of her surroundings and the weight of the shackles on her wrists. She reaches for him, pulling his already blistered and raw hand into hers. A rush of energy surges through her, and heat waves over her as she directs her focus on his hand locked in her grasp. As quickly as the pain had come, it vanishes. Tears in his eyes, he breathes a sigh of relief, and when she releases him, he inspects everything with awe.

"Why the King hates you so I am not sure, but I owe you a debt of gratitude," he says in the most sincere of ways.

Davina stands so close to Americ he can see the fine details in her eyes and smell the salty air clinging to her skin. Chest thumping, he leans slightly closer to her until their arms brush lightly. Finding the touch electrifying, he craves more, inching closer as she allows it. Stuck in a trance, they find themselves frightened as a guard crashes through the door.

"Your H-Lord uh-Meric Sir. Letter for you from the King."

Americ shoves away from Davina and, gathering his composure, moves to retrieve the letter.

"While you are here, you can remove the shackles from my prisoner." Americ reads the note, expression hard in secrecy. "Very well. I need to address this, so please take the prisoner back to her cell. Be sure wood is always available to her, and see that she has food and drink." Americ nods at the soldier as he follows orders, leading Davina down the stairs.

Shaking off the feelings that had consumed her moments before, she wanders behind the soldier, embarrassed yet longing for Meric's presence. Colliding at the bottom of the stairs with a passerby, she moans in pain before looking to see if the other person is alright. Face draining of all life, she ceases her movement and chokes on her own breath.

The man, carefully standing, has the face of someone she once knew and believed dead, a man she mourned over every day.

"Father," her whisper, only meant for the man, could be heard by the guards nearby as well. Eho looked triumphant.

Throwing herself into the man's arms, she weeps. Overwhelmed by her presence, Brien can do nothing but hold her tightly, overjoyed she was alive but also fearful of it. A million emotions pass between them in the short time they have together before the guards break up the reunion, dragging Davina away, kicking and screaming.

Sobs echo in her den as she pounds her fist heavily against the door, screaming for her father and begging for just another moment with him. She fights until her hands are numb with bruises and the skin torn and bloodied. Voice hoarse from her despair, she sags to the floor in defeat, ignoring the failing fire and wishing for the first time she could die.

* * *

The dark, cold room is stale and silent as Americ enters, the door clicking harshly behind him. The sharp sound echoes momentarily, and he fights to find his bearings, hoping Davina isn't planning to attack him again. Terror seizes his body as he searches the darkness for her, inching across the rough floor.

Where are you?

Frantically, he stops, closing his eyes to calm himself and listen. The waves stand out strong, with the rhythmic whoosh and crash as well as subtle drip reverberating through the cavern. And then a steady breath, just ahead of him. Opening his eyes, he staggers backward, terrorized by the woman standing before him, eyes piercing the veil of black. His chest throbs with anxiety, and his body shakes with fear as he falls to the ground. Without a word spoken between them, Americ could feel her anger and, for the first time since knowing her, felt afraid.

"I hate you. Leave and let me die." Her whisper shatters his heart.

Slipping back into the darkness, Davina returns to her place in the corner of the room. Fumbling around the space, Americ finds the flint stone and any burnable material he can find. Striking over and over until a spark catches, he steadies his breathing and regains his composure. Light flickers across his face as he builds the small flames into a hot rolling fire satisfying him enough to face Davina.

Crouched in the corner of the room, she sits with a tear-streaked face and tattered clothing. Her bruised hands from pounding on the door look painful, dropping his heart further into despair.

"I didn't know," Americ speaks without thinking.

Davina shoots a glare at him. Her jaw clenched as she bites back words of anger.

"So you have come for penance then?" she says crisply.

"No. Nothing I can say would make up for such a transgression as this. Instead, I come with news I wish I didn't have to tell you." Davina sits, eyes wide and trained on Americ. With no reply from her, he continues. "Your father has been sentenced to death. He will be shackled in the lower chambers where the tide will take him. I'm sorry." Averting her gaze, he swallows with difficulty.

"He gave his life to save me, and I wasted it. You don't get to tell me sorry. Just show me mercy and take my life." Americ's gaze shoots back up to hers, tears erupting from her eyes in agony.

He shakes his head, stomach lurching with the thought of her death, and repulsed by it being from his own hand, he turns his back to her, rushing for escape from the room.

"I need to speak with Rheyhas. Now." Turning to the guard as the cell door shuts, he demands him away harshly, feeling daring enough, at last, to make his escape and free the girl.

TWENTY

——

Wind whistles outside and in through the tiny window in the wall of Davina's prison. Barely able to see out with both eyes, she peers into the void of spiky waves beyond them and out into the horizon, the rich, vibrant sky fading into nothingness. Davina, lips puckered, as tears well up in her eyes, finds her hope all but lost, fallen heavily with the news of her father. The tide came and went. She wonders if he suffered and hoped with all her heart, he had forgiven her. Tears glistening on her cheeks from the last beams of light. She watches as the sun disappears under the vast ocean, leaving its residue smudged along the horizon to fade.

Keys jingle crisply and scrape at the door in a scuffle. Bursting open, Americ flies across the room at her, surprising her with his ferocity. Throwing himself against her, they slam into the wall, and in the chaos, he whispers two little words only she can hear, "Trust me."

Searing pain rips across her scalp as she is drug from the room, Rheyhas voice trailing behind them, "This is not a good idea, sir. What can you gain by this?"

"She will tell me what I want to know, or her father will suffer far worse than high tide." Americ's grip releases her hair and moves to her arm, fingers digging into her skin, leaving bruises.

Rushing down the corridor, the three of them wind through the maze of stairs and halls, digging deeper into the frightful prison. Frantically searching around her, Davina's eyes fall on faces peering from peep holes and cages, sick and filthy, mumbling as they pass. A guard calls out before them, and they stop.

"Cadison," Americ orders him with a nod to take his place.

Shoving Davina to the wall, Rheyhas watches Americ speak with the guard whose face falls to a sick ash color. Waving them forward, Americ falls back, taking Davina once again by the arm, marching past the soldier. Down another stairway, they reach a cold and damp corridor, salt from the sea stinging their eyes as they approach a door covered in deep black moss.

Rheyhas steps to the door, turning to Americ and looking at the two of them sweetly.

"Take care to leave immediately. Go directly to the ridge below. I have a man waiting who will take you as far as the town of Dorvague. A man named Yrin will meet you in a tavern overlooking The Serpents Tongue. Give him this." Pulling from beneath his vest, Rheyhas gives Americ a letter, sealed in navy wax.

Davina, realization sweeping over her, looks from man to man, dumbfounded.

Returning focus to the door, Rheyhas shoves it open then nods to Americ before running up the corridor they had come from. Releasing her, Americ walks inside before Davina, who closely follows. A man sits perched on his knees in the middle of the pungent room, wrists shackled to the floor on either side of his body.

"Father?" Davina scrambles to her father, kneeling before him and pulling him to her to rest.

"Davina." His voice is weak, and his body is heavy against hers.

"I can heal you. We can escape, be free. Let me heal you." Davina runs her hands over his body, sensing where the greatest damage could be.

"No." Pulling away, Brien grunts in pain as he looks up, his eyes swollen into slits, search her face desperately. "I swore to your mother I would make sure you survived no matter the cost. You have a destiny to fulfill, so you must go. Leave my old, damaged soul behind. Death is my only freedom." Hacking suddenly, he crumples, swaying in place then regaining his posture.

"You need to go, my child." Leaning his head forward, Brien kisses her forehead as tears trickle down his face onto hers. "You are more like your mother every day," he whispers.

Unable to catch a breath, Davina freezes before him, speechless. In the background, Americ stands watching, desperate to run from the distressing reunion. When Brien's eyes meet his, chills run down his spine as his face is full of recognition.

Fear he knows Americ's true identity, he moves to Davina, placing a hand over her shoulder. "We have to go. There isn't much more time."

Davina throws herself at her father, grasping him tightly around the neck.

Brien turns his face into her cheek, kissing it sweetly, then murmurs something into her ear. Americ watches her pale face back away and, with a quivering lip, rush away from him to the door. Meeting Americ's eyes once again, he slightly motions for him to come nearer, so Americ bends down to his level.

"It is by no accident you are here. Protect her. Your fates are bound and have been since before your lives began. She is the answer to your reign." His voice is soft and weak yet full of confidence. "Now go."

Without a moment's hesitation, Americ sprints across the room to Davina in the doorway. Closing the door tightly, Americ takes her by the arm and runs to the first set of stairs winding up two floors. Shooting down the corridor, Davina has no time to think or process what is happening. Like a stone wall, the fresh sea air hits them as Americ forces through a door. Releasing his grip on her, Americ lunges forward with all his might, and they continue through the night air, enemies fleeing together as allies.

* * *

Dorvague reeks of dead fish, salt, and alcohol, all wafting up from the cove and grungy pub along its banks. Davina and Americ walk along the muddy streets in silence, searching for signs of danger. The homes, made of stone, are worn and crumbling over the flowing grass, attempting to mimic the nearby sea. Stumbling through the night, Davina follows closely behind Americ, not wanting to be separated from him until they are safe. Moving along the path leading down the embankment, the two make their way to the tavern. Voices float from the open windows along the pale rays of light.

Americ, suddenly stopping, looks over his shoulder at Davina. She stops, too, curious as to what would be so important to stop in the freezing cold.

"If anything goes wrong, run. Go as far from here as you can." Americ looks at her with concern. "I mean it."

"Alright," Davina replies, surprised.

Gently, Americ opens the door, smoke from the fire enveloping them in clouds of heat, and the smell of gammon fills their lungs, sending their stomachs ablaze with hunger. All eyes fall to them when Davina enters, her dress torn and dirty alongside Americ, clean and well put together. Stepping across the room, Americ finds himself before the barmaid while Davina takes a seat at the nearest table that stands empty.

Davina glares at the eyes peering at her around the room, full of lust and drink. Wary of her situation, her eyes flip back to Americ, now speaking with a tall man, draped in a deep russet cloak and furs at the collar. Handing him the note, Americ nods in Davina's direction then, once finished speaking to the man, he returns to her side. Davina sees the man slide two coins across the wooden surface before pursuing Americ.

"Are you well enough to continue? There are still a few hours yet to go." The man's golden eyes meet Davina's green ones, and she nods.

"This is Yrin. He will take us to Dune like Cadison said." Americ looks at her, speaking with relief and excitement.

Beginning to regain feeling in her fingers, she looks out the nearest window and grimaces. Her clothes, thin and ragged, barely provided enough to cover her, let alone keep her warm in the night. Observing this, Yrin steps away back to where the barmaid stands, overlooking her customers. Following Yrin, the woman full of concern, prances to Davina, taking her by the arm and leading her away from the men and room. Up the steps to the second level, Davina finds doors line the hall. Turning sharply into an open room, Davina finds two more women, scarcely dressed, lounging across the bed and floor.

"Leave us."

The girls jump, running immediately from the room as the barmaid commands.

Davina rubs her arm once released from the woman's attachment, turning her attention to the room and its simplicity. Simple drapes hang over the window, made from the same cloth as the bedding. A small chest sits in the corner, and candles riddle every ledge available to be propped onto. Suddenly overly aware of the warmth of the room, Davina looks for the fire and finds it ablaze behind her, crackling and spitting vigorously. Drawn by its intensity, she crouches, falling to her knees, soaking in every bit of its protruding warmth.

"This should do nicely, I think." The woman's voice is cheery behind Davina.

From the corner of her vision, Davina sees blue fabric flutter through the air. Interested, she pivots around, remaining seated on the floor to see a dress laid out across the bed. Standing now, Davina reaches for it, the soft wool comforting and warm in her hand.

"I am Esrin. Yrin is my brother, and he has asked me to care for you before you leave for Dune. I have to agree you are in great need. Come." Waving her hands in the air, Davina obeys without question, folding herself into Esrin's care.

Stripping the ruined clothing away from Davina's filthy skin then wrapping her in a blanket, Esrin leaves the room in search of a basin and water. Davina finds herself embarrassed and ashamed, allowing a few tears to shed and dry unseen. Returning with hot water and a rag, Esrin takes to Davina's skin with the gentleness of a mother. Heart swelling with gratitude, Davina begins to cry, and Esrin accepts it silently without question. Once cleaned, Esrin dresses Davina, slipping each article over her head and tying it securely at the back.

"Thank you," Davina whispers as Esrin leads her from the room after a long while.

Esrin doesn't reply. Instead, she smiles, taking Davina's arm in her own and leading them back to the tavern room. Yrin and Americ sit drinking ale across from each other, a plate of gammon between them. Rising at Davina's appearance, Americ's cheeks flush slightly, and Yrin nods his approval, handing her a savory piece of meat.

"Tell mother and father I am well and will bring Maory to visit in the spring," Esrin speaks over Davina to Yrin.

"Mmmhmm," he grumbles to her.

Handing Davina a cloak, Esrin watches as her brother leaves the tavern, slamming the door behind him making the walls rattle. Clenching her jaw, she shakes her head after him before storming away in the other direction.

Looking to Americ, Davina's concern is obvious, but he only shrugs, taking the same path outdoors to an unknown future.

TWENTY-ONE

Dune's high walls seem to touch the rosy sky as they enter through the gates, weary and weak. Guided through the streets, they found themselves in the center of the city before a large home. They swept inside to beds located in the upper rooms, where they fell into a dreamless sleep. Waking late into the evening, Davina wanders from her room to the main room below, finding Yrin, a young woman perched on his knee, and an older woman sitting across from him before the fire. Their voices are quiet and serious as she enters the room, sending the young woman to her feet to serve Davina.

Motioning to an open chair, the older woman nods curtly, and Yrin leans back into his seat, looking toward the door the young woman disappeared through. Taking a seat, Davina settles into the warmth, searching for Meric, hoping to see a familiar face.

"If you are searching for the young man, know he is resting. I am Elra, Chieftess of this place and its people. You are safe here." The older woman says genuinely, her voice deep and rich like thick molasses.

The wooden planks creak lightly from above with movement, and after a few moments, Americ appears in the doorway of the stairs. Just as he descends, the young woman returns with a tray of food and drink, settling it on the table near Elra before resuming her seat upon Yrin's knee.

"This is Adyra. She serves my house and is the wife of Yrin." The girl's face flushes pink as Yrin places his hand around her small waist.

Davina nods in Adyra's direction then sees the tray of delectable goods, her mouthwatering with the scent.

"Come and sit, my children. Eat your fill while we speak about my nephew who so kindly sent you to my care," Elra says, following her own words by taking food herself.

"Rheyhas is your nephew?" Americ speaks, voice cracking from sleep.

"Yes. My brother came to this country for peace in the war with Uutithea. He remained in the Great King's court after treaties were signed and the war ended. The King favored him, allowing him to marry one of his daughter's ladies. I tried to convince him to join us here when we came upon Omideon's shores, but his wife served the princess, and they could not leave. Remaining in the guard, he kept power and position at the king's right hand. When Cadison was but a small child, a plague swept the country, taking his wife. Cadison became Agnai's companion as his father had become obsessed with the prophecy spoken by the Nasinreth visionary. When Agnai had become of age, he appointed Cadison as the commander of his personal guard once my brother passed. Soon after taking the throne, my brother died, insuring Cadison's place." Gazing past Davina, Elra's face becomes solemn and distant.

Americ remains at the door of the stairs, arms folded as he takes in the story and scene before him. Davina thinks of the man's kindness to her and his protection, and now she understands why he would send them there. Searching Elra's face, she recognizes something else but is unsure why. Her honey eyes, deeply salted hair enmeshed in her thick black locks, and the hard lines of her jaw makes Davina feel as though she knows her.

"Why would he stay in Aldhorran if his family is here? I know him well enough to know he has no wife or children." Americ asks, searching for answers to unimportant questions.

"He had two valuable reasons to stay. When I came to Omideon, it was not by choice but rather necessity. Romathe and Drumidia were at war because of the King's own selfishness, taking our bride. My husband became the Chieftain as he was the only survivor in his line, and so to keep his lineage safe, he sent me away with our three children. My daughters died on the journey, but my son survived. As an adult, he left home chasing after a girl, and they settled in Aldhorran. He refused his birthright for the Chieftain Seat, so when his wife bore him a son, we knew he would be the last line of Tamlik.

Cadison remained in Aldhorran to watch over him as I could not remove him from his father's devilish care. The poor boy nearly died on multiple occasions had it not been for Cadison's intervention. Hoping he would return here after Daventh's death, I had a marriage prepared, but he arrived with his heart intended for another." Elra watches Davina's face as her expressions change from interest, to recognition, to shock.

"Ascher is next in line to become Chieftain of Romathe?" Davina's voice is excited, forgetting any others present in the room.

"Your sister will make a good wife and leader to the Aulik if they so choose." Elra smiles at Davina's childish reaction.

Remembering Yrin, Adyra, and Meric, she looks at each person, smiling ear to ear.

"You said there were two reasons," Americ speaks impatiently, searching the faces of each person.

"The Crowned Prince. If there came a day when he began seeking release from the King, Cadison would be there," Elra says, watching the blood drain from Americ's face. She looks to Davina, then back to Americ, tilting her head slightly. "I think he kept his word seeing as you are here, alive and well, Americ, son of Agnai."

Americ holds his breath, panic rising in his chest as he watches expressions change across the faces before him. Stepping backward, he glances into Davina's eyes, cold with anger. Before anyone can stop her, Davina dives for the poker near the fire, sweeping it up from against the wall and swinging it at his head. Ducking, Americ rolls across the wooden floor out of harm's way. Tossing a glance behind him, he sees Yrin taking Davina by the waist, hauling her back to her chair while Adyra replaces the fire poker.

"Yrin, please take Americ out while I speak with Davina," Elra says calmly, looking at her, huffing in her chair.

Watching the men and Adyra leave, Davina settles slightly in her chair, glaring at Elra. The two of them sit, watching one another closely. Davina wants nothing more than to follow the small party and fight the man who deceived her, not because he is the child of her greatest enemy but because he lied repeatedly.

"Ascher sent word to me not long ago, and it reached us just yesterday. They are safely in Aldara along with Sirien, your other sister. They asked me if I could find your whereabouts or fate. I sent a messenger this morning informing them of your safety," Elra announces happily.

"Why would you allow him to stay?" Davina asks between gritted teeth.

"Because of Cadison. He has become fond of the boy and assures me he is nothing like his father. I never met Amesah but had heard of her gentleness and goodness, which is what Cadison sees. The horrific things the young man has witnessed and been a part of are enough to turn one's stomach. My nephew is wise, and if he says Americ is trustworthy, I believe him. Give him a chance." Elra sounds motherly in her words, and Davina cringes at the simple thought.

"I need rest. Is that all?" Rudely, Davina rises, not waiting for an answer as her feet thunder up the steps and across the hall above.

Elra listens to the door shut with a snap, then reaches to the hearth, taking a small log and throws it into the fire. Taking the abandoned ale beside her, she drinks, pondering over whether Yrin needs to remain for the night and watch over Americ or if she should take her chances with the free spirited Nasinreth.

* * *

The moon shines bright through the window, sitting at its highest point. Crackling, the flames of the fire lick at the wood, digesting it slowly into ash. Davina holds her knees tightly to her chest, propped against the end of the bed, watching the logs deteriorate. The house, silent other than creaking from the wind, is peaceful, yet Davina cannot find sleep. The conversation with Elra sits heavy on her mind, and she thinks of Rheyhas then Americ, heart pounding erratically.

Even with the knowledge Americ is the crowned prince, what bothers her most is the fact he lied to her about who he was, pretending to be lesser than his title. Davina fought herself daily to not care for either men who constantly stuck their necks out for her. She entertained the idea of becoming friends if they escaped together and his character remained the same, but could she still do so now? Would doing so be the greatest betrayal to her people and father?

Soft steps pat past her door, boards creaking as the individual inches away down the nearby stairs. Gathering what warmth she could from the fire, Davina pulls a heavy quilt from the bed, wrapping it around her shoulders to cover her shift. Peering out her door, she finds the hall empty and dark. Carefully, she takes the same path as the person before her, sneaking to the main room below to seek out the person still awake.

Just as she had suspected, Americ is crouched before the hearth, poking the smoldering coals underneath a fresh log. His eyes catch her, following Davina's movements as she finds a chair near the low heat. Moving away, Americ sits across from her, preparing for a fight or simply to run, but she makes no advances. Instead, Davina tucks her feet up underneath her, wrapping tightly in the quilt.

"What did my father say to you before we left?" Davina's eyes bore into his, making him uneasy.

"He said to protect you and our fates were bound." Americ looks to the fire, avoiding her gaze.

Davina slips into silence, looking down at the blanket around her, confused yet intrigued. She feels hope again that maybe they could be friends. She adjusts in her seat, annoyed with the childish thoughts, chiding herself.

"Why did we leave so hastily?" Davina breaks the silence again, shoving her thoughts aside.

"Rheyhas saw a letter from my father to another guard. He

ordered your death and expressed his disappointment in me, which is great, warranting some new punishment I cannot endure." Americ wipes his face with his hands.

"Does it keep you up at night?" Americ looks at Davina, unsure of what she is asking. "Elra said you have witnessed a lot of difficult things. Does it haunt you at night, keeping you from sleep?"

"Oh. Yes. I don't sleep well." Americ looks down at his feet shyly, the fire light flickering across his face.

Curiosity sweeps over Davina, and suddenly she feels the need to know this man, to understand him. She stares at him, taking in his appearance, remembering his actions and what he has said to her. Never in her small crypt of memories has she witnessed his cruelty purposefully, and she begins to wonder if Elra was right.

Perhaps I should give him a chance.

"Tell me about them. Sometimes it can help." His eyes meet hers again, but this time with fear.

"You hate me already. Why would I tell you anything to give you more of a reason?" His voice trembles.

"I was angry. I will admit that. But I am listening now. Tell me the dream that woke you." Davina's eyes twinkle genuinely.

"It's not a dream. It is a memory that will haunt me for the rest of my life." His whisper is full of sadness.

He clenches his hands into fists, setting his jaw tightly together a moment before moving to tend the fire. Kneeling before the burning embers, he stirs them before placing another log over them. Watching him relaxes Davina, and she finds herself happy to be with him.

"A few years after my mother disappeared, my father's rampages worsened. The council had told him that favor did not lay in his hands any longer. To ensure his strength, he made an alliance with Divanthra, betrothing my twin sister Charlotte to their prince. When the ambassador arrived, he did not like what he saw as she has always been strong-willed and open with her opinions. He called off the alliance with his King's permission, leaving Omideon without a treaty. Castah was pledged to Netheis and I to Uutithea, leaving Charlotte to still be desired and useless. In his rage, he sent her away with one of his advisors to train her properly.

Two years later, she returned home, telling father stories of her teacher's violence and acts. Enraged, my father had him beheaded. Loyalties still uneasy in the council chamber, father promised them anything they desired if only they would commit to his rule. The discussion turned quickly to Charlotte and how she was tainted by the dead council member, thus no longer worthy of having a blessed union with any man. They saw her beauty and enjoyed her company, so they asked for her.

After careful thought, he agreed. We were thirteen, and I remember it being the only time I stood up to him. He smacked me around some, telling me I had no part in such matters. He said Charlotte is his property, and he will do as he wishes. For my insolence, he drug me to Sir Hathen's chamber to witness..." voice cracking, Americ stops, staring into the fire.

Rising from her chair, Davina goes to him, pulling Americ into her arms. She doesn't have to think to know his immediate need. Instead, she gave into herself, allowing the hatred for him to empty, filling its place with gentleness and care. Her skin feels electrified as she sits, holding him tightly. Americ, shocked by the action, gladly curls up, laying his weight against hers.

"It wasn't your fault," Davina whispers to the top of his head as he shudders, tears breaking free in his pain, no longer locked away.

TWENTY-TWO

———

"Has something happened to them?" Amalie asks, her breath fogging the window before her.

Amalie stands, arms folded over her chest, watching Sirien's still figure at the end of the path. Snow glides down from the sky, dusting her hair and cloak in the frozen flakes.

"I doubt it, not with Yrin there." Ascher says, a sharp whistling ring coming from his direction.

Amalie peels herself from the window, her steps taking her to the hearth where Ascher sits sharpening his ax. She watches as he guides the small round stone in his hand along the blade's edge. His focus makes her smile, because in that moment he is at peace, in his element.

"How do you know Yrin?" Amalie asks, fascinated by his technique.

"I have known him since boyhood. My father and I had travel papers for trading. The King liked my father's work and rewarded him with the ability to come and go as he pleased. I spent a few summers in Dune, then took over the trade runs for my father. Yrin and I essentially grew up together when I was around." Ascher grins at the memories flashing across his thoughts.

"I didn't realize you spent so much time there," Amalie says, amused, sitting back in a nearby chair.

"After my mother left, he didn't want me, so I spent a lot of time with Elra. When she asked him to officially give up his rights, he became angry, and I didn't go back until the trade runs." Ascher runs his finger along the blade's edge, checking the smoothness before turning it over to begin on the other side.

"If he didn't want you, why wouldn't he?" Amalie questions, confusion in her voice.

"He left for specific reasons, and he wouldn't be passed up by his own son, which is what she wanted." He stops, looking up at Amalie, suddenly nervous. "There is a lot more to my family than you think. Things I haven't told you, Amalie. Secrets I thought I buried until we went to Dune."

Taking a large breath, Ascher resettles himself in his chair, but before he can speak again, they hear a shriek from outside. Shooting up from their seats, they rush to the door and bolt outside, dagger in Amalie's hand, drawn from her back and ax still in Ascher's grip. To their surprise and excitement, their sight falls onto four riders. Face alight, Amalie sheathes her dagger and runs forward to Sirien, clutching her arm as Davina dives from her horse and into her sister's arms.

Squealing and crying, they embrace tightly until Amalie's gaze floats over the two heads onto Adyra's sweet face. Releasing herself from the sisterly love, she marches to Adyra, embracing her and thanking her for bringing Davina home.

"Yrin!" Ascher heartily laughs as he claps Yrin over the shoulder, smiling widely.

"It is sure good to see you, brother. It has been a long journey, and as you likely suspect, we have much to discuss." Yrin raises an eyebrow, glad to see Ascher.

"I did figure as much. Bring the horses, and we will settle them." Taking the reigns of all four horses, Ascher sees the fourth rider, a young man with every physical trait of a Drumidian.

His silver eyes meet with Ascher's golden ones for a moment before his attention draws to Davina. Pulling the horses away, he takes another look in the other man's direction, then hustles away to the stable with Yrin.

The strong, pleasant scent of manure and hay fills Ascher's lungs as he enters. Stopping before three plump horses, he pats each nose before moving past them, opening the gates to the stalls. Slowly the horses make their way to the opening at the end of the structure that leads into a corral. Waving a hand in the direction of the empty spaces, Ascher moves aside to allow the new horses in, led by Yrin.

"When you go back, you can tell her no," Ascher says strongly.

"You know she will never take no for an answer. Does your wife know?" Yrin asks, loosening the straps of the saddle on the first horse.

"No. I almost told her, and I will. I just…" Ascher sighs, moving to remove the saddle from a different horse.

"Ascher, this is your birthright. When your grandfather dies, it will be you, the people want. The homeland needs the Tamlik to remain their Chieftain." Yrin peers over the blank horse's back, marked with sweat from the leather.

"I may be Aulik, but I was born and raised in Omideon. How could they want me? I am a foreigner," Ascher says with irritation.

"You are more Aulik than you credit yourself. Besides, if it were to ever be questioned, Amalie would put an end to that immediately. Are you sure she is in Nasinreth?" Yrin smiles obnoxiously.

"It's hard to believe, but she is. She would be better suited to lead than I." Shaking his head, Ascher carries away the saddle, laying it over the stall edge. "I thought it was just you and Davina coming. Why did Adyra come along, and who is the Drumidian?" Ascher turns to the next horse while he speaks, loosening the straps quickly.

"As I said, your grandmother doesn't take no for an answer." Yrin laughs lightly. "It's a good thing I already had an eye for Adyra because she is now my wife."

"Ayy!" Ascher smiles, walking away from the horse to Yrin. Taking his hand, they pull each other close, patting roughly on the back in a manly hug. "I think it is a well-made match. You are a lucky man. Her meals are delicious." Yrin slaps his stomach.

"There is no hunger with her around." The men laugh heartily together before falling into silence. Yrin works quickly with the straps, thinking over the next part of their conversation.

"Yrin!" A shrill scream from the house sends chills down the spines of the men, sending them in a flurry for their weapons out the door and across the yard.

Adyra, standing in the door, is pale as yelling shatters the barrier of the cottage walls. Yrin reaches the house first, pushing inside, followed by Ascher.

"Amalie, no! Sirien put the fire rod down!" Davina yells at the two women positioned and ready to strike.

"What is going on here?" Ascher's voice booms, looking to the fractured room.

"You have brought a traitor into our home!" Amalie points her drawn dagger at the man standing behind Davina.

Turning to Yrin, Ascher looks to him for answers. Returning his weapon to its place, Yrin rubs his face before answering.

"This is Americ, son to the King."

Ascher becomes rigid, drawing his ax tightly in his fist.

"He is not like them! Don't ask me to explain because I can't. I don't understand it fully myself, but he is different! He is good. Please, put your weapons away," Davina pleads with her sisters, glancing at Ascher then back to her sisters.

Ascher looks back to Yrin, whose eyes are trained on his wife. He looks to Amalie, her fist clenched around the hilt of her dagger, ready to throw in an instant.

"Why did you bring him?" Ascher speaks calmly, watching Amalie carefully.

"Because Elra asked me to. It is a long story, Ascher. One you may find interesting," Yrin replies curtly.

"I'm not interested in stories, Yrin. Why?" Ascher demands.

"Because my father is a tyrant, and I want to be free," Americ speaks for the first time, looking at Ascher, his cold eyes piercing.

"Amalie." Ascher breaks eye contact with Americ to look at her.

Looking at him for the first time since he entered, Amalie bites down, stalking past him to the door, but stops before leaving.

"They may think you are different, but you royals are all the same. If you betray any of us, I will cut out your heart and allow it to beat its last in my very palm, and I will watch the light dim from your eyes." Reaching for her cloak hung on a peg by the door, Amalie leaves.

Ascher, sighing heavily, chases after her, and life itself stands still, her threat eerily saturating the room.

* * *

"How dare she bring him here? People we know and love have died by his father's hand, Sirien!" Amalie nearly shouts as she paces the small room.

Ascher watches from a distance, arms folded as he leans against the wall across from the home's door. Sirien sits in the armchair, staring into the roaring fire, while Adyra and Yrin find comfort at the table, a good distance from Amalie.

"I don't know Amalie, but we should be trusting of Davina, and if not her, then the woman Elra you speak of. Perhaps there is a greater purpose," Sirien sighs, perplexed.

"I don't care if he has a greater purpose. I don't want him here or to be a part of it." Amalie continues pacing.

"Elra spoke of a man, her nephew, who claims this prince only wants peace. If he says this and she believes him, so shall I, as should you," Yrin's deep voice rumbles.

Amalie stops, looking him square in the face. Suddenly she grabs a mug from a side table nearby and, with great force, throws it into the fire. The liquid inside bursts the flames into insanity for a moment, causing the entire room to become uneasy.

Leaning his head back against the wall and closing his eyes, Ascher speaks with a tone of agitated humor. "And what does this *Nephew* suggest we do?"

"Cadison believes the King is weakening in power and may soon be overthrown," Yrin replies, watching Ascher's eyes pop open and body stands rigid at the name.

"Rheyhas? One of the Kings guard?" Ascher asks in shock.

Yrin nods and watches Ascher's hand go instinctively to his ribs, eyes shifting to the floor. Amalie sees it too, looking from Ascher to Yrin then back, hoping for an explanation.

Sirien looks into the fire, oblivious to the looks of the others.

"She asked him to watch over you and keep you alive. If she couldn't raise you, she needed to watch over you," Yrin says in an attempt to settle his mind.

"If this is true, I owe them both my life. They have earned my trust. The boy stays." Ascher whispers, overwhelmed by the new information.

"So that's it then? They woo you with one simple act?" Amalie snaps.

Instantly regretting her anger, she watches as Ascher closes the gap between them. Pulling his tunic free, he rips it from his body, his scars illuminated by the firelight. The shirt still in one hand, he stretches his arms out to the side, looking directly at her.

"All of this. You have seen it. You have cared for it and cared for me. That man, that soldier saved my life more than once, pulling me from the brink of death. He stopped Daventh the night I knew I was to die. Someone had seen us, Amalie, in the woods that day, and when I came home, he was determined to have you killed to teach me a lesson. If he trusts the boy, so will I. He stays." Moving past Amalie, he hurtles himself up the steps, his tunic whipping at his side.

Jaw clenched, Amalie stands still in the place he left her, eyes of the others focused on her. The room is silent while the world outside howls and flurries. Nodding, Amalie turns to the stairs, taking a step up the first one before stopping again and peering over her shoulder.

"He stays for now. But if he is any trouble at all, I will kill him." Heading up the stairs, she leaves the others behind and wanders to her room directly across from the landing.

The door opens a crack, sending light into the dark hall. Pausing, she looks down the long stretch to the other doors, dark and cold other than Americ's. Shaking off the frustration, she prepares herself for Ascher's anger before slipping through the door.

Ascher sits on the bed. His body turned to the door. Shutting it quietly behind her, Amalie steps toward him, overly conscious of the dozens of marks across his back. Slowly she makes her way around the corner until she stands before him.

"I don't trust the boy either, but I owe it to Elra to give him a chance," Ascher speaks defensively.

"I know, and I respect your decision." He looks at her with relief. "Why didn't you ever tell me?" Her sight slips down to the wide patch of skin, distorted by a healed injury.

"I never wanted to burden you. If you knew why you might have walked away to save me, which would have been worse than death."

Her eyes are tender, listening to his every word. "Tell me now then," she whispers.

"I fought him. Throwing fists, grabbing anything within reach to use as a weapon, but when I turned on him, he had a hatchet. I have no idea where he found it, but it was there in his hand and then in my side. He stood over me laughing, and when Cadison broke in, he nearly killed Daventh by beating him. I kept saying your name, and when he came to my side, he listened. The neighbor cared for me, nursing me back to health even though she swore I would die. When Cadison visited again, he told me you were safe, and so was I. That's what killed him. Whatever that man did to him was permanent. He never touched me again." Ascher closes his eyes, leaning back to fall against the bed.

"Come to bed, Amalie. You need your rest." Obeying, Amalie strips down to her shift, crawling onto the bed beside him and curling in close.

TWENTY-THREE

———

Laying in the dark, Davina listens to the voices below, angry with her for bringing Americ and confused by her actions as well. Davina, eyes wide, focuses on the beams above her, waiting for the noise to calm itself and hoping Americ is hearing less of them. Suddenly, silence cuts the air, and footsteps tromp up the stairway. Not long after, a second set of feet trail the same way, closing a door gently. Thankful for the quiet, Davina rolls to her side, hoping sleep will take her quickly, but she finds disappointment in the idea as she tosses and turns in discomfort.

As quiet as a scuttling mouse, Sirien slips into the room and sneaks to her side of the bed. Carefully, she settles under the quilt so as not to disturb Davina and falls asleep quickly. Davina waits for the sound of her heavy breaths before rising, scooping up a blanket from the end of the bed, and rushing across the floor in her bare feet. As silent as Sirien had come, Davina goes, shutting the door with a subtle thud. Searching the hall, she finds she is alone, giving her the ability to freely go where she chooses.

The last door in the hall is closed, but light streams from underneath, and she can see a shadow move across it. Tapping lightly, she waits until the door slits open, and she smiles at Americ peeking out. Allowing her inside, she immediately crosses to the open hearth where she can warm her toes, but Americ doesn't move from the door.

Why is she here? Americ wonders, nervous she brings bad news of his unwelcomeness.

Listening to the ruckus below, he paced the room, remembering the threat Amalie had given him and is terrified of its reality. When the knock at the door came, he hesitated, afraid to find the evil woman on the other side. But he did answer, and to his delight, found Davina, and now he stares, confused by her presence as she squats down to the floor before the fire.

Reminding him of her imprisonment, she sits, blanket wrapped around her shoulders, knees tucked into her chest, hair loosely falling over her shoulders, and sight trained on the fire. The only difference is that she looks alive here, happy, fulfilled. Observing this, his prior thoughts feel even more prominent and right. Turning her head, Davina smiles at him, eyes glimmering in the firelight.

"What is it?" she asks.

"Nothing," Americ shakes his head, walking to the bed to pull a blanket from it and join her on the floor.

"Liar." Davina raises her eyebrows and tilts her head, looking at him in the face.

"I was thinking you look alive here." Americ's face flushes with heat, and he is thankful for the fire so close to blame.

Biting her lip, Davina nods, looking into the flames. Awkwardly, they sit against the foot of the bed, watching the orange spikes flicker.

"It is said if you look hard enough, you can see your fate," Davina speaks quietly, enthralled in the crackling light.

"What is it you see?" Americ allows his gaze to dive into the hearth, ablaze with fire.

"The restoration of this kingdom by your fair hand." Davina's eyes are black, her face sober.

Taken aback by her observation, Americ shudders, shaking his head in disagreement. Folding his arms over his knees, he rests his chin on the bony platform. He thinks a moment before speaking, hoping his voice isn't too weak to make a sound.

"No."

"Why not?" Davina huffs.

"Because I am never going back." Sitting up, Americ leans back against the bed, forearms resting on his knees. "I have always wanted freedom, and now I have it. I will leave tomorrow if the weather is fair."

Davina stiffens, looking at him, stung by his betrayal of their friendship. She opens her mouth to speak but falters, wordless, shutting it hard enough her teeth click loudly together. Reasons of why he would leave so suddenly rush through her thoughts, as she considers every possible way to convince him to stay. Americ waits for an answer, but nothing comes from her.

"Your sisters don't want me here. Nobody trusts me, and I don't blame them. I don't wish to be King because of this same issue. It is not just you and your family Davina. It will be everyone. It's time a new family steps upon the throne."

"I trust you," Davina's voice is a whisper, so low Americ is unsure he heard her right.

"What?" Americ says.

"I trust you, Americ, and I don't want you to leave," her eyes are sad as she speaks, the glimmer absent and blank.

"How can you trust me?" Americ looks at her softly, heart skipping.

"You saved my life. You are kind and good. I see what Cadison sees and do not share the fears or views of my sisters." She looks at him. Concern etched deep in her forehead. "Don't leave me."

"Then come with me. We can make a life anywhere in the world. I will be good to you. Perhaps this is too hasty, but I feel it in my soul Davina that we are fated." Reaching for her hand, Americ looks at her with a longing in his eyes. Never had he felt such a passion as this or could ignore it any longer.

"Americ, your place is here. Your kingdom is here, and if your father is overruled, then the crown is yours. You can't leave. You have to go back." Pulling her hand from his, Davina looks questioningly at him, abashed by his words.

"I can't." Americ, shaking his head, stands suddenly, face distorted by rejection. "My father will kill me. He made that clear the day I left. I failed him, Davina, and I am replaceable." Anger begins to burn behind his eyes, so he walks past her, his back turned, shielding his face from her.

"He has no other sons."

Americ heaves a curt sigh.

"He has bastards. One, in particular, he fancies above the rest. His firstborn child before marrying my mother and is highly honored as a soldier in his guard. He is an animal like my father." Gripping the bottom edge of the open window, Americ leans into it, feeling the wintry sea breeze and smelling the mixture of pine and sea in his lungs.

Davina sits, silently staring after him, his broad shoulders hunched in defeat, red hair a tangled mess lose over his shoulders, and fine clothes tattered from travel. He didn't look much like a royal but rather a wayfaring stranger lost to himself and the world. Americ is worn. His face reads tired and bedraggled from the burden of being the King's son.

Intrigued by his character, Davina had spent the weeks in Balaoug to study him, and with each passing day, she noticed the subtle changes which drew her to him. Watching him now is no different. He is the boy, drug down by the weight of the war waging within himself, slumping in the window, body slack in defeat. Compassion waves over her resolve, and like a shadow, she rises to her feet, crossing the room. Instinct taking over her, as if not in her own consciousness, she places her hands on him, one flat between his shoulders and the other around his upper arm, her slim fingers gently grasping the flesh and muscle.

"We are fated, therefore where you go, then so will I," Davina whispers in his ear.

* * *

The warmth of the morning sun peaks through the small window of Sirien and Davina's room. Sirien stirs, a pleasant dream still on the edge of her drowsiness, and for the first time in a long while, she feels rested. Stretching, her hands find the cold blankets around her, and opening her eyes, she sees the emptiness of Davina's place. Taking in the soft brilliance of the room, Sirien lays on her back, peacefully reminiscing the dream she just woke from.

The stillness of the home is everything she has ever wanted, liberation in exile. The soft laugh of a woman drifts from below, so Sirien rises, feet dangling over the side of the bed as she reconsiders, leaving the warmth of her wool cocoon. Shoving the urge to rest longer, she forces herself up, bones cracking with each stretch as her body comes to life. Rubbing a hand over her slightly raised belly, she whispers good morning before slipping her gown over her head, concealing the little bump.

To Sirien's surprise, the pregnancy was easy and concealable. The small child flutters, stirring a love inside of her she could not manage, knowing she carried a part of Castor within. She sorely missed her husband, thinking of him without end, but her mourning was over as her sisters were there with her alive and well. Completing her morning routine, she pulls a shawl around her shoulders before wandering from the room and down the stairs, expecting to find Davina among those risen early, but to her surprise, she finds both her sisters absent.

"The morn to you." Adyra, bright-eyed, speaks softly to Sirien as she descends the steps.

Perched near the fire, Adyra and Yrin sit, huddled together in the chilly air as the heat slowly radiates from its flame.

"Have you seen Davina? She wasn't in our room," Sirien asks, taking a seat in the rocking chair near the hearth.

Adyra and Yrin look at each other, smiling as they shake their heads in response. Unsure by their reactions, Sirien sits a moment in hope for an explanation. Without one, she changes her focus, moving from the chair to the large stove in the kitchen. Taking care to fill and light it, she takes to the barrels and jars placed around the home, filling a large bowl with the contents.

"May I be of assistance?" Adyra appears at the edge of Sirien's vision.

"Yes, actually. There is salt pork in the cellar outside. Would it be too much to ask?" Sirien scrunches her face, aware of the cold and difficulty a trip through the snow would be.

"I will take care of that." Yrin nearly jumps from the couch, groaning as he arches his back.

Before either of the women can say a word, Yrin is out the door. Smiling with admiration, Adyra looks in the direction of the door before turning her attention to Sirien. Admiring the couple, Sirien thinks about Castor, the looks she used to give him, and similar actions he performed for her.

"Right. What can I do?" Adyra claps together her hands, looking over the wooden platform strewn with ingredients.

"I am making buns. I have everything here to do so." Sirien motions at the mess before them. Taking instantly to the chore, Adyra begins mixing the concoction into a dough.

"Davina visited Americ late in the night. Her footsteps woke me." Adyra naturally begins to knead the dough as she speaks. "If she was absent this morning, then perhaps she never returned?"

"If that is the case, then she and I will be having a discussion this very day." Sirien's face flushes at the thought and hopes Adyra is wrong.

After a while, Yrin returns with the pork, placing the slab on the table, tossing wood into the fire, and then heads back to the door, this time reaching for his cloak hanging off to the side before exiting the house. Before long, the steady crack of an ax striking wood sounds around the home. Working quietly, Adyra and Sirien form each bun before setting them into the oven, hot from the rolling fire in its belly.

"Good morn Davina, Americ." Adyra's voice rings cheerily beside Sirien, and she turns to see the both of them descending the steps.

Both rosy-cheeked gives the air of guilt as they avert either of the women's gazes. Slipping past Davina, Americ glides light-footed across the room to the door, mumbling about wood and help. Davina, now alone, edges her way to the fire, and Adyra smirks at Sirien, brows raised slightly.

Sirien takes in a heavy breath, leaving Adyra to the food as she makes her way to Davina. *Oh, mother, help me.*

TWENTY-FOUR

———

Eyes focused on the plates of food on the table, the lot of them eat in awkward silence. Knowledge of Americ and Davina's indiscretion in the night had spread, and even though it was a simple conversation and nothing more, it is the fact they stayed the entire night together that is looked down upon. Sirien's words to Davina that morning were harsh in the most gentle way.

Americ, sitting quietly opposite Davina, barely ate, stomach churning at the thought of a talk with Sirien, wishing he could run away and never look back. Scolding himself wordlessly, he listens to the smacking of lips, occasionally glimpsing at the pile of meat and bread as it shrinks in size.

"Yrin and I are going out hunting after this. Would you join us, Americ?" Ascher speaks huskily down the table to Americ.

"Oh, I uh-No, sorry. I am afraid I need to remain here to rest and prepare for my journey." Despite his lack of an appetite, Americ shoves an entire bun into his mouth.

The faces around the table shift to look at him, then to Davina, whose face is calm and not surprised. Sirien and Amalie exchange looks while Yrin continues to chew the food in his mouth with slow intensity. Adyra sighs, leaning back in her chair while Ascher shoves away his dish, folding his arms over his chest, and glares at Americ. No one speaks a word, assessing the general mood among them before proceeding. The air is tense.

"Your throne," Yrin grumbles before taking another bite of food.

"I don't care about a crown or title. If I return now, my father will kill me anyway," Americ replies irritated.

"Killing you would be a mistake. He has no power without you, no heir," Ascher says with confidence.

"He has other sons. Sons he could give a title to if he so chooses to," Davina speaks up, watching Americ closely.

"Are you going with him then?" Amalie speaks, her voice strained and tense. Davina swallows, hands shaking in her lap.

"No. Neither of them are leaving. Americ, I have seen it. You will take the throne, and Davina will be by your side. There is no running. You were born to rule, unite the people, and set them on a straight path. It is time you accept your place and focus on the legacy you will create." Sirien's focus is distant, looking down at the fine grain of the wood of the table.

All eyes shift to Sirien, nodding in agreement. Americ's heart skips, and the words of Brien echo crisply in his thoughts. *She is the answer to your reign.*

"Hunting it is then." Bolting to his feet, Americ shoves away from the table, rushing to the stairs.

Leaving the others below, Americ climbs the steps by two to the upper level and tromps loudly to his room. Panic overwhelming him, he finds the corner of the bed where it meets the wall and sinks to the floor. His breath, heavy and rapid, he curls into himself. Paralyzed with anxiety, Americ closes his eyes, angry with his weakness and lack of control as sweat peaks across his forehead. The room begins to spin, so he shoves his head between his knees, hoping to only stay upright.

Time passes slowly and painfully as he begins to take back control of his mind and body. His eyes droop, and he feels lifeless, but the sound of footsteps nearby force him to come back to reality. Expecting Ascher or Davina, he is surprised to see Sirien appear at the door, eyes searching for him. Finding Americ on the floor, his head peering out over the bed, she becomes concerned, rushing to his side.

"Are you ill? What is it?" Sirien bends down, touching Americ's damp forehead, looking him over in a motherly way.

"No. I, uh, I get light in the head sometimes. It is not often, but it does happen. I'm fine." Americ pushes away her hands, pulling his weight up from the ground.

Stumbling slightly, Americ rests on the edge of the bed, catching his shallow breath. Sirien watches, concerned with his well-being. Standing erect, Sirien folds her hands, careful not to rest her hands under her belly, exposing the hard bump.

"Well then, I need to speak frankly with you, Americ. I knew by what Davina had said your desire to escape Omideon was great and seeing you now, I would say she did not express the severity of it. However, we need you. Davina is destined for greatness, fated to wear the crown. By what Viala has told me and what I have seen, I am confident in this." Sirien watches Americ's face closely as the color of his face drains to a deadly gray.

"Americ, I cannot feel what you feel and know the damage the past has done, but I do know you are strong, and you love deeply. I have seen you with my sister and know the connection is there. I need you to stand with us, fight by our sides and take what is yours and give my sister what she deserves."

"She is the answer to my reign," Americ hisses so quietly Sirien barely hears him.

"What?" Sirien looks at him with surprise and confusion, his blank face staring past her.

"Your father told me she is the answer to my reign. We were fated." Americ rolls his eyes to look at her, watching her expression of surprise cross her face. "I will help you. I will stay." Americ slumps, leaning his elbows on his knees and wrapping the back of his neck in his hands.

Sirien watches as he submits himself to her will and feels guilt from his pain. Biting her lip, she tosses the idea back and forth in her head, deciding whether now is the time to request one last thing from him or not. Turning away from him, she makes it to the door before the flood of pressure in her chest stops her, and she walks back to him.

"One last request." His head rolls up to look at her, his eyes full of moisture and the color in his cheeks slightly returning. "Marry Davina, here, in our customs. What happened last night cannot happen again, even if it is only friendly and not intimate."

"I would be happy to," Americ replies without hesitation.

Sirien smiles, nodding as she turns from him and leaves the room, proud of her little triumphs.

* * *

Standing at the door, Yrin and Ascher gather their weapons and gear to face the cold and hunt. Waiting impatiently for Sirien and Americ to appear, Ascher glances up the stairway regularly, hopeful she is making headway so he wouldn't have to. Davina and Adyra sit near the fire, sewing and chatting, while Amalie makes herself busy gathering food for their day's outing. Ascher can see the frustration in her face at not joining them and chuckles under his breath, looking away from her at the sound of footsteps. Sirien descends the stairs, a smile spread across her face, nodding.

She's done it. Now we plan. He thinks excitedly, looking back to Amalie, who sees the short exchange.

Moving to him with a wrapped bundle, Amalie lays it in the empty satchel on the floor. "I should be going with you," she remarks under her breath. "There are things to be discussed."

"Like what?" Ascher asks, obnoxiously grinning at her.

"Like what you were telling me yesterday before my sister came home with the devil's offspring." Looking down at her, his stomach twists, and he clenches his jaw.

"It can wait and don't call him that. Amalie, you are going to have to accept he is not our enemy." Turning to Yrin, Ascher nods to the door. "Tell Americ we are outside." He says, playfulness absent from his voice.

"I'm here. Let's go." Americ appears, pale and bundled like the others in two tunics, a cloak, and furs.

Nodding back to him, Ascher and Yrin shove outside, followed closely by Americ. Slowly, they march in a line through the snow. The forest around them is cold and wet, a fresh blanket of snow covering the ground and weighing down needled branches of evergreens. Trees growing thicker, Americ takes a glance back at the cottage, now barely visible between gaps between branches.

Will she reject me? Have I made a mistake?

"Americ, let's go!" Ascher's voice rings through the air, and Americ obeys him, turning his back on the women inside the house.

Her cheeks hot, Davina stands, arms folded before the fire. She couldn't believe Sirien could suggest such a thing as marriage to Americ, let alone she had already spoken with the man who agreed to it. Appalled, Amalie disagreed with Sirien, and now they stand across the room, harsh whispers tossing back and forth.

All sound to Davina is muddled, underneath an ocean of complete fear. She trusted him to a point but still had her doubts digging far deeper than corruption, but rather soundness of mind and soul. His kindness far outweighs the fact he is heir to the throne, and his kindness overshadows the darkest parts of him. Marriage is for those in love, and Davina is not—mutual respect, yes, but not love.

"Davina." A hand grasps her shoulder tightly, swinging her around to face Amalie. "Do you want this?" Amalie's face is strained, eyes bulging with terror as she asks.

Frozen in time, Davina doesn't answer, only stares, blank-minded.

"You've broken her, you see. Sirien, how could you suggest this? Are you out of your mind? The vision was wrong," Amalie speaks hastily, hand still grasping Davina's shoulder.

Perking at her words, however, Davina pulls from her sister's touch and steps forward, looking directly at Sirien.

"What vision?"

"You will rule Omideon, unite the people. It's not the only vision of this. Viala spoke of another one pointing in the same direction." Sirien speaks clearly and carefully.

"I need to see her." Davina rushes past Amalie to the door, reaching for her boots.

"Now?" Amalie asks, shocked with her haste.

"Yes, Amalie. Now. I need answers. I don't want to marry Americ, but I also will not ignore fate seen by the seers." Slipping the boots on, she begins lacing them tightly.

Amalie and Sirien look at each other, then, remembering Adyra's presence, look to her as well. Adyra smiles, waving her hand to shoo them away. Grabbing her cloak, Davina flings open the door, heading to the stable. In a rush, Amalie and Sirien fight their boots and cloaks, hurrying after her to seek out Viala.

* * *

The dense smell of herbs sit in the air, the fresh stalks and bags hanging from the poles of the roof. The hut, tall in stature is dim and stuffy, smoke from the fire rising to escape from the opening above them. The short ride to Aldara gave each of the girls time to render their minds fresh and open to the truth. Now in the comfort of Viala's hut, the sisters sit and wait for her to arrive. Refusing to speak a single word to one another, Davina sits tapping the table, Amalie paces the floor, and Sirien finds comfort in the solid oak rocking chair in the corner of the room.

The intensity of emotion in the room overshadows the calmness of the crackling fire and soothing scents wafting from above. The door swings open, and a harsh cold sweeps into the room, startling the occupants. Viala enters, smiling to see them all and greeting each with a nod. Sitting across from Davina, Viala settles herself, motioning for Amalie to join. Refusing the invitation, Amalie continues pacing, so Viala looks to Sirien.

"What can I do for you, friend?" Viala's words are a gentle hum in the air.

"Tell them what you told me about our mother. The visions our grandfather saw," Sirien speaks calmly.

"As I told you, Sirien, your grandfather foresaw your birth. It was seen you would be the last visionary of the Nasinreth. The other child…" She stops, looking to Davina, then Amalie, and back to Sirien, who motions to Amalie. "The other child had a strength and wisdom far surpassing any Nasinreth to have lived. He only saw two."

Viala, looking at Amalie, now shifts her gaze to Davina. "But then he saw her, your mother as a young woman standing before the people, crowned in golden roses. Maeda knew it wasn't her he saw, and he knew too. Who he saw was you. You look just like her. The answer to the old prophecy to reunite the people."

Viala's eyes shine as she reaches for Davina's hands, gripping them within her own tightly. Davina's heart sinks as the realization comes over her. She would need to marry Americ to secure her fate before the people, and they would need to take the throne.

"Did our father know this? Was he present when the visions were spoken?" Amalie stops pacing and turns to Viala.

"For the first, not the last. If he knew, it was only through Maeda," Viala replies confidently.

"He knew. I never understood until just now he knew more than he was telling me. He always asked if my visions ever had Davina involved, and when they did, he took them very seriously." Sirien spoke, eyes glazed over.

"I always knew he loved you, Davina. You look most like her. But it was more than that. You had a greatness about you, a grand future. Sirien was a means to an end, and I, his weapon, his safety." Amalie's voice quivers with rage as her face grows hot and red.

"He loved us all, Amalie," Davina interjected.

"No. I'm afraid Amalie is right. It's time to accept what is and always has been. Amalie and I have been your guardians, and we will continue to be. It is time you succumb to your purpose by marrying Americ. It is what our father raised you to become, so you must follow fate rather than your heart," Sirien speaks in a motherly tone, demanding her submission.

Throwing the chair back with the force of her body wrenching from it, Davina flies away from the table and out the door. Amalie shakes her head, chasing after her, so Sirien follows the pursuit. Davina's horse, already absent from the two other ones who remain tied to a tree. They stop, searching rapidly in all directions. An elderly man raises a shaky hand, pointing into the shadows of the forest, and without hesitation, Amalie mounts the stallion, racing away. Sirien, out of breath, watches her fly away and suddenly can't move.

The world around her falls silent. People walk, talk, and laugh, but not a sound escapes their lips, and then she appears. The white woman, pale skin, white hair loose and tangled with a few braids at the front and her eyes, silver as the moon. Her lids are smeared in black, and she is looking past Sirien, her hand outstretched, clenching a large staff. The shadows begin creeping in around her until there is nothing to see, the woman fading into oblivion.

Noise erupts, screaming and crying from behind her. Sirien, searching for the light, turns to find a ray piercing through the branches. Pushing her way through, a door opens and she stumbles, falling to her knees. A crowd stands before her, violent and angrily throwing rocks and food in her direction. Trying to move, she finds herself shackled, and she panics. Searching the crowd, she sees Amalie, a small boy she recognizes in her arms, crying. A man groans as he is forced to his knees beside her, and as she looks, she gasps. Americ, bruised and bloodied, wears his father's crown, staring out among the people.

A voice rings out, "Kill them," and she hears the sharp ring of iron drawing through the air. A whistle rings out then a great force slams into the side of her neck. Suddenly, she is standing behind the two bodies, beheaded before her, the heavy sword in her hand. But its weight is not what sickens her. It is the head of Davina staring back at her on the floor.

TWENTY-FIVE

———

As the sun hides below the horizon, Amalie paces the room as they wait for the men to return from their trip. Sirien's vision had come so rapidly and strong she could not return home and asked Davina remain in Aldara with her. The vision she had terrified both Sirien and Amalie, and together, they agreed Davina would never know.

"Davina and Americ must marry, but it most certainly will kill them both unless he sends her away at the first sign of trouble. But how will we know when the time has come?" Amalie moves, pulling at her fingers with anxiety.

"Perhaps Yrin can convince one of our clansmen or Cadison to be their ears," Adyra voices a thought.

"Or Ascher could take his place and command it," Amalie vents.

"You know?" Adyra's body becomes rigid.

"You think Elra would keep that a secret? She wants what she wants, and honestly, I don't blame her. Your clan is relying on her to deliver their successor to Romathe in place of her husband who is very old and dying." Amalie laughs, seeing the shock on Adyra's face.

"You haven't told him, you know?" Adyra asks, taken back.

"It is not my place. He will tell me in time, and I will continue to hint subtly." Amalie shrugs mischievously.

Hearing a roar of laughter outside, Adyra and Amalie rush to the window to see the men carrying large bundles over their shoulders, laughter thundering out from them. Patting the wrinkles from their dresses, the girls rush to the chairs by the fire, hastily grabbing up their needles to not be caught spying. The men bust through the door moments later, loudly showing off their health and lively spirits.

"I see you have returned empty-handed?" Adyra teases, looking over their bloodstained clothing.

"Oh, wife, you know me better. We put it all in the meat shed where it will stay cold till tomorrow when we can properly do the butchering," Yrin bellows in reply.

Amalie, setting her needles down, hops to her feet, going to Ascher. The smile on his face shows her a joy she has never seen from him, and her heart warms with the thoughts of him rejoining his people. Swooping down to her, his icy lips brush hers, sending chills down her spine. Taking his face in her hands, Amalie looks Ascher over closely, inspecting the bloody streaks across his clothes and skin to be just that, and not from injury. Satisfied, she moves to Americ, overshadowed by the large Romathan men, and looks him over as well.

"We have things to discuss. You will all need to get these filthy clothes off and get cleaned up. Supper is still hot," Amalie says, staring at Americ.

Grabbing Ascher by the arm, Amalie drags her husband up the stairs leaving a trail of mud and snow behind him. Once safely in the comfort of their room, she shuts the door and turns quickly on him.

"We have a problem, Ascher. We went to the village today, and Sirien had another vision." Gravely, Amalie tells him about their meeting with Viala, chasing Davina then returning to find Sirien recovering from her curse. She recounts the vision and Viala's translation, being sure to include Davina being oblivious to it all.

"She knew Sirien had a vision, so how could she not know?" Ascher pauses, looking at her wide-eyed. Snapping back into focus, he replaces his breeches with fresh ones, dazed.

"Sirien told her it was the same vision from the past. Davina and Americ are fated." Amalie sits on the edge of the bed.

"So Sirien still believes they need to be wed?" Ascher asks, pulling his tunic over his head and throwing it on the ground.

Amalie nods, handing him the new one laid across the bed beside her. Taking her hand, Ascher pulls her up from the bed, placing it over his chest and wrapping his arms around her. Setting into his embrace, she finds comfort in the warmth of his skin, the odor of pine, animal, blood, and sweat lure her closer, reminding her of the wild outdoors. His heat pounds gently beneath her cheek, and she begins to lose her thoughts, melting into the steady drum.

Moving her fingers along the muscles in his chest, Amalie finds the raised scar over his heart. Tracing it, she wonders what it is and why Daventh did it. She knew his reasoning was flawed, but she is still curious. Amalie never asked, though, never stirring the memories that tortured Ascher.

"What are we going to do, Ascher? I can't leave her knowing she is fated to die. I should stay and protect her, become one of her ladies. I…"

Ascher jerks away from her, holding her at arm's length.

"No, you will not. Someone in Dune will do it. We will ask them to watch over her." Ascher's honey eyes look at her fiercely and sternly.

"Why would they? They have no interest in us or our quarrels. We have no money to pay." Amalie presses away from him, moving to the smoldering fire.

"They will listen to me, Amalie. There is something you need to know." Ascher huffs, looking at his feet only to be startled by a light giggle.

Looking up, Amalie turns to him, thoroughly entertained. Ascher searches for whatever it is she sees, making her laugh harder. Brows furrowed, he finds himself confused and annoyed at the turn of her mood.

"I was being serious, Amalie. I need to tell you something."

"I already know. Elra told me before the oath." Jaw-dropping, Ascher looks at her in shock as she laughs heartily again.

"You knew? Why didn't you say anything?" Ascher says, raising his voice slightly as it cracks.

Walking back to him, Amalie cups his face in her hands, reaching up on her toes to brush his lips with hers, then falls back on her heels, patting his cheek lightly.

"It wasn't mine to ask. I have no expectations, Ascher. If you wish to become Chieftain, I will be by your side, and if you choose to turn your back on the people and live a simple life, so will I." Her eyes glance back to his chest over the brand over his heart.

Seeing this, Ascher touches it, the raised bump.

"It is the mark of an outcast, exiled. He put it there to be sure I never took my grandfather's place. My father didn't want to be Chieftain, nor did he want me to be." Reaching for the tunic that had fallen to the ground, Ascher slips it on, covering the mark and scars. "We should go downstairs. There is a lot to discuss with the others. Our decision over the clan can wait." Taking Amalie by the hand, Ascher guides her from the room, and together they join the others.

* * *

"You spoke of another son, your half-brother. Do others favor him in the court?" Yrin asks in a burly voice, a mug of ale gripped in his large hand resting on his knee.

The room is dim as they huddle near the fire. Ascher, arms crossed with a mug in one hand, stands leaning against the chimney, its warm stones thawing his icy bones. Americ sits directly before the smoldering flames, elbows on his knees, while Adyra sits in the crook of Yrins arm as they lean back, relaxed together. Amalie finds her comfort on the floor, knees folded up into her chest, feet bare resting on the hearthstone.

"No one knows. My father has somehow kept him a secret. I only know because of overhearing them once. Cadison knows, and when I told him, he warned me to never speak of it again." Americ shrugs.

"Would he pose a threat to you if you were to take the throne?" All eyes turn to Yrin as he speaks.

"Most definitely. Baldur has a roughness, but he also has a kindness toward a woman, one I know well. Together they would be my greatest enemy." Americ nods, shuddering at the thought.

"Baldur? Second in command? The guard everyone fears?" Amalie leans back, remembering the man towering over men and women in the market, plundering and beating any and all for no reason.

"And the woman?" Ascher speaks up, eyes focused on the drink in his grip.

Americ pauses, avoiding the faces peering at him. The flames of the fire flicker ravenously, devouring the air and wood fueling its rage. His stomach twists, aching with threats of expelling its contents. His brow beads with sweat, and his fingers go numb from clenching his fists so tightly. The sickness of his family had gone beyond repair, and he knew that. The killing, torture, manipulation, and hunting prisoners in the woods didn't compare to this indiscretion. In his mind, the greatest sin of his father and sickest downfall would be his sister and how his father bartered her innocence for the council's favor. How he used and destroyed her for his own selfish gain.

"My twin sister. She has an affinity for him. No matter what. I have tried to tear her from him, and yet, she remains oblivious, running into his arms." Americ buries his head in his hands, ashamed to admit such a transgression.

The room falls silent, horror-struck and repulsed by Americ's revelation. Amalie's hatred for the royal family has always been subjective to the people and the hardships they endure daily under the King's rule. Never had it crossed her mind the brokenness of the kingdom actually stemmed from the brokenness within the royals themselves.

"This union will not be without its costs," Amalie whispers, eyes glued to floorboards, rough and worn beneath her.

"Amalie is right. Americ, there are things you need to know before you fully commit to this course of action," Ascher begins, stepping away from the wall, taking a long swig of his drink before setting it aside and sitting behind Amalie. "Sirien has had another vision which frankly has put us all in a foul mood and general unease."

Ascher sets his hands over Amalie's shoulders, drawing her back against the chair between his knees. She settles, putting her right hand over his left, resting on her shoulder. The group becomes somber, looking at each other with hesitation. Americ glances from face-to-face, suddenly feeling nervous at the changes in their expressions.

"My eldest sister has had another vision, and it was very disturbing." Amalie pauses again, tension rising in the room, and she looks at him with hesitation. "You will die after becoming King. You will be overthrown, and we can only assume it to be by your very sister if what you say is true. But not only you. Davina as well, and that cannot happen. She is meant to be the bridge for the people and the royal house. If you choose to follow through with the marriage, you will have to be willing to die for your wife and child." Amalie speaks carefully, watching Americ's face drain of color.

Standing suddenly, Americ moves away from the others, pacing the open space between the chairs and table. Hands folded behind his back like a prisoner, he moves, face-changing expression as quickly as water in a running brook. Panic, fear, anger, sadness, and what they can only guess to be the urge to flee his downcast future controls his body language, unsettling him in his seat. Pulling her attention from him, Amalie shuts her eyes, resurfacing herself from nausea overtaking her by Americ's rapid movements.

Suddenly, the clicking of footsteps stops, and when Amalie opens her eyes. She sees Americ leaning over the back of a chair at the table, turned away from them. He looks so small and childlike like this, which makes Amalie feel pity toward him for the first time. She still doesn't like the man or the presence he holds in their home, but now she has to accept it.

"I will continue through with the plan. If it is as you say and a child is in our future, I will do what I must to ensure Davina's safety. A heir would stabilize the country and complete the prophecy, even if I fall." Americ's voice is low and quiet as he speaks.

Stepping back from the table, Americ stretches, his open hands cradling the back of his head. Sudden relief spurs over the room, and the small group realizes they all had been holding their breaths, afraid he would refuse, and they had to use him for what they needed. Yrin and Adyra have begun to grow fond of Americ and Ascher, and Amalie knew Davina has as well, unwillingly. Returning to his place before the fire, Americ stands, biting his lip, considering whether to speak again or not.

"I care for her more than I care for my own life, even if she never returns the favor." His eyes slip to Amalie, hoping his words would give her confidence in him.

Batting her eyes, Amalie is taken by surprise, speechless. Nodding in reply, she watches Americ nod multiple times before stepping away, folding into the shadows of the evening up the stairs into loneliness. Amalie, never questioning herself before, wonders if she had been wrong about this man, and part of her is sad at the prospect of losing him.

TWENTY-SIX

The bustling of busy feet outside the hut wakes the occupants inside. Not accustomed to the noise, Davina tosses and turns in the small bed, ruffling Sirien from her peaceful sleep. The sound of stone grinding against stone in a rhythmic pattern pushes Davina past her final nerve, wrenching herself from the bed and dressing quickly. Pushing past the large tapestry separating the single room into two, Davina finds Viala working quietly.

"Good morning, my dear. Did you rest well?" Viala asks, looking up from her work briefly.

The whole space smells of lavender and wood rose. Garlands of winter jasmine and foxhale vine float across the table in preparation for the binding ceremony. Davina makes her way to the center of the room, sitting before the fragrant jasmine blooms, still waking from the restless night. Chuckling lightly, Viala watches Davina's expression, knowing she hadn't slept hardly at all.

"I suspected as much. Here, drink this brew, and it will put you in higher spirits." She places a carved cup at Davina's fingertips returning to her work once more. "I have your dress. I found it last night after you had gone to bed. It is just as I remember it. Your mother wore it," Viala speaks casually.

"My mother? You kept it?" Davina perks up, interested suddenly.

"It has been worn by many of the women here. It is a ceremonial dress." Viala smiles as she crushes the lavender buds with the pestle into the large, round mortar.

"Would you do it? Marry someone because of fate's design?" Davina spits out the words before she swallows her courage.

"Yes, and I have. I have grown to love my husband greatly without regret. We are fated for a reason. Our God does not make false choices. But you are afraid, and I cannot blame you, for I was too. But tonight, you will seal the prophecy in your union, fulfilling the path of greatness set for you. All you can do is trust."

Sitting in the chair, Davina holds the hot mug within her grip, the scent of the steaming liquid wafting up. She imagines what life will be like in the castle, standing where her enemies once stood. Carefully, Davina sips at the liquid, burning her tongue with the sweetness of honey and bitterness of lavender, relaxing instantly as the aroma takes hold of her consciousness.

"The ceremony is tonight?" she asks, her whisper touching the liquid, pushing it into ripples.

"Yes. I already sent word this morning to prepare the others at the cottage. We will start the procession just before dusk," Viala speaks without looking up from her work.

Silently, Davina watches the dried leaves turn to granules then dust in the little stone bowl. Her body feels heavy from the weight of the prophecy on her shoulders, and she wishes she had run from Americ when she had the chance so he would have never come with her to Aldara. But then again, her heart skips at the thought of leaving him behind, and she wonders what he would have done without her.

Why do I care?

* * *

Small flakes flutter around them in the cold night as they stand in the front of the house waiting for Davina, Sirien, the high elder, and his wife, Viala. As is tradition, they ride the distance on horseback where the people wait to greet the bride and take her to her betrothed. Men and women crowd together in the cold to share body heat until the first sign of Davina's arrival. A torch burns lightly in the distance, slowly etching its way through the black.

Amalie and Ascher stand next to one another, not acknowledging their presence or touching, afraid to show affection around other's watchful eyes. Americ stands in the doorway of the house, the Nasinreth people shielding him from her view. Yrin and Adyra stand on the crowd's edge, warily watching with confusion at the calm and quiet, very unlike their own ceremonies of Aulik.

Without notice, a low rumble hums in the air, followed by another and another. A woman beside Amalie suddenly opens her mouth, and a sweet high voice flows from her lungs. Gradually, the yard fills with a beautiful hum, morphing into a song. A woman walks through the crowd to the front, words forming on her lips as she sings what would seem more like a lullaby to the group buzzing. The sound is surreal, and Amalie feels as if she is floating on it as she watches the torchlight grow closer until Viala and the Elder's faces can be seen clearly, the torch carried between them.

Craning her neck to see over the crowd, Amalie searches

for Sirien and Davina. Stopping, Viala and the Elder pass down the fiery rod to another, waiting before dismounting, opening up the space to see Sirien, her pale figure on a dark horse, looking fragile and tired. Amalie's heart sinks, worry filling her chest over Sirien's declining health.

Behind Sirien sits a figure cloaked in a silver veil giving her the essence of mist in the air. Men from the crowd step forward and assist them both from horseback, and as if parting of the great sea, the people move, making a path to Americ. Davina walks slowly behind Sirien, Viala, and the Elder, her figure thin, young and beautiful under the veil, her dress flowing like waves behind her. The hum around them grows until Viala and Sirien lift Davina's long veil, shrouding Americ underneath it as well. The voices dim until the hum is silenced, allowing the Elder to speak.

"You have chosen to be bound under our God and custom. This commitment to each other is meant for the duration of your lives together." Davina and Americ look at one another for a moment before Davina's eyes droop to the floor. Viala appears beside her husband, a silver bowl in her open palms, full of a rose-red liquid. Lifting the edge of the veil, she gives it to the couple who hold it, hands entwined together.

"The cup you hold represents the fullness of life in love and spirit. If either of you removes your hold even slightly, it will falter, and the wine may spill from it. You can never regain the contents. This is the same with your faith in one another. You will uphold one another in times of triumph and failure, joy and grief, support, reason, compassion. Honesty will be your greatest challenge but will carry the greatest rewards." The Elder motions to Americ, who guides the cup to Davina's lips so she can take a small drink of the sweet wine inside. Looking to Americ, the Elder speaks again.

"In this world, we often blindly follow each other's lead. May you never break that trust and lead wisely. Live with truth and grace, giving abundantly of love and honoring your wife in all ways. May you be blessed under our God, living out his word." The Elder motions to Davina to do the same, guiding the bowl to Americ's lips to drink as well. The Elder speaks to her.

"In this life, our days are numbered. We are not given too much or too little time, only what our God has provided us. Cherish each moment, live thankfully and appreciatively, honoring your husband in all ways. Be slow to lambaste, instead remain gracious. May you be blessed under our God, living out his word."

Viala steps forward, removing the cup and replacing the veil once more. Sirien takes a turn, bringing forward another silver bowl for the Elder and a willow switch brush, the end bound in leather. Dipping it, he pulls it into the air, flicking it at the tented couple, hands now joined between them.

"With this, I bind you." Dipping again, he flicks the liquid at them, circling around them slowly, continuously showering them in tiny droplets. "May you guide each other on a virtuous path, support each other in all ways, defend one another in trials and troubles, comfort each other on your darkest days, and become one mind and soul, steadied in faith in our God. May your love last an eternity, never faltering beyond the end of your days."

Completing a full circle around them, the Elder sets aside the bowl and switch, then turns, walking into the house. Viala and Sirien walk to the door's edge, taking a corner of the veil each and pulling it up from the newly pledged couple. Davina and Americ walk together through the door as Sirien and Viala hang it over the frame and walk through it together.

One by one, the Nasinreth cross the threshold through the veil until Yrin, Adyra, Ascher, and Amalie remain. Standing in the snow, they listen as the voices inside cheer and laugh in the joy of the union and future.

"That was different," Yrin says, breaking the silence, and the other three nod in agreement.

"But quite beautiful," Adyra voices.

"We will need to leave for Dune in the next few days if we are going to continue with our plan. I will need the support of our people and a pledge of their fealty to my wife and me. They need to know the Tamlik legacy continues." The light from the house shines in Ascher's eyes as he speaks, his expression calm.

Reaching for Amalie, he wraps his arm around her waist, pulling her close to him. A smile erupts across Adyra's and Yrin's faces, pride at being the first to know his decision. Pulling his dirk from his belt, Yrin steps forward, taking a knee before Ascher and raising his blade, laid flat in his palm.

"I pledge my life and soul to my Chieftain, my clan, and our people." Yrin closes his eyes as Adyra falls to her knees beside him, submitting to her new leader.

Ascher takes the dirk from Yrin. Taking the tip of the blade, he draws it along the side of his palm, where a light scar was visible. Blood trickles from the open wound, pooling in the crater of his open palm. Dipping two fingers, Ascher draws them across their faces, creating a line over their eyes and brows.

"It is customary for the wife or husband to tear the bandages." Ascher looks at Amalie, hoping she will comply.

Without hesitation, Amalie stoops, taking a piece from the hem of her dress, and begins caring for Yrins' wound. Standing, Yrin and Adyra bow their heads, and Ascher returns the dirk to its owner. Taking Yrin by the shoulder, Ascher looks him in the eye with extreme gratitude.

"When we return to the homeland, I want you by my side. I will need you to bridge the gap between our people and us. You have lived the ways far more than I, and even though I know them, I need someone I trust." Taking his hand and slamming it down on Ascher's shoulder, he nods, honored beyond words.

The cold begins to seep through the heavy cloaks. The four find the path to the house, making their way quickly, passing through the veil into the stuffy room packed with people. The garlands of flowers hang draped around the room beautifully. Going straight upstairs, Yrin and Adyra disappear for the night as Amalie and Ascher join the exuberant crowd in search of the new couple and Sirien to inform them of Ascher's decision to join his people and their plan to leave for Dune soon.

Following Yrin and Adyra's lead, Ascher and Amalie retire soon after finding the others, followed by Sirien leaving Americ and Davina to the guests. One by one, the Nasinreth vanish back into the woods until they are alone and the house is silent. Standing at the foot of the steps, Americ watches Davina, her gown a silvery blue in the light angelically flowing around her. The gown is loose other than the sash tied around her waist, the neck shaped like a crescent moon, and the sleeves long to the floor, tight only to her elbows before dropping gracefully.

Davina, a goddess of elegance in Americ's eyes send his heart into a chaotic flurry. He watches her glide around the room, tidying it slightly, avoiding the task of going to bed for the night. Americ, aware of her thoughts and nervous himself, slips away to the room they would now share. Preparing throughout the day, he scoured the house for extra blankets, thieving straw from the stable and making space in the small room, preparing himself a place to sleep other than the bed in the center of the room.

Unable to speak with her prior to their union, Americ had not set her mind at ease by assuring her he had no expectations. He recognizes their union is not conventional but rather a duty to the prophecy and the people. Settling himself on his makeshift cot, he waits for Davina, hoping she will find enough confidence to come to him and see the respect he has for her.

Eyes drooping after a long period of time, Americ feels defeated and alone in Davina's absence. However, setting his mind to speak with her in the morning and settle the delicate situation properly, he decides to allow sleep to take him. Unexpectedly, the door whines as it opens, and his eyes burst wide to see Davina sneaking in. Seeing him on the unruly cot sends guilt explosively through her body.

Davina had avoided his touch and gaze most of the night and ignored his absence when he left. Now seeing the length he went to make her comfortable, she regrets her actions and scolds her childish self. Americ smiles, rolling over, so his back is turned to her, and she feels his compassion unyielding and respect for her modesty appreciated. Slipping her gown off, leaving her in her shift, she rushes into bed, covering herself in the warm quilt. Looking at his figure hunched in the small bundle of old blankets, Davina finds herself burdened by her neglect and, after hesitation, speaks.

"Americ," she whispers. He rolls onto his back, turning his head to look at her. "Come sleep here. It's more comfortable, and after all, we are wed."

"I am willing to sacrifice my comfort for your well-being."

She blushes, grinning at him.

"I don't want you to sacrifice. Please come and get some rest." Davina pats the bed beside her and he hesitates for a moment before gratefully sliding out of his poky bed and moving into hers.

They lay under the quilt. Each other's body heat was radiating in the gap between them. Neither speaks as they listen to one another breathe alongside the crackle of the dying fire. Slowly, exhaustion overtakes their bodies, and they both begin to drift out of consciousness, leaving the day's events behind them.

TWENTY-SEVEN

——

"I won't say I'm displeased to see you but quite surprised. What brings you home grandson?" Elra asks, astonished to find Ascher and Amalie on her doorstep on an early evening.

Stepping back to admit them, they stomp inside, tired and cranky from the long trip. The five days Yrin had said it to take extended into eight. The snow, much deeper than anticipated, made the trek for the horses much more difficult, Sirien suffered yet another vision, and a raging storm blew in overnight on the third day, keeping them housed in the small village of Orivang.

"We have come to ask for help." Ascher shakes the snow from the shoulders of his cloak, showering Elra in the cold melting flakes.

Seeing their soiled clothing, Elra moves to the fire, stoking it with another log and yanking a quilt from a nearby chair. Drooping it over Amalie's shoulders, she hugs her curtly before returning her attention to Ascher.

"What is it now, Ascher? Is there trouble?" Elra asks.

"The King seeks to kill his son, but we seek to end Agnai's reign, putting the prince in his place. He has married Davina, and once he is on the throne, he will fulfill the second part of the prophecy by reuniting the people." Tired, Ascher slumps into the nearest chair, resting his head on his hand.

"If he is going to be King, he needs to raise an army himself. I will not ask our people to follow him blindly into battle, Ascher. You know that is not our way." Irritated, Elra turns away, sitting in the chair across from him.

"They will not be following blindly, Grandmother. They will be following their Chieftain and avenging the treachery of the crown's betrayal to us. He took our bride, sending our people into war. I want to pay him what is owed." Ascher looks at her, eyes red from exhaustion.

"My grandson has truly returned home." A crooked smile spreads across Elra's face.

"I need men and a promise from you. A few will need to remain here and serve in Americ's guard. He and Davina will be in ever-present danger, and I need our best to keep her safe." Ascher closes his eyes, rubbing them with his fingers.

"Only her?" Elra looks to Ascher, then Amalie, brows furrowed.

"He knows and has accepted his fate," Amalie speaks blandly.

"Very well. I will speak with Cadison in the morning about such arrangements. He is staying here as well. I assume the prince and your sister told you about my nephew?"

Ascher and Amalie's heads droop.

"Now, you both look exhausted and need rest. When will the others join us?" Elra stands, moving to Amalie and guiding her to the stairs.

"Everyone is here in Dune. We stopped by Yrin's home. He agreed to shelter them for a time." Ascher rises from his chair, dragging his feet across the floor to the stairway.

"You can stay in the same room as before. It will be cold,

but there are plenty of quilts I will bring up to you. I will be sure you are not disturbed."

Without a reply, Amalie and Ascher miraculously climb the steps and dress for bed, falling asleep immediately, dreaming of nothing.

* * *

Ascher breathes steadily beside her, chest rising and falling calmly, the scars prominent in the moon's faint light. Sleep abandoning her in the moment of need, Amalie watches him for a while, face relaxed, mouth parted slightly, his dark hair a mess around him. Rolling from under the heavy woven blanket, Amalie sneaks across the creaking floorboards, escaping the room to leave Ascher in a dreamy peace. Walking tenderly barefoot down the stairs, she hopes to find a warm fire to rest before, and as she rounds the corner, she finds a figure occupying the main room.

Stopping cold in her tracks, she looks, recognizing him immediately. Commander Cadison Rheyhas, a tall older man sits, staring blankly into the flickering light. Heart pounding, she steps back, hoping not to disturb him as the board beneath her toes squeal loudly.

"I'm sorry to startle you. I didn't expect anyone to be up at this hour." Amalie's voice floats through the darkness as he jumps to his feet.

"Nor I. But please join me." He motions to the chairs around him, returning to his seat.

Amalie tucks her feet up underneath her as she sits across from him, wrapping the blanket tightly around her. They sit in silence, staring at the fire. Had they ever met before Americ told them of Rheyhas true purpose to serve the King,

Amalie would have killed him or died trying. Now however, she sits with questions that need answers, ones she hopes to get in the future.

"Elra said you were here. Have you decided to abandon your post then?" Amalie looks at him, curious about the man.

"I no longer have a reason to stay in the King's service. His son is safely away, and Ascher is here. But I assume you already figured as much." A wry smile forms on Cadison's lips.

"Yrin mentioned your part in their lives. And I remember the times with Ascher you were somehow always around. I could never figure out why or how, but it made it that more exciting, sneaking around." Amalie's mischievous gaze makes him smile, knowing the look all too well.

"I never told Elra about you, afraid she would find her own way of protecting him by getting rid of you. It was the right decision, and I am proud to stand by it. You always intrigued me. The Nasinreth are normally more cautious and gentle." He smiles, looking in her direction.

"You knew about my family and our lineage?" Amalie asks hesitantly.

"I had my suspicions of your eldest sister and tried to keep my men from noticing as well. I may serve the King but do not agree with his tactics or beliefs. When you began seeing Ascher, it made things more difficult." Cadison shifts in his chair, groaning with discomfort.

Sitting in quiet, Amalie watches him rub his chin and face, trying to wipe away the pain and exhaustion that follows. She thinks over the past memories, and a question rises in her mind, one she has always wanted to ask but never had the courage to.

"What happened to make Daventh leave Dune and his

rights to lead?" Amalie jumps to the next thought, looking for answers she never wanted to ask questions for.

"He became infatuated with a woman. Elra refused to bless the marriage, so Daventh left and settled in Aldhorran. Elra sent word, asking me to remain in the King's graces. She wanted me to find his weakness so they could enact revenge. Much happened in that time, Agnai's power grew, and when Ascher was born, Elra pleaded with me to watch over him. Daventh had become mean with age and drink, his wife wrote Elra often, afraid for her life and her sons. Suddenly, the letters stopped, and when I called, I found her bedridden. Ascher was small, told me his father hit her, knocking her to the ground. He was in tears. She died in bed days later. Daventh knew nothing of raising a child, raising Ascher like a slave, refusing to release his rights. Elra tried as did I, but the law was in his favor, giving us no other choice but to watch and hope for the best." Cadison shifts in his seat again, his hand balling into a fist and wincing.

"Why didn't you kill him? You had the means to do so," Amalie blurts, startling him again.

"I tried. Had him imprisoned for a while, sending Ascher here, but the King pardoned him because he was the best blacksmith in Aldhorran. We had no choice but to return the boy when the King commanded it."

Amalie listens, evaluating his thin, aged face speaking emotionless

"Do you think Ascher remembers his mother's death?" Amalie looks away, saddened at the thought.

"Possibly. However, he was very young, so I am unsure. Americ remembers his mother, and they were around the same age when they lost them. It is a possibility." Wishing he had said no, Amalie grimaces, hoping Ascher's silence on the matter is because of unawareness rather than trauma.

"I think I will retire. It was good to finally meet you under proper circumstances, Amalie, and I am glad you are safe."

Nodding, he pushes up from his chair, face going pale as he clenches his teeth together, fighting pain. Limping, he heads to the stairs, stopping at the bottom of them, heaving a sigh of exasperation. Lifting his left leg first, she watches as he drags himself slowly, thumping up the stairs. The house creaks with every step until a small tap of his door shutting echoes down the hall.

The night passes by slowly, and light begins to skirt over the horizon. Quietly, Amalie returns upstairs, tired once again. She slips under the quilt and falls asleep.

* * *

Giggling like children, Adyra and Amalie race their horses along the sandy coastline. Amalie's dark hair was flying freely behind her while Adyra's auburn hair bounces over her back in the long braids. They ride in freedom, and Amalie revels in it as she takes in the salty sea air. Never had she been so happy in her life, nor unburdened. Hooves splash in the tide as it rolls in and out in small waves. Stopping slowly, Amalie stares out over the endless sea, imagining the adventures beyond it at the next shore. Adyra, falling beside her, looks in the same direction, scanning the horizon.

"I don't want to go back, Adyra. I never want to leave this spot," Amalie speaks, sounding breathless.

"Back to Dune?" Nervously, Adyra replies, hoping she is not thinking of leaving the clan.

"No. Aldhorran. I know we must overthrow the King, but I don't want to."

Relieved, Adyra sighs with relief.

"It will be quick. Then we can return to the homeland."

Adyra looks at Amalie, glad to be in her company. "Ascher is a good and strong man and a Tamlik, but if I can speak frankly, he is hesitant around his people. If you want the people to accept him, they need to see you beside him, strong and powerful. Women are revered here and are not expected to stand back and submit. They need to know you can lead if he cannot."

Amalie meets her eyes.

Elra had informed them in the early hours she called for a meeting this afternoon to give Ascher a chance to present himself before his people and declare his birthright. Nervous, Amalie nods to Adyra, then looks out over the water for a moment longer.

"We should head back. Race you." Digging her heel into the horse's side, Amalie breaks the serious moment, laughing as she flies away.

The few-minute ride from the coast to Dune is exhilarating. Once through the gates, they stable their horses and walk briskly together through the streets. Making their way to the lodge, they begin to hear voices thundering from the large building, and they look at each other in surprise. The meeting had begun early, and they were late. Angry with herself for leaving town, Amalie shoves through the doors to find the crowd agitated as they call up to Ascher standing before them.

"What if he is untruthful?" A man yells.

"It is likely a trap!" Another man calls out, the crowd erupting in agreement.

"Quiet, please!" Ascher replies to the unsteady congregation before him.

"Why should we listen to you! You aren't a warrior. How can we trust a newcomer?" One person yells, men and women howl, cheering in agreement.

Amalie looks at Ascher, overwhelmed by the commotion of the people, which fills her with rage. Shoving through the crowd, she makes her way to the front, stopping next to a man she overhears call her husband weak and unworthy. Her fist, flying through the air meets the side of his jaw, knocking him off balance. She grabs his hair, a single thick braid at the back of his head, dragging him roughly behind her as she mushes forward.

Confused by the sight of her, the crowd parts, allowing her through. She looks to Elra as she steps onto the platform Ascher is occupying and sees her amused look. With force, Amalie shoves the man to his knees on the ground.

"This is an outrage! You know who this man is, who his relation is, yet you refuse him! He is your future, your present. He is your blood. You do not deserve his mercy and should be exiled when he returns to the homeland. My husband is far from weak as he has endured a life of pain and torture, surviving so he can stand before you today!" Looking at Ascher, she pulls the dagger from her belt, and understanding without words, he lifts his arms to the side, allowing her to slice his shirt open and ripping it from him.

Gasps from the crowd sound as the scars that riddle his body become visible, especially the burn in his shoulder.

"His own father tried to break him, brand him an outcast and traitor, yet he is stronger than ever, stronger than all of you. He beat death countless times, and his name is Ascher Tamlik. He is the son of Daventh, Grandson of Adenus and Elra, Chieftain of Aulik of Romathe, Chieftess of Dune, next in line, here to claim his birthright. If you follow him, your loyalty will be commended, and you will have the right to serve alongside him when he assumes his place in the homeland! Join us to remove a king and instill a new one, then let's go home!" Crouching to the man before she takes the dagger in her hand and places it before him.

"Pledge your allegiance, or be branded an outcast and remain in Omideon the rest of your days. And if you ever betray us, I will kill you." Hesitating a moment, the man takes the dagger and turns, kneeling before Ascher to swear allegiance to his new Chieftain.

TWENTY-EIGHT

"When will you leave?" Cadison asks, meeting the others in the front of the lodge as the people of Dune disperse.

"A group will leave each day starting this evening. We will leave the day after tomorrow, meeting together in the forest in a week's time," Ascher replies, arms folded across his chest.

"And what will you do when you get there? The castle is unbreachable." Cadison squares his shoulders, looking at his newly founded Chieftain.

"I will infiltrate the castle, taking Davina as my prisoner. I will be sure to keep her close, and my father wouldn't dare kill me with witnesses. This gives me the opportunity to find a way to either distract the guards or disable the gate, allowing Ascher to have the upper hand." Americ speaks with confidence.

"And if they don't make it in, then what? Your father will already know you have betrayed him. You know he won't fall for any tricks, Americ," Cadison says, concern apparent in his voice.

"I know my father well enough to know what to say, so he will believe me." Americ looks at Cadison, eyes narrowing at him.

"Your father will see right through you, Americ. If you are stuck on this path, allow me to help you. I can train you to deceive him as I have for a long time," Cadison speaks irritably.

All eyes turn to Americ, watching as he considers the idea, then nods in acceptance. Cadison, satisfied with this battle won, moves on to the other parts of the plan, speaking with Ascher and Yrin over the men they will need and the plan of attack. Surveying the small map roughly drawn, he suggests changes and ideas for infiltration as well as scouting positions for the days before. He informs them of the borders the soldiers patrol each day and the times they pass by.

Ascher and Yrin take his words gratefully, soaking in the information with pleasure, asking as many questions as they can possibly think of. Cadison takes joy in his part, finally feeling useful to the longtime goal of destroying Agnai. He had done his part keeping the two boys alive, and now, a united front will help them thrive in the world.

As the night draws, the group slowly dissipates until only Ascher, Cadison, and Yrin remain. Patting Ascher on the shoulder as he passes, Yrin yawns heavily, leaving the two men alone. Tired as well, Ascher rolls up the map and stands, stretching to his full height, stepping after Yrin.

"There is one detail I would like to discuss with you," Cadison says to Ascher, stopping him in his tracks.

"Of course, Cadison. You have my full attention." Ascher looks at him gladly.

"I would like to stay in Omideon, serve Americ, and protect Davina. Elra told me your request, and I would like to fill the position."

Ascher nods, giving Cadison a peculiar look.

"Very well. If you choose to stay in this horrid country, be my guest. At the first sign of trouble, you must leave and take

Davina with you. Americ knows this, and he is prepared to face death." Watching his face, Ascher sees the weight of the future rest on his mind, displeased, however understanding.

Nodding, Cadison rubs the back of his neck before standing, grunting with pain.

"How were you injured, and have you seen Davina? She can possibly heal you." Ascher grimaces, hating to see him hurting.

"I went on patrol in search of Americ and Davina after they left. Elra sent men to lie in wait for me and one of my men. They beat me, allowing him to escape with his life, giving the impression I was dead. Nothing I won't survive or heal from, but still very unpleasant," Cadison laughs, wincing as he steps.

"I will ask Davina to see you tomorrow. Please do not refuse her."

Cadison nods, huffing with each step.

Ascher walks slowly through the dark streets by Cadison's side, casually talking as they go as if old friends and yet apprehensive about speaking what is truly on his mind. Elra's home is visible in the distance, and he stops. Cadison, unsure of Ascher's sudden pause in his step, turns to look at him.

"I remember every time you came to us, Cadison. The night my father nearly killed me, the times he beat me until I couldn't stand the branding. You were there every time, stopping him from continuing. You were there for her too. I saw the tears in your eyes when you found her dead and the sadness you had when you brought me home to him. I never thanked you because I thought it was just odd timing, but now I know it was by design. You saved my life, and I can never repay you." Ascher's eyes fall to his own feet, not wanting him to see through this vulnerable moment into his damaged soul.

"Be the man our people need. That will be payment enough." Meeting Cadison's gaze, Ascher smiles sheepishly.

Motioning Ascher forward, Cadison resumes, limping to Elra's home. The house, still and quiet, puts Ascher instantly at ease. Leaving Cadison in the main room, Ascher moves up the stairs to the upper level and down the hall to his chamber. The dim fire sheds a flickering light over the bed where Amalie lays fast asleep. Creeping to her, he stoops, kissing her forehead gently, causing her to stir.

Amalie lifts a hand, touching his arm lightly, and puckers her lips, searching for his face with her eyes closed. Kissing her sweetly, she smiles, then rolls to her other side, slipping out of consciousness.

Moving to the hearth, Ascher stokes the hot embers, watching sparks fly in all directions as the flame erupts, engulfing the new log. He thinks back to the time in his life where it was never simple and the fight to survive was never-ending. The memories swarm him, Cadison's face emerging in each one, realizing he had seen him but didn't always realize it. Then the memories freeze, stopping at the one moment in time he knew was the end of his struggle.

Ascher sees Cadison's face looking down at him in terror as he bleeds from the gaping wound across his chest and ribs. The man, pale and his words muffled as Ascher loses his battle, falling into a dark sleep he may not wake from.

"Hold on, Ascher. You can't die on me. Your people rely on you. I rely on you."

TWENTY-NINE

The creek flows steadily over rocks, ice crystals attempting to net across its ever-changing surface to no avail. The bitter cold has reached Aldhorran, the ground frozen solid and frost clinging to the trees. The fog settled overnight, giving the small grove an eerie ambiance. Standing over a fresh mound of stones, Amalie looks at it, bare compared to the one beside it, grown over with moss and vines, weathered with its age of existence. The last time she visited the stones of her mother's grave was the day Davina showed signs she possessed the blessing of a healer, begging for wisdom over the matter.

This time, she came to add new stones, giving her mother companions. Castor had also been family, and though Sirien spoke little of him, she saw her grief and the illness it caused her. It took four days of travel after leaving Dune to reach the farm. Careful to only come and go in the night, they stay within the home, knowing it will be overlooked in the darkness. No one would expect traitors to return home, thus the perfect plan to elude the guard.

Today would be the final day of preparation. The clan will gather in the towns bordering Aldhorran, moving to the forest in the evening. Exhausted from the journey, Amalie sits at the foot of her father's grave, scowling. Her stomach was growling with hunger twists and turns, making her nauseous from its fury. Reaching behind her, she grabs her satchel, pulling a small cake from within. Adyra, her talented hands never ceasing in the kitchen, was sure to supply them with enough food for a week's time. Now stale, the sweet crumbly loaf is all they had, but no one complained.

"We've done it. Davina wed the Prince, dear father. Davina did not marry the King and Amalie is speaking aloud to her fathers grave. She will become queen, uniting the people. I've done my duty as you trained me to do. I see that now. But I have a new path, a future at the head of the clans of Romathe. Aulik is only the start, and reunification will be tricky, but I believe we can do it. And maybe one day, we will make peace with Drumidia and call ourselves Eporiae once more." Taking another bite, Amalie sits, staring at the stones.

"He would be very cross with us if he were here now," a low voice sounds behind Amalie.

Startled, Amalie jumps to her feet, seeing Sirien walking through the trees behind her.

"What are you doing here?" Amalie speaks softly, mouth full of food.

"I came to pay my respects to our mother." Sirien stops beside Amalie. Her eyes fixed on the two new stone markers.

"Castor deserves a place," Amalie whispers, seeing the tears well in Sirien's eyes.

Unable to speak, Sirien nods, moving in its direction to touch the carefully placed rocks smoothed by the creek's water.

"Do you think he would scold us for coming here?" Amalie asks, looking at her father's grave.

"Absolutely. He would be most angry Davina came and is in a dangerous position. He loved her dearly." Sirien touches the smooth surfaces of Castor's mound.

"I know we have had our differences, and father may not have cared for us as he did for Davina, but I did then as I do now. Without you, I don't know how I would have gotten through life. You have been my voice of reason, as you always say, and I'm thankful." Amalie averts her eyes, feeling vulnerable.

"What do you think he would say to us now? Would he approve of this?" Sirien asks, pulling Amalie's gaze back up to her. Sirien now faces her father's fresh memorial.

"We have become what he raised us to be. He would be happy to know we are fulfilling his plans of protecting Davina. It's what he wanted," Amalie says with a tone of annoyance.

"It is funny to think we were born enemies of the crown, and now the youngest will sit upon its throne. We will have to exile if we survive." Sirien looks at Amalie, pain in her eyes.

"I know. We will be traitors to the Kingdom, but not its people," Amalie speaks softly, looking up to the treetops. "We should go. The fog could lift soon, and we need it as cover to return home." Holding out a hand, Amalie waits for Sirien.

Kissing her fingertips, she places it over the stones of her husband's mound before taking Amalie's hand as they leave the grove for possibly the final time.

✳ ✳ ✳

Davina lays on the bed huddled in a quilt pulled from the chest in her father's room. Without the luxury of a fire during the day, they bundled heavily in layers and cloaks to keep themselves warm enough to function. This morning, however, the chill had set into her bones it seemed, and she shivered constantly.

Ascher and Americ sit across the room, speaking with seriousness. Davina blinks her eyes, looking over the room slowly, not finding her sisters, Adyra or Yrin anywhere present. She wonders if they all left already to rendezvous with the others traveling in, or had something happened?

Sitting up, Davina looks to the men, questions swimming in her eyes. Seeing the movement, Americ looks in her direction and stands, moving to her immediately. Seeing her shaking body, he removes his cloak, tossing it over her.

"Where are the others? Have they gone?" Davina looks frantically at Americ, searching for answers.

"Yrin and Adyra have. Sirien and Amalie will be back, and hopefully soon." Rubbing his arms with his hands, Davina watches Americ closely, trying to hide his chill.

Scooting over on the bed, she makes space for him and, slipping an arm free, pats the bed invitingly beside her. Looking at her, Americ feels cautious, not wanting to overstep her boundaries, yet finds himself longing for her closeness. Slipping in beside her, she shoves the quilt and cloak over him, pressing up against his side. Heart throbbing, he forces back a grin as he swings an arm behind her and gently pulls her closer. Not fighting it, Davina rests her head on his shoulder, burrowing her face in the blankets.

For comfort or his body heat, Americ had no idea what made her want this, but he doesn't care. In the weeks of their marriage, he wished for more from her, but promising her patience, he acted as a friend only, keeping his distance. It had worked in many ways as her touch became more frequent and conversation light and easy, but Americ could still sense her discomfort, so he waited.

Now, sitting on the bed with her is like a dream and very easily the happiest moment of his life. His arm, wrapped around her back and hand resting on her waist, keeps her tightly held close to him while his chin sits on the top of her head. Feeling her hand move across his stomach, he freezes, muscles tightening as her fingers meet his, winding together tightly.

"Americ?" her voice is soft and low as she tilts her face up toward him. "Even though our marriage was out of necessity, it doesn't mean I want to lose you. We are a part of each other now, so promise me this will work. Promise me you will be alright." Tears shine in her tired eyes, and Americ feels sick with dread.

Without a second thought, Americ leans down, kissing Davina on the forehead. She doesn't recoil but rather leans into him. Panic surfacing, Americ regrets coming back to Aldhorran, walking into the line of danger, and giving up the future with her he so badly wants. The little time they have would never be enough. He will die, the others were clear, but Davina doesn't know because they plan to save her.

Americ never questioned Amalie when she told him he had to sacrifice himself, he just accepted it. But should he have? Could he have changed both of their fates by running away with her in the first place or leaving her behind altogether? Cursing himself, he fights his mind, shutting out the worries and instead focusing on the rare moment they are sharing.

The door flings open swinging wide as Amalie and Sirien walk through it. Davina, sitting bolt upright, brightens at the sight of their faces, relieved to see them safely back. Splitting away from one another, Amalie walks to Ascher, and Sirien heads to Davina and Americ.

"Amalie and I have been discussing the plan, and we have decided to make an adjustment. You will be taking both

Davina and I with you to the King. Together we will be stronger and safer." Sirien looks down at Americ, voice commanding.

"I will not argue that. It may sway my father slightly more to have you both. But are you sure?" Americ looks at her, concern swelling as he takes in her pale pallor and fragile appearance.

"Yes. I need to be there." Sirien's voice is firm, her decision unrelenting.

Nodding, Americ looks at Davina, her expression thankful yet worried. Sirien reaches out, pulling her sister's arm from the warmth of the covers and taking her hand. Squeezing Davina's fingers tightly in her hand, she gives her a small grin, attempting to reassure her. Releasing her grip, Sirien pats Americ's shoulder before walking away and shutting herself in her father's room.

Looking across at Amalie and Ascher, Americ grows uneasy, knowing the time grows close that they will need to leave. Pushing away from the warm quilt, he tucks Davina in tightly, moving to the closed door between Sirien and him. Knocking lightly, he hears the rustling of skirts then the door opens.

"Can I speak with you for a moment?"

Sirien opens the door wide enough for him to slip through, closing it softly behind him. The room is bare. Only a bed and trunk occupy the space.

"Amalie told me about the vision you had in Aldara. I didn't question her then, and I hate to now, but I need to know why you pushed forward with this union if Davina were to die because of me?" Americ speaks hastily.

"Viala told me it was seen before her birth. She is destined to be on the throne, and I saw you. There is no changing fate." Sirien sits on the edge of the bed.

"Then will you be able to save her? If we leave now, could we both escape death?" Americ steps toward her, anxious for answers.

"I don't know. You need to be crowned to pass on the title to your son. Your deaths are linked, Americ. If you are together during your fall, she will go beside you. She has to leave at the first sign of danger to save your son and to raise him to take back the throne," Sirien sighs, speaking impatiently.

"But there is no guarantee she will be able to escape soon enough." Sirien looks at him with tired eyes.

"Americ, you have to do your best to save her. I cannot tell you anything more because I do not have the answers. I'm sorry."

Americ watches her shift her weight finding a new position of comfort. Not speaking, he leaves, returning to the main room and Davina's side.

* * *

"He's here." Ascher peers out the window, watching a man sneak to the house and lightly tap on the door.

Allowing him inside, Amalie grins widely, seeing it to be Mungar, and Ascher embraces him tightly, overjoyed to see him.

"Did anyone see you?" Stepping back, Ascher looks him over, barely recognizing the grubby appearance.

"No. There is a cart waiting for us, so we need to hurry. I will be waiting for you on the inside." Mungar beams, speaking with excitement apparent in his voice.

"Eager for a fight?" Ascher chuckles, seeing a smile spread across his face in reply.

"Till tonight." The men take one another by the forearms, nodding in farewell. "Stau Haulo im Sempt." Mungar says with intensity.

"Ado Naie," Ascher replies.

"Ado Naie." Mungar releases Ascher, turning to face Americ, Davina, and Sirien.

Motioning them to follow him, they slip from the house into the daylight, embarking on the start of their coup.

* * *

Shouts rise from the top of the sturdy walls, yelling Americ's name and title. The gates screaming as they open send chills down everyone's spines. Wrists shackled, Sirien and Davina huddle together in the bed of the cart, terrified of this moment and their time residing here, praying all goes according to the plan. Americ sits by Mungar as they ride in, soldiers converging on them as they pass through the gates.

Faces Americ recognizes pass by, crossing his line of vision, and he shrinks in his seat, wishing to turn and sprint away rather than face his father. But as promised, he bites his tongue and forces a strong look over his face, preparing to confront the tyrant he calls father. The guards stand alert, looking over them as they halt in the courtyard and wait to be approached. Expecting to see Baldur, Americ is surprised to see Jonas acting as the commander instead.

"My Prince, welcome home." Jonas greets him joyfully, surveying the other three with Americ.

"I need to speak with my father immediately. This man needs to be fed and cared for. He has been a great help to me these last weeks and deserves recognition for his acts."

Mungar looks at the commander, nodding with respect in his direction.

"I have gifts for the King. Where is he?" Americ motions to Sirien and Davina in the back.

"Of course, sir. I will fetch servants for your companion and seek out the King's location." Bowing, Jonas turns, tossing orders around to the various bystanders.

In a flurry, Mungar is whisked away, and with help from Jonas' men, Davina and Sirien are pulled from the cart and led behind Americ into the fortress where they will face the beast and be condemned to misery if their plan fails.

THIRTY

———

Agnai glares at the women, looking over their angry faces as they stare back. Americ watches him closely while speaking to Jonas, laying out the plan of his captive's imprisonment. Accepting his orders, Jonas bows, leaving Americ to speak with the King.

"I'm curious to know how you were taken in the first place," Agnai speaks without looking at Americ, his eyes set on the women.

"I feigned rescuing the girl. She wasn't giving me what I wanted, so I gave her what she did—freedom. However, it backfired on me. When we reached the Nasinreth villages, I was taken captive." Americ walks around the two women, kneeling before his father.

"And how did you escape?" Agnai's brows raise in question.

"I befriended another prisoner, promising him riches if he helped me escape. The idea worked seamlessly, and when these two followed me when I ran, and I had the upper hand, taking them as *my* prisoners." Americ smiles victoriously, keeping his focus trained on his father.

The king sits, rubbing his stubbly chin, and Americ

watches, afraid he may not take the bait, but he keeps his resolve as steady as possible.

"So what now, son? What is it you want?" Agnai asks curiously.

"I want to take a regimen of men to the villages and eradicate these people once and for all. I know the terrain and their secrets. I would also like to continue my questioning with them for further revelations."

Narrowing his eyes, Agnai looks at his son with disbelief.

Heart skipping under his father's scrutinizing gaze, Americ thinks quickly, flitting his eyes to the table where his father's dagger sits unsheathed next to a whetstone. Reaching for it, he takes the thick hilt in his grip and reaches for Sirien. Stepping behind her, he takes her chin in his other hand and lifts it, exposing the tender flesh of her neck. The newly sharpened blade pierces the skin as it touches her, a small trickle of blood running down her fair skin.

Agnai laughs, clapping his hands, and Americ looks up, legs quaking behind her. "Enough, son, you have earned my trust. Let her live so we may question her. I will grant your request and allow you to question them further."

Americ releases Sirien, avoiding the urge to look at Davina with apologetic eyes.

Americ bows, replacing the knife on his father's desk. Pulling Davina and Sirien from the floor, he guides them toward the door. Steadying his walk, Americ holds himself tall and gives off the illusion of dignity and satisfaction over his catch.

"Son." Americ halts, holding his breath as he turns his head to look at Agnai. "Well done."

Agnai's voice speaks with genuine pride over Americ's accomplishment, and for the first time in his life, Americ feels accepted. Pushing out of the door, he walks quickly, taking the girls away. Once a safe distance away, Americ sighs with relief, apologizing profusely to Sirien.

"All is well. It was necessary," Sirien whispers quickly.

"This is where we must part ways. I will see you both soon." Americ says to Davina, speaking behind her head to conceal his words from Jonas, who stands ahead of them.

Meeting the guard at a large, closed door, Americ releases Davina and Sirien into his custody, instructing him to take them to the pit. Obeying immediately, Jonas takes them away, moving through the large doors he had been standing before and disappearing behind them as they thud loudly.

Leaving with his stomach in knots, Americ worries about leaving them alone, but for Ascher to breach the castle, he must find Mungar and set the stage.

＊ ＊ ＊

As the sun falls behind the horizon, Amalie and Ascher set out to rendezvous with the others along the forest edge. Cadison had prepared them for all of the routes and times the guards take. Timing is key, and everyone knows it. The countryside sits calm and quiet as they travel the hour's distance to the northern side of the castle. By dark, they reach the forest's edge, diving into it in search of their gathered men and women.

Not a spoken word between them, they ride, eyes peeled to any movement or sound alerting them to the location. Finally, in the heart of the gathering of trees, they see a dim light glowing in the shadows, and they advance until the thick forest breaks into an open space, crowded with their people. Blackened faces turn in their direction, standing abruptly from their seats one by one, honoring the arrival of their Chieftain.

Seeing this, Ascher is moved, speaking fiercely from the depths of his soul. "I see you and honor you all. Americ is not of our people, and this is not our home, yet we stand here ready for a fight. Tonight we will free this Kingdom from the terror it has witnessed and accepted for far too long and place a new ruler at its head. Tonight we enact revenge for the bride stolen from us and pay back the losses we suffered. Tonight we rise mighty and unbroken as we have waited far too long for this, and with success, we will ride the sea home to Romathe! Follow me as your Chieftain, accept me as your brother. May the messengers take favor on us, protect us, guide us and bring us glory. Show no mercy. Stau Haulo im Sempt!"

The people thump their chests, men and women alike echoing the call of the Aulik. A tall man moves from the group toward Ascher and Amalie as the others settle back into their seats, resuming the conversation they had been in prior. A thick black line covers over the bridge of the man's nose and both his eyes, making him unrecognizable and terrifying.

"Inspiring." His tone of sarcasm makes them chuckle, knowing the voice belongs to Yrin.

Sliding from his horse, Ascher takes his friend by the arm, embracing him roughly.

"Yrin! Are the men ready?" Ascher asks.

"Beyond. They have been waiting for this day." Looking to Amalie, Yrin stretches out his hand, allowing her to take it as she slips from her own saddle. "You will need to see Lauden for painting. It will set you apart from the soldiers in the dark and mark you for safety." Yrin doesn't wait for a reply before walking away toward the warriors gathered together.

They lead their horses to the camp's edge. Amalie and Ascher hand off the reins to a woman standing waiting for them.

Yrin's tall, broad frame is easy to spot, towering above most of the people, and when they finally catch up to him, they find him speaking with a woman, covered head to toe in markings etched into her skin. Her unusual blonde hair draws Amalie's curiosity to a peak, the golden strands braided away from the woman's thin and strongly boned face.

"This is Lauden. She will prepare you." Yrin pats Ascher on the shoulder, taking him away to the nearby fire, where a group of men sit chatting fiercely.

"Sit, please. I will first tie your hair. What you have will not do in battle." Moving to Amalie's loosely braided hair, Lauden unties the leather strap, running her thin fingers through the dark strands. Weaving into a complex set of braids trailing from crown to base of her skull, Amalie begins to feel antsy and tired of being fussed with. Loose behind her ears and the back of her head, her hair falls in wavy locks while smaller braids line the sides of her head. Finished with her hair, Lauden moves back into Amalie's line of sight, scooping up a wooden bowl in her hands and settling herself before Amalie. Dipping her fingers, Lauden begins marking her face with a black paste, circling the eyes first before dragging two fingers from the eye down Amalie's cheek to her jaw. Next, she takes a twig, and tilting Amalie's head to the side, begins writing down her neck, starting below the ear.

Stepping away, she looks over her work, nodding with approval. "Now you are Aulik."

"She looks more Aulik than me," Ascher says behind her. Turning to look at him, she is shocked at first, seeing half of his face is gone, blending into the shadows beside and behind him, only a golden honey eye appearing in the void. "We need to go. The guard just passed by and are in our custody. It won't be long before they are missed."

Looking around her, Amalie sees fires being doused and feels the energy of the people course through her. Marching through the trees, they walk like phantoms haunting the forest, horses snorting as they pound the ground with their feet and the thirst for blood running rampant through the air.

Stopping at the edge, concealed in the darkness, they can see the castle, torches lining the upper wall, and figures walking the edge, patrolling the outer world. Amalie reaches out beside her, taking Ascher's hand and squeezing it. Looking down at her, Ascher looks deep into her eyes, pulling her close to him and bending down to kiss her.

"I love you." His breath is hot on her face.

A scream bellows from the castle walls, tearing Ascher and Amalie's attention apart. A man falls along the outer edge of the wall and crunches at the base with a deafening pop. A cry from the wall pierces the thick cold air.

"Ado Naie!"

The voices of the Aulik rise like a howling wind, their shrieks shrill, penetrating the calmness of night, sending fear into the bones of their enemies.

"For honor," Amalie whispers, mounting her steed and following Ascher into chaos.

THIRTY-ONE

———

"Really? Could you not have been more subtle?" Americ yells back as the two men running down the stairs carved into the side of the wall.

"I am Aulik, Americ. We like to throw the enemy off their game. It's more fun that way," Mungar calls back, chasing after Americ.

"Just get to the pit and release the women. We need them!"

Stopping at the bottom of the stairs, Mungar looks out into the space, becoming overrun with soldiers as hell rains down on them. The clashing of swords, yelling and screaming, thuds from body hitting body, blood spilling, and weapons flying through the air strike with great intensity. Mungar flings himself into the chaos, charging for the door leading inside.

Americ moves into view of the courtyard, watching Mungar make his way through the fight. A guard, crumbled a few feet from him, has a bow and quiver strung across his back. Reaching for it, Americ takes it and searches again for Mungar. Seeing him in a battle before the door, Americ aims, praying he hits his mark.

Loose. The first arrow flies, hitting one of the men in Mungar's path, freeing him up to advance. Watching him disappear at last, Americ tosses aside the bow, stepping down into the chaos himself, keeping his back to the wall. Ascher's men all look frightening, features disguised with black spread across their faces, some so much you can only see slits as eyes and bold white teeth. Standing in a shadowy section, Americ watches the fight, hearing the shrieks of pain and cries of victory as bodies fall to the ground in defeat. Pushing away from the wall, Americ shoves through the fighting, taking a sword from the hand of a fallen soldier, and runs, knocking into guards, sending them to their deaths.

"Surround the Prince!" a voice rings out, yelling in Americ's direction.

Five men surround him immediately, shoving away from the fight toward the Castle. One by one, they drop, overtaken by the ferocity of the intruders leaving only one man to his aid. Jonas. Grabbing Americ roughly, he shoves him forcefully back, taking a step forward to shield the Prince. Standing still for a split moment, it seems time has slowed, Americ's heart dropping to see Jonas' body slump to the ground, a dagger sticking out from his neck.

A woman stands a few feet away, looking Americ in the face intensely. A soldier appears to her left, and without hesitation or hardly a glance, her ax slices through the air, marking him in between the eyes. The noises Jonas makes as he chokes and suffocates on his own blood overpower the sounds of war surrounding them. Stepping backward, Americ stumbles over a body forgetting the Aulik are allies and not enemies. The woman advances toward him, her face covered with the same black markings around the eyes and stretched down her cheeks as if she cried the black paste. Squatting before him, Americ sees her eyes and knows them, a sigh of relief escaping his chest.

Raising her brows at him, she reaches forward, taking him by the hair at the top of his head, ripping him from the ground. "I will spill his blood!"

The soldiers nearby stop, and a few begin to rush them until she jerks a dagger from her belt, shoving the point of it against Americ's throat. Surrendering, the soldiers call out an order to cease the fight. Dropping the men to their knees by force, the Aulik stand victorious over their first battle, knowing full well the fight was far from over. A man walks menacingly from amid the wall of fighters, face half black, a hatchet in one hand and sword in another, and blood splattered across his face. Walking backward, the man and woman move to the door, slipping inside. Immediately, Amalie releases him, and Americ takes a second to gather his wits.

"Where do we go now, Americ?" Another man slips inside with a voice like rumbling thunder. Yrin.

"The guard will have alerted my father, so we should go to the inner court where the garden is. If Mungar made it to the dungeon and freed Davina and Sirien, they should be on their way back, and we can catch them."

Nodding, Yrin looks to Ascher for instruction.

"Kill the guard, and let's get moving." Heartless, Ascher speaks to Yrin, turning his back to the door as the world outside erupts in a howl of painful cries.

* * *

As instructed, Mungar weaves through the halls in search of the place they call the pit. Hiding in doorways and shadows to avoid the guard rushing to the courtyard, he makes his way slowly yet efficiently. Finding the entrance to the castle dungeon, he sneaks inside, finding a line of closed doors down the dreary, damp hall. Americ had said the pit would be at the end, and he wondered in the back of his mind why it would be called that.

At the end of the hall, Mungar stoops to pull out a key from his boot, and with a steady hand, slips it in the hole unlocking the door with a click. The room is pitch black and noiseless. Reaching to the left of the door, Mungar grasps a torch from the wall and slips inside. A winding stair surprises him, understanding why it was named the pit. The stairway winds around the outside of the room to the bottom, and he can just barely make out two figures.

"Let's go. We haven't much…" The crack of a step surprises him. As he spins around, he finds a soldier stooping over him.

The blade of the soldier's sword pierces through him, and he grunts at the sharp pain. His body grows cold as life flows from him, and submitting to the weakness, Mungar falls to his knees. The echo of screams floats up the cavern walls as the torch falls to their feet, breaking into a billion sparks.

Boots clicking down the stone steps haunt Davina and Sirien. Huddled together, they back into the wall away from the base of the steps, and as the man moves closer into the light, their hearts drop, knowing they are as good as dead. Davina watches Baldur's face as he laughs.

"I knew we would meet again, darling. And you brought a friend." His voice booms, rattling them to the core.

Crouching before Davina, he takes her chin in his hand, turning her face so he can get a good look at her. Angry, Davina spits, showering Baldur's face. He doesn't flinch, staring at her as he wipes his face on his sleeve. Reaching up he grips the top of Davina's head, hair wound tightly in his fingers as he pulls her to her feet.

Crying out, she grabs his thick wrist, relieving the strain on her scalp slightly. Sirien jumps to her feet, throwing herself at Baldur, only to be smacked away, the room spinning around her as she falls to the ground.

"As much as I enjoy these games, I am afraid we haven't the time." Baldur smiles as he looks at Davina's face, agony etched into her skin.

Releasing his grip, she falls to the ground. Black spots floating across her sight as she crawls to Sirien.

"Get up before I make you," he threatens.

Pushing up from the cold stone, Davina steadies herself, helping Sirien up. Pulling an arm over her shoulder, Davina takes both their weight, climbing the stairs slowly.

Baldur snickers at their struggle, pushing them hard to move faster. Toward the top, they stumble over Mungar, his body still warm, giving light to the fragility of life. In the dark corridor beyond the pit, Baldur moves ahead of them, checking for enemies before advancing out into the open.

Dragging Davina by the arm, they move quickly, up sets of stairs and down halls until they stop before a room lined with shelves of books and scrolls. Moving to the back of the room, Baldur kicks back a rug concealing a trapdoor. Peeling it up with a screech, Baldur looks at the women, expecting them to go inside. Hesitant, Davina takes the first step into the black hole, finding a step not far inside. Taking them by feeling, Davina descends, holding Sirien's hand as she follows on unsteady feet.

"My son, I always knew you would betray me." Sound echoes through the tight space from the end of the narrow tunnel.

"Give up now, Agnai. My men will kill everyone here if that's what it takes to get to you." Ascher's voice gives Davina a sense of hope as she makes her way to the light ahead.

"I am your King!" the man screams.

"Look around, father. Your men have failed, and you are surrounded." Americ's voice is strong in the near distance, and Davina's heart leaps at it.

Sirien, close behind her, the two hustle into the light, entering into a moonlit room full of candles, flickering against the cold air. A man stands on a balcony off the room, looking down at the party below.

"I knew the moment you set foot in this fortress you had a new vendetta. You think you can outsmart me by playing my own game. What I didn't expect was for you to escape Balaoug. You were meant to die there along with that Nasinreth witch. But now you are here, and I have a second chance." Agnai throws his hands in the air, stepping back from the edge and moving inside just as an arrow pierces the wall behind where he stood.

Seeing Baldur he pauses, looking at him with pride, shifting his gaze to Davina and Sirien.

"He tried to make me believe he would kill that one. I am going to assume she is not the one he cares for the most, but her." Agnai walks to Davina, taking her throat in his hand.

Gasping for air, she claws at his arm, his eyes a dark brown staring into her pine green ones, watching the light slip from her eyes. Sirien tries to lunge for Agnai, only to be held back by Baldur. Releasing Davina just before the world goes blank, she gulps air into her lungs, burning as they inflate to their full capacity.

"You coward! Face me! I am your son, heir to the throne. I will not be tossed aside or replaced! You will look me in the eyes when we defeat you and see me rise in your place. Face me!" Americ's voice trails up the wall into the small room.

Annoyed, Agnai grabs Davina around the waist, hoisting her up and carrying her toward the balcony, stopping briefly "Kill her and bring me Americ." Agnai looks to Baldur, motioning to Sirien.

Sirien backs away from Baldur, panic rising as Davina moves from her sight. Trying to fight, Sirien hits and kicks, reaching for the sword at Baldur's side. Frozen, her body in shock, she watches the man back away, the knife in his hand smeared with blood. Her hands move to her belly, feeling the warm wetness spread over her dress. Hands shaking, she looks to see the red staining her skin. Sirien's knees strike the ground with a bone-breaking heaviness, and she can feel her child writhe inside of her. Falling to her side, she hears a voice, muddled and distant.

"I will give you one chance, my son. Give yourself over to me, and I will spare her life. Your execution will be with a royal's honors. If you do not comply, I will kill her."

Sirien moves her hand over her belly, heat filling her body. She coughs and sees the blood spatter from it. The child, its kicks and movements weakening, breaks her heart.

"No. You will release them. They have no part in this. I will give you one chance. Surrender easily and keep your life, or die. It is simple." Americ's voice drowns in the ringing in Siriens ears.

"Americ, don't!" Davina screams, Americ yelling, pleading for his father to stop.

With all her might, Sirien drags herself across the floor, the unborn child's writhing stopped and numbness overtaking her as she has nothing to lose or live for. Seeing Davina, arm twisted behind her back. The King has her bent over the wall's edge, tantalizing those below. Forcing herself to remain conscious, Sirien pushes herself up to her knees, heaving blood and bile as she fights the trauma to her body and soul.

Looking up, gathering her wits, she stops, body cold and the world absent of sound. In the shadows of the tunnel stands the mysterious woman, clad in white, pale, and marked across her body. Her eyes black as night, and for the first time, she hears her speak, the sound so sweet and consoling.

"The time has come."

Sirien has no questions to ask or need to wonder what she meant. Releasing all of her built up rage and suffering, she musters the remaining energy she has, forcing herself to her feet. Screaming, Agnai turns to see her lunge toward him. Throwing Davina aside, he tries to move out of the way but doesn't succeed. Toppling over the edge of the balcony, they fall, a sickening crack as their bodies meet the cobbled path.

Sirien lays, eyes wide, staring up at the sky, a tear sliding down her temple. Her head slowly falls to the side, and she sees her hand outstretched in a pool of blood and his crown at her fingertips as her sight dims, and she falls into an everlasting sleep.

Shock runs rampant through the men and women standing in the garden, looking at the crumpled bodies on the ground. Amalie looks at her sister, sprawled across the ground, and freezes as chills course through her at the shrill cry from above. Looking up, she sees Davina, leaning over the edge at the bodies below, terrorized and brokenhearted. Americ stumbles back, reaching for the nearest living soldier, and leans in, speaking harshly in his face.

"Where is the entrance to the balcony? Tell me now!" Americ shakes the man, his panicked response to Davina's strangled cries.

"The library," the man sputters.

Jumping to his feet, Americ sprints away, the clicking of his boots moving until silenced by distance. Thankful for Americ's absence, Amalie allows the white hot rage to overcome her. Stepping to Ascher, she slides the ax, slick with the blood of their enemies, from his hand and propels herself forward.

Hacking away angrily, Amalie huffs with each blow until Agnai's head is free of his body and she is out of breath. Dragging the head by its hair from the courtyard, Amalie trails through the winding corridors out into the main courtyard and up to the top of the wall, posting it over the edge of the wall for the world to see. Over the mountains, a dreary gold and rose color stain the clouds as snow falls sweetly skirting the ground. Amalie envies its beauty and hates the serenity. Broken in the farthest depths of her soul, she screams, crumpling to her knees and submitting to her vulnerability.

"Amalie. We have to go," Ascher speaks behind her. "Americ is bringing Davina out, and she needs you. You need her. Our men are already dispersing, and now we need to do the same."

Biting her lip, Amalie pushes herself up from the ground. Without looking at him, she brushes past him, rushing down into the courtyard.

Yrin stands holding the horses, antsy to leave the horrid place. They wait for Davina and Americ, looking wildly around them in search of the lost couple.

Finally, Americ comes running out with Davina cradled in his arms. "You need to go. Hurry." Handing her over to Ascher, Americ kisses her head briefly before running back inside. The trumpets blaze, and shouts ring out.

"The King is dead. The King is dead!" Mounting their horses, Yrin, Ascher, Amalie, and Davina take off after the remaining clansmen across the road and into the open fields as light crawls across the open space, heading for home.

THIRTY-TWO

———

They refuse to speak Sirien's name or mourn together openly, acting as if she simply disappeared or never existed at all. Davina spends much of her time on the wall's edge watching over the open expanse, waiting for a sign of Americ calling her to him. Waiting hour after hour in silence, hoping and praying. Days, then weeks pass without a word and the worry over his credibility and rights to the throne rise in all of their minds.

"He will come." Amalie's voice is quiet behind her, startled by her silent arrival.

"If he doesn't?" Davina asks, fearing the worst.

"If he doesn't, then you come with us." Amalie looks out in the same direction as Davina had been.

The days are shorter this time of year. Early evenings like now are already dusk and will fall dark before supper reaches the tables. The forest edge beyond them transforms suddenly, glowing with shimmering lights, then a form cloaked in white appears holding a lantern followed by many more.

"What is that?" Davina asks, peering out at the curious sight.

A low rumble sounds from a distance. Then a high hum joins in. More white figures appear, lanterns glowing in their hands. A song, lamenting the lost, one Amalie remembers as a child standing before the funeral fire for her mother.

"They are paying respect to Sirien," Amalie whispers as she takes Davina's hand, a silent tear sliding down her face.

"After all this time?" Davina's voice is soft and uneven.

"There is never a wrong time," Amalie replies.

The voices blend naturally, floating across the winter breeze through the duration of the beautiful song. Clansmen make their way up on the wall as well, searching out the sound and joining the sisters in remembering the lost. Peace falls over the town, and they watch until the last Nasinreth recedes back into the trees, their lanterns absent, leaving behind shadows.

Pulling Davina into her arms, Amalie weeps, finally allowing herself to mourn the loss and let go of the pain. Together, they allow the night to fall on them, draping their figures in the shadow of night before heading back to the home of Elra's. Taking their time, the women make their way to their beds, hating sleep and the dreams it brings.

* * *

The morning is quiet and dull, wind nudging at the window, the house creaking in response. Winter is in full force now in the lowlands, making travel difficult for even the most experienced. Laying in her bed, Davina's chest aches from her losses and loneliness, and she wishes for a reprieve from such pain. A tear slides down her temple, temporarily staining the linen underneath her head. Stiff from the night, Davina brings her body up from the bed, moving slowly to dress and brush out her hair. Dragging her feet down the hall, the voices of Amalie, Ascher, and Elra float up from below.

"Three months. Travel across the sea into Netheis would be your best and safest route. Then travel by horse to Romathe. Go through the Noruwah pass near the Vale," Elra says, pointing to the map sprawled across their laps.

The thought of Amalie so far away is hard to fathom, and the throbbing becomes worse. Joining them in silence, Davina soaks in the luxurious heat resonating from the fire. The sudden sound of the horn blowing outside startles them, sending Elra to her feet immediately. Snatching up cloaks and shawls, they rush outside, flying through the streets to the stairs that climb the wall. Heaving from the climb, they force themselves through the small crowd of onlookers and glance into the white expanse.

Flags wave vigorously, holding the King's Crest, a parade of soldiers in tow, and at the head rides Cadison. Heart leaping, Davina races back down and out of the opening gates. When she's in his sight, Cadison gallops faster ahead of the caravan, stopping before her. He jumps from his saddle and walks the few feet it takes to close the distance between them, kneeling before her.

"My Queen. I have come to bring you home." He rests on his knee, bowing his head.

Throwing herself at him, he looks up just in time to catch Davina as she cries with joy on his shoulder.

"Americ?" She shoves away, concern suddenly filling her eyes.

"He is King. He waits anxiously for you," Cadison says, a smile stretching over his face.

Offering his horse, Cadison sets her high in the saddle as he walks her back to Dune. Butterflies fill her chest thinking about Americ and how much she misses his presence and the comfort she finds in it.

"Long live the Queen!" Cadison bellows as he enters the gate and the gathered crowd inside raises their voices in celebration. Elra, standing high on the stairs, smiles with pride down at them and silences the crowd with a raise of her hand.

"We will feast tonight in celebration of victory over the throne of Omideon. We will honor the warriors who brought down the mighty Agnai and thank them, for we will be going home in the spring now vengeance is served!" Elra raises her voice, the crowd roaring exuberantly.

Stepping down from her platform of steps, Elra meets Cadison and Davina in the street. Leaving Davina with Ascher and Amalie when they make their way to them, Elra takes her nephew by the arm, and they walk together back to her home.

"When will you leave?" Elra asks.

"Day after tomorrow. I don't want to leave Americ too long. Baldur has gone missing, and Charlotte is imprisoned for now, but it will not last. They will need to reunite and produce a heir as quickly as possible if they are to stabilize their reign," Cadison says, an urgency in his voice.

"I see. Amalie and Ascher are in the same light, and I do not believe they see the severity of the situation. Romathe is not a gentle country. They rely on guarantees, not promises." Elra looks to Cadison, eyes weary with age.

"Let's just focus on tonight and the banquet we now have to prepare. Ascher will do the right thing, and together, Amalie and him will flourish alongside the clans," Cadison reassures Elra, patting the hand she has wrapped around his arm.

Smiling, Elra grips his arm tighter as they round the corner to her home, finding women huddled near the door awaiting their orders to prepare the feast.

* * *

The lodge is lit brightly, doors open wide to the festivities inside. Music rumbles the timber walls, food fills the space with a mouthwatering aroma, and families riddle the area, leaving hardly any space to walk.

Immersing themselves in the crowd, Amalie and Ascher talk and laugh excitedly, accepting congratulation and words of wisdom for the days to come. Davina, subdued in her merriment, hangs along the wall, accepting a goblet of ale as clansmen pass by, offering it to her. She watches her sister, her face lit with purpose among her new people, fitting in here far more than she had in their own family.

The lodge is large enough to fit over four hundred people shoulder to shoulder. Two large pits of stone sit in the center of the room, harnessing large fires within. Surrounding them are tables stacked high with dishes and food. Tables also line the inner edge of the space, leaving just enough room between them and the walls to walk and stand. Torches line each pole supporting the sides and giving light to the joyous faces.

Ascher and Amalie move slowly through the crowd toward the front of the room where another table stands, and behind it, two chairs draped in furs are elevated above the rest of the room. Elra sits upon the one on the right, watching happily over her people. Seeing Ascher and Amalie draw closer to her, she stands calling out over the roar of voices.

"Silence!" The room quiets slowly. "We are gathered tonight to celebrate the coming home of my Grandson and his wife, who have vowed to return to the homeland and take the right of Chieftain, which is his by birth. He fearlessly has led you into his first battle, surfacing victorious, instilling a new ruler over this land. He has taken up his oath in marriage and to me, pledging his fealty. But the time is now that I stand aside with great pride, pledging my own fealty as he leads us forward." She looks at him and steps away from the seat, leaving it empty.

Ascher steps forward, taking a goblet from the table, and stands in her place facing the people.

"I stand here, vowing to take my place when the time comes. Our people came to serve, advise and forge an alliance with the King long ago, and in turn, he broke our trust, splitting our lands and scattering our people." Murmurs run through the crowd excitedly, nodding to each other. "But no more. We have rid this country of the vile disease and given it new life. In the spring, we will sail, and we will return to our homeland. I swear to you I will work tirelessly to restore unity among the clans, and one day our sisters to the West may ally with us once more." Raising his ale before him, he searches the people for Amalie, and when he sees her glowing face, he yells at the top of his lungs, "Stau Haulo Im Sempt! Ado naie."

The room simultaneously raises their cups and repeats the phrase back to him before gulping the amber liquid from within.

The drums begin to beat, and the people disperse into animated conversations lasting late into the night. When they stumble from within the walls, they find the sun peeking over the horizon in its splendor.

* * *

"Never lose your faith, and remember the people you came from," Davina says to Amalie as she walks toward her horse.

The cloak Americ sent is a beautiful, thick Emerald color, with a collar of rich chestnut fur. She looks royal, sitting high on the horse, hood drawn over her head. Looking at her, Amalie knows Davina was always meant for this, for greatness, and a tear slips down her cheek.

"I wish I could come with you, be by your side every day, and keep you safe," Amalie says, standing at Davina's feet looking up.

"I know. But you have your own King to stand by and protect. I can take care of myself." Davina grins at her, and Amalie knows she is right. Stepping back as Cadison rallies his men to ride onward, Ascher slides up beside Amalie, wrapping his arm around her waist.

"We are ready," Cadison says to Davina.

"You watch over her." Amalie reaches for Cadison's hand.

"With my life," he replies strongly. Letting go of him, he takes off, leading his men away.

Davina leans down and grabs her sister's hand, giving it a small squeeze before taking the reins up. Patting the horse firmly in the hindquarters, he jolts forward. The procession leaves an overwhelming dread left in their wake where Amalie stands still, staring in the direction they are headed. Ascher never leaves her side, allowing her the time she needs to say goodbye silently.

"Cadison will not allow any harm to come to her." Ascher tosses his arm and cloak around her, which she finds warm and comforting.

"I told her Sirien foresaw her to have a son. I hope I wasn't wrong. I look forward to sharing the joys of motherhood with her through our correspondence one day." Amalie speaks tenderly, her mind on a distant thought.

"They will. I spoke with her as well. It is vital they have a son as Elra reminds me daily of the importance for us as well." Ascher grins, swiveling them around heading back to the town.

"How long will the voyage be again? To the Aulik village?" Amalie asks, keeping a tight grip on him by wrapping an arm around his waist.

"Three months until the spring thaw and another three with good seas and a few weeks on horse." Ascher's face crumples deep in thought.

"Good. Our child will have a stronger claim if born among its people."

Stopping suddenly, Ascher looks at her, eyes wide and brows raised. Giggling at his expression Amalie watches his face as a tear slips from the corner of his eye, running down his cheek. His hands move to her sides, looking down at her small flat belly then back to her face. Saying nothing, he kneels, placing his forehead just below Amalie's ribs. Running her fingers through his hair, she hears him whisper delicately, meant only for the unborn child.

"I choose to be the father you deserve. This is my promise."

THIRTY-THREE

———

FOUR MONTHS LATER

"King Americ, we have orders to arrest you on the charge of regicide."

Americ turns to see Baldur at the head of the group, speaking with a smile.

He has worked closely with Charlotte, the true force behind all of this. Her hunger for power has gone beyond her restraint, and now she gropes at every opportunity to achieve it. Walking tall to the door, Americ, surrounded by men, is escorted to the pit. Steadily, they make their way to the lower level, and as the door swings wide to the deep chamber, Americ sees another who already occupies it.

"Where is the Queen?" Charlotte looks at Baldur. Her eyes slit like a snake's.

"She wasn't present when we arrived. I have men overlooking the grounds now."

They won't find her. Cadison would never allow it. She will live. Americ thinks to himself, grateful for the man's selfless decision to remain in Omideon and serve him.

"You may go. I would like to speak with my brother alone." She waves her hand at them, ushering the men away.

"Where is Davina? You say she has been unwell, confined to her chamber the last month, yet the servants say she is not there and hasn't been for a time."

"I'm not sure. She left when we found you were no longer in your cell," Americ growls.

"You are lying. We shared a womb brother, I know you better than anyone could, and I can see it in your eyes. Where is the one we call Queen? Where is Davina?" She is angry, frantic for an answer. She knows if Davina is with child the line is secured and could rise again even with her on the throne.

"Even if I did know where she had gone, I would never tell you."

Charlotte looks at him long and hard.

"We will find her. My men will comb the ends of the earth if they must. She will be found." Charlotte turns her back to Americ, walking to the stairs that wrap around the cell. Americ laughs, and she turns, eyes wide and wild. "You married the very thing father despised and have ruined everything he built. I have always been the better choice, but being the second daughter, I knew I had to fight for it. When you were born moments after me, I became nothing. Castah was admirable and easy to mold to his needs, and you were the only boy, and me? I was father's toy. It is my turn Americ. My turn to be important, and you are in my way." Charlotte dusts off her shoulder with her hand, then pushes her hair back over her shoulder as she calms herself.

"The people will never love you, Charlotte. Not if you follow in father's path. There will be a coup and another one after that, and someday you will lose," Americ spits angrily, annoyed by her logic.

"I am cunning, perhaps even more than father was. I have proved it over again, and I am unafraid to make those tough choices." Charlotte takes a few steps up the stairway. "You see, when I found mother trying to leave here long ago and take us back to her country, I stopped her. Father wasn't too pleased with that, and well..." She plucks a piece of debris from the same shoulder, flicking it away. "She never had a chance to run after that, and for a while, he favored me."

"You are a monster." Americ feels disgusted, body shaking with rage.

"No. I am strong and ruthless. I am exactly what a ruler should be. You may have thought you were hated most, but father was hard on you because he had to be. I was unwanted as a wife, too strong headed, they said, so I was a gift to his men. Pacify their needs, sway them into submission. I was a pawn in his game, and now you are one in mine." She smiles sickly. "I promised myself I would be Queen, no matter the cost, and now I am." She walks up the steps, stopping at the door. "The council is taking over your charge, but I am sure it will be resolved soon. The executioner has already begun to prepare his blade," she calls down just before leaving the room.

If anything can be worse for the people, it will be her.

Full of rage, Americ slams his fist into the stone walls, breaking open the skin as he cries out in anguish. The only wish he had for his life would be to have the chance to enjoy it with Davina and his child by his side. She had never admitted it to him, but he knows deep down she loves him, and even unspoken it means the world to him.

* * *

The King is going to die, and his wife has fled for safety. She will not have gone willingly but is truly the best she has. Ascher and Amalie sit in a tavern outside of Aldhorran, designated for travelers between cities carrying goods. At dawn, he will be executed and his sister crowned in his place. It took time for the news to spread and charges announced, delaying their travels to Netheis, where they should be by now.

It is a dreary spring, raining often and chilly, plant life springing up in every direction. Adyra and her husband have gone ahead to ready a place on a ship leaving in two days to cross the Sea Of Kings. Sitting in the main room of the tavern, Amalie and Ascher drink and eat late into the night, hearts too heavy to sleep.

"Will she ever recover?" Amalie looks across the table at Ascher, breaking the silence. Ascher looks around the room and sees no one nearby.

"It is hard to say. She may." Gripping his mug tighter within his fist, Ascher brings it up to his lips, taking a long swig.

"Would you two like a room upstairs?" An old woman appears, wiping her hands over her shabby apron.

"No. We will take more to drink, however," Ascher replies politely.

"Very well. You will need it, seeing as there is an execution in the morning. If you are here, you are sure to be a witness to its horror. Poor soul, the young man was a promising King. Regicide, who would have thought." She stammers on then walks away still shaking her head.

Looking out the window, Amalie sees the skies are still dark with only a tinge of light on the horizon. Exhausted from their travels, they want nothing more than to rest and sleep, but with the need to leave immediately for Netheis, the two decide to push on directly after Americ's sentence is carried out. Leaving a small pile of coins on the table, Ascher shoves from the table, giving Amalie a hand as she stands, the little bulge in her midsection throwing her off balance.

Making their way into the subtly lit night, Amalie mounts her horse, Ascher helping her into the saddle. Taking his place on his own stallion, they ride slowly, wishing they did not have to witness such a tragedy. The city's main cobbled court is set specifically for the day's agenda. A platform freshly built sits high in the center, and around it, a crowd has already begun to form. Remaining in the saddles, Amalie and Ascher sit at the edge of the crowd, watching over their heads as they wait for Americ to be towed out before them. Sighing with exhaustion, Amalie stretches, rubbing an ache in her low back. Ascher looks at her with concern, but brushing it aside with a convincing smile, Amalie sits tall.

Their height gives them the advantage because when the procession starts, they are the first to see him. Walking before it all, a guard to each side dressed in clean linens, a crown on his head—the carriage behind Americ carries the new Queen, hidden from the curious eyes of her people. Once at the platform, Americ steps up, men following him as he plants his feet in the center, looking out at his gathered people. A sadness is in his eyes, longing for a face he knows will not be in the crowd. A man rises on the wooden planks behind Americ, masked and carrying his monstrous sword at his side. The new light reflects from its sharpened and shined surface.

Ascher looks at Americ with pity, an ache in his chest over the loss of his new brother, friend, and ally. Their eyes meet like the first time they met, and Americ is stricken rigid. Charlotte rises from the darkness of her carriage, and the crowd bows simultaneously, her silky golden hair blowing in the breeze. She steps toward him, taking the crown from his head and turning back to the carriage. A man slips from its depths, and a chill inches coldly down Amalie's spine. Baldur walks to them, the boards creaking under his weight, and kneels on one knee before Charlotte. Placing the crown on his head, she grins, as his dark hair bunches up below its rim.

"God save the King!" Rising from the ground, the crowd echoes her words.

"God save the Queen!" Baldur's deep voice rolls through the crowd, and they return the words in unison.

"Do you have anything to say, brother? A confession, perhaps." Charlotte looks to Americ.

Clenching his jaw, he looks out into the crowd once more, finding Amalie's face mouthing ever so slightly Davina's name. Nodding, his posture and attitude shift immediately, reassured by her reply of his wife's safety.

"Today, I will die an innocent man, usurped by my own flesh and blood, one whom I shared a womb with. But my reign will not be at its end. I have united the kingdom as the prophecy had declared it to be, and my son will rise, returning one day to his throne to bring the kingdom to glory." Looking at Charlotte, he smiles victoriously. "You will always live in fear, dear sister, until the end of your days."

Pale and boiling with anger at his words, Charlotte frantically looks at the soldiers and people, then back to Americ, nodding harshly for the execution to take place. Taking Americ's arms, two soldiers shove him to his knees. Looking up into the eyes of Amalie and Ascher, he waits, listening to the rustle of feet behind him as the executioner takes his place.

The whack of the blade against Americ's spine brings a lump to Amalie's throat, threatening to shove the liquid contents of her stomach back into the world. Silence falls over the people, disheartened but not shocked. The Queen, swift as a fox, hides away in her carriage, demanding to return to the castle. Ascher and Amalie pull the reins, leading themselves from the city. A tear slides from Amalie's cheek, and she thinks about their time in the forest near Aldara and the pressures her family put on his head.

We wanted him King, we made him King, and I have now watched him die a King.

* * *

"The ship won't leave until the morning after next. We could stop here for the night and allow you to rest." Ascher says with concern standing over Amalie as she heaves. His hand sets between her shoulders, holding her long wavy hair back and consoling her best he can.

"No, we should continue on. I am well. This is simply the woes of childbearing." Amalie stands, wiping her mouth on her sleeve as she pats him on the arm, walking away. The ache in her lower back nags, tugging at her insides, making it impossible to keep anything down. Rubbing with one hand over her belly and the other at the small part of her back, she walks and stretches, trying to ease the pain.

"Maybe we should wait in Halidor for the time you have left. In your condition, you need rest." The concern across Ascher's face grows in intensity, watching her pace and sway.

"Ascher, I am with child, not dying," she laughs, looking at him sweetly. "I know you are concerned, but there is no need." Mounting her horse, she stares down at him, patiently waiting for him to follow her lead.

Taking the day in stride, Amalie and Ascher ride quickly, arriving in Halidor by early evening. The small town is a simple trading post. Homes are rough stick-built huts and stone cottages. Boats overcrowd the harbor, smell of rotten sea life, and look worn and untidy. Yrin and Adyra already arrived in the days prior and wait in a pub near the docks, the ship they will take in clear view from the bedroom window above the main room of the establishment.

"The Captain said we could leave tomorrow. He has all he needs, and if the passengers were all accounted for in the morning, we would be able to cast off." Adyra's face is alight with the excitement of coming adventure to a land she has longed for her entire life but has never known.

Talking late into the night, Ascher and Amalie recount Americ's death and the uneventful journey between Aldhorran and Halidor. Submitting to her heavy eyes, Adyra leans into Yrin's side at the table. Taking her into his arms, Yrin scoops her up, cradling her as he carries her up the narrow stairs to their room, where he bids Ascher and Amalie goodnight.

Falling asleep instantly, Ascher's deep breaths keep Amalie awake. Giving up on sleep herself, she moves about the room, her aching back and hips unsettling. The jarring motion of riding for days on end from Dune to Aldhorran had been difficult, and Amalie knew she was simply paying the consequences of those actions. Pressing the spine of her lower back, she wishes for relief, feeling the pain spread to her thighs.

"Amalie, what is it?" Ascher's tired voice raises from the shadows.

"I just can't sleep. It's nothing." Amalie moves to the window, seeing a dim purple haze along the horizon, hovering over the vast ocean.

"Is it the child?" Ascher slips from the bed, moving to her and resting his warm hand over the hard bump.

"He makes it difficult to sleep comfortably." Amalie exhales, placing her hand over his.

A jab in her side startles them both as a lump pops out from within her abdomen into the hand stretched over her belly. Ascher reels lost for words at such strength and beauty. The reality of being a father had only just begun to settle, but now, feeling the strong life within Amalie wiggling about fills him with a love beyond explanation.

"Are you sure we shouldn't stay here a bit longer? We can find a new ship and captain. Have the baby here. You seem pained," Ascher speaks, his gaze set on the roundness under his hands.

"My body aches in protest, that I will confess. I can rest on the ship where I won't have to ride a horse, fight a battle, or work." She rubs her back again out of a newly formed habit.

"Are you sure?" Ascher's eyes meet hers, and they look at one another, sharing a tender moment as the baby kicks and flutters about between them.

Amalie nods, surveying the dim morning light drawing through the grimy window as it enters the room. Dressing slowly, they go through the motions of preparing for the day and journey ahead. By the time they make it to the dock, the morning sun is brightly reflecting off of the water, heat radiating against the morning chill. Adyra and Yrin appear on the dock shortly after Ascher and Amalie, leading the way to the ship and its captain. Ascher and Yrin follow the captain away as the women stay in place, watching as men above hoist supplies aboard.

"Are you ready for this?" Amalie asks Adyra, a hesitant grin on her lips.

"Are you?" she asks in reply.

Calling to them, Ascher waves them in his direction, Yrin already halfway up the ladder slung over the side of the immaculate ship. A swing slung over next to the ladder waits for Amalie and Adyra to hoist them up to the ship's deck. The crew welcomes them with toothless smiles, escorting the women below deck and shaking the hands of the men. Amalie, making her way back up top just before setting sail, finds Ascher, watching over the edge as the waves lap the sides of the fine wooden structure.

"Home," Amalie whispers.

"A place I never dreamed of going to, but yes. Home." Wrapping an arm around her, Ascher kisses the top of her head, and together they see the shore grow small behind them until it is all but gone.

THIRTY-FOUR

——

The corridor echoes with every step. White marble laced with golden trails hold portraits and grand paintings along the ceilings and walls, statues etched in stone line the walkway, and fresh air flows in-between each column, giving sight to the large fjord the city sits in. Eketria, the Nethian Capital, is carved into the cliff sides and stretches across the flat land above, surrounded by lush greens and bountiful flowers. Its beauty is beyond comprehension. One could almost call this place heaven if it existed on earth.

A servant leads Ascher and Amalie to a pair of large, closed doors. His fist clenched behind his back while the other swings at his side. He is dressed in a loose tunic, green sash wrapped around his waist, pants, and boots up to his knees. His hair bounces, curls freely hanging just to his shoulders. Coming to a stop behind him, the man knocks twice, and the doors slowly swing wide, opening to a large bright room. Pillars reach to the sky supporting a beautiful domed roof, and three chairs sit at the front of the room, two larger and one smaller, golden frames draped in blue silk.

"The King and Queen of Netheis," the servant announces,

jolting Ascher and Amalie to a stop looking to see a man and woman enter the room.

The King has dark blonde hair, golden brown skin, and is tall, towering over the Queen who walks beside him, her red hair and silver eyes like Americ's. The woman, gowned in a low-necked dress, looks like an angel floating across the marble floor. Moving directly to the chairs at the head of the room, Ascher and Amalie watch them sit elegantly before motioning them forward.

"What can we do for you, Romathan travelers?" Ascher looks at the King curiously, wondering if it is often his people grace the King and his fine kingdom.

"My wife and I have traveled for many months now from across the sea. We seek out a woman, a relative of my wife's, and we hear she resides here." Ascher bows his head as he addresses the King.

"And this relation you speak of? What is the name?" the Queen asks, her voice quiet and gentle as she looks at Amalie.

"My sister. Davina. She fled here for sanctuary along with a Cadison Rheyhas, her guard." Amalie curtsies the best she knows how as she addresses the royals before her.

"I thought Davina was Nasinreth, yet you stand before us as Romathe." The King ponders with hesitation, looking over Ascher's tired and unruly appearance.

"My wife is Nasinreth. She chose to marry me and join my people."

Nodding slowly, the King looks them over, searching their eyes for any sign of mistrust.

"Trinity! Please prepare them a room and send word of their arrival to the Queen of Omideon. She will be delighted at such news," the King orders a young girl suddenly, startling all in the room. "There will be food and wine on the veranda and fresh clothing in the room for you. Anything you find a necessity for, you need only ask." Rising from his chair, the King turns, holding a hand out to the Queen, and together they leave the room.

Confused by the suddenness of their arrival and departure, Amalie nearly misses seeing Ascher leave the room to follow the servant girl.

Leading them through a maze of immaculate corridors, the servant stops before another large doorway, opened wide to a bright, airy room. The sun shines through the high arches that draw the eye to a balcony overlooking the fjord. Drapes blow in the breeze, drawing giving life to the other elements of the room. A pool of water sits in the corner, reflections dancing across the ceiling, while vases of flowers adorn the walls, the plants drooping like waterfalls to the floor in variants of greens and purples. The bed is covered in fine silks and piled in elaborate pillows, and intricately woven rugs spread across the floor. Amalie turns her face away from the bed, searching for Ascher.

He stands on the balcony overlooking the gardens surrounding the palace, his eyes glazed and distant as he stares. Taking this time of loneliness, Amalie moves to the pool, the fresh scent of gardenia and rose lifting from within the steaming water. She dresses down, sinking into the water up to her nose, and leans back. The sounds are muddled, but her heart beats loud and steady, resonating through the warmth surrounding her. The few month's journey across the sea had been the hardest months of Amalie's life. Not only did she have no escape from the crew and those around her, but she was also forced to face a slew of emotions in her idle time. Soaking in the warmth and freshness of the bathing pool, Amalie relaxes, leaning into her frustrations and heartbreak of the near past.

"I am leaving to find Cadison. I just wanted you to know."

Amalie slips up from beneath the water quickly, causing it to splash over the side, drenching Ascher's feet.

Amalie nods silently, watching him leave the room, shutting the heavy doors behind him. Closing her eyes, Amalie allows a tear to break past her lids, shaking away the emotion immediately after to continue her bath ritual. Cleaning away the grime and salt from the voyage across the sea gives Amalie a sense of herself again, something all but lost to her. The two have been distant, talking very little and not touching at all in the last weeks, sorrow too deep in their hearts to care. Amalie stares up at the golden veined ceiling, replaying the death of Sirien and Americ over in her head, and her skin crawls as she feels the demoralizing voyage between kingdoms animate over her body. Now they are here, on Netheis' shores here to see what death has made of her sister.

Once feeling sufficiently human again, Amalie drags herself from the steaming water and walks to the ornate wardrobe in the corner of the room, hidden by trailing plants. Water pools at her feet in a steady drip while she sifts through the clothing to find every dress inside, made with the same delicate materials that are too revealing for her taste. The only one that has less neckline drop in the front but cuts low in the back and flows loosely to the ground is the one she chooses. It is a clean white color, resembling wholeness and completion, two things she completely lacks. Finding her sandals, she leaves the room in search of a servant to lead her to Davina, the only piece of her heart left that hasn't shattered.

"Oh, Americ. The arrival of Amalie and Ascher can only mean you are gone, and I am a widow. How could this be with such a little amount of time together." Davina whispers to the willows below, dancing in the gentle, warm breeze.

She could sit for ages watching the limbs sway, the leaves rustling, and birds flitting in and out. Davina's heart aches, and she wilts in her chair on the balcony, allowing tears to creep from her eyes.

"You loved so deeply and heartily, caring for my every need. You were more to me than I could have ever expressed. Our bond was not of fate or marriage but friendship and human nature. I cannot thank you enough for saving me in my darkest moments and if you can hear me, know I am sorry I couldn't be there for yours. Americ, I need you. You have been by my side, and now I don't know who I am or my purpose without you." She clutches her arms tightly around herself as her body racks with sobs. "Oh, Americ, I am so sorry. We should have run when we had the chance. We could have had more time, grown old together. Why are the fates so cruel to this world? I never got the chance to tell you what I needed to. I need you and want you by my side. I never told you I..."

The cough behind her startles her. Davina bolts from her seat, wiping away the tears quickly before turning to see the servant in the center of her room. The girl bows, turning her head to the door. With sudden delight, she sees a familiar face, one she has known her entire life.

"Amalie!" Hurrying to the door, Davina holds her arms open wide, the dark dress parades around her gracefully.

"Little sister." Amalie takes her in her grip, squeezing the small woman with a gentle tightness.

"It is so good to see you, Amalie. I missed you so," Davina whispers, tears falling freely once again.

"I am so glad you are safe. I worried for you. Are you well?" Amalie releases her grasp, stepping away to look her sister over.

"As well as I can be. I assume you came because Americ is..." Davina begins, choking on her words.

"He went with honor, fearless, a King's execution." Amalie looks at Davina, watching her face go pale at the thought.

"It's not fair." Davina clears her throat, wiping tears from her cheeks with a shaky hand. "He never met his son."

"You are with child. Sirien's vision has come to pass." Sadness shows in Amalie's eyes as she speaks her sister's name, and Davina nods, closing her eyes firmly.

"I am confident even though it is early. I can sense it." Davina lays a hand over her waist, eyes closed as she breathes deeply.

"You are sure?" Amalie asks, her heart leaping with pain and joy.

"I have sensed it before, but I didn't realize what it was." Opening her eyes, Davina looks at Amalie, biting her lip while considering what to say next. The revelation she hadn't realized she made the night they stormed the castle would come as a shock and devastation to Amalie as it had herself.

"I could feel its heartbeat, but I thought it was her own, so fast like butterfly wings in flight. Sirien was afraid when Baldur came to the dungeon, but it wasn't her I felt."

Amalie looks at Davina, shaken by the news.

Stumbling to the side, Amalie sits on the bench at the foot of the bed and stares. Speechless, she sits, trying to summon some form of emotion, but can't. Davina watches this, soul aching to see Amalie in such distress.

"You are absolutely sure?" Amalie asks after the silence had become too much.

"I am. I felt the same thing the day I left Dune, and you told me of your own. It was then I knew. Sirien was with child the night she died."

Amalie inhales sharply at her words, turning her face from Davina. Her body shudders silently, her shoulders folded inward and face buried in her damp hair. Davina could feel her pain and the brokenness she carries. Never had she seen Amalie in such despair, and she had no notion of what she could do.

"I will find Ascher," Davina says, turning away quickly.

"No!" Amalie yells, making Davina jump.

Amalie's face is tearstained, red, and blotchy, her eyes glazed and tired. The fiery young woman Davina had always known was absent, and in her place, a being wounded so severely she may never heal. Gliding to Amalie's side, Davina takes her in her arms, pressing her sister's head into her chest. Amalie fiercely weeps until there is nothing left in her. Soothing her, Davina strokes Amalie's hair, watching the light stretch across the marble pillars and walls.

"She was so small," Amalie whispers. "She had so much hair and the tiniest toes. She was perfect. So perfect I couldn't let go." She hisses numbly. "He had to take her from my arms, and now she belongs to the sea." Her body convulses, gasping for air between sobs.

Davina runs her fingers through Amalie's hair, tears escaping her own eyes.

"Amalie, I'm so..." Davina begins.

"Don't. I can't have you feeling sorry for me. What's done is done." Sitting up, she wipes her wet face on her dress then stands.

"Did you give her a name?" Davina sits, smoothing the wrinkles in the silk.

"Eira." Amalie folds her arms over her chest. "Davina, we won't be staying long. Maybe a few days to rest and replenish our supplies. Thank you for listening, and I'm sorry about Americ." Nodding curtly, Amalie rushes from the room, leaving Davina to her thoughts once again.

THIRTY-FIVE

———

The few days Amalie had spoken of turned into weeks of recovery from the arduous journey between kingdoms. Davina, relishing the unaccounted time together, now finds solitude in a dreadful and lonely place in life. With grave word from Elra, who had completed the journey home, sparred the small group of clansmen to gather and leave immediately. The Chieftain, Ascher's grandfather, has fallen ill, and to claim his birthright, they had to leave in hopes of beating time itself.

To say farewell this time proved to be difficult for Amalie and Davina. They feared it would be their last moments together but hoped for happier times ahead and vowed to write often. But even now, Davina's heart is heavy, knowing it will never end happily for her.

Down a dark, airy hallway, Davina walks, a silver candlestick in hand, as she makes her way to the sanctuary in the heart of the palace. The summer air is warm and damp. Crickets chirp loudly, moths and sun flies riddle the landscape and hallways. Her bare feet touch the marble softly, melting into the cool stone as they guide her by muscle memory. So many nights, she has taken this same path to pray and ponder over her life.

The heavy oak doors open a crack, allowing any who wish to enter to do so easily. Glancing around her, she sets her candle by the door before slipping inside. The long room is empty except at the end, where a large golden chest sits, candles covering every inch of space on top, the large center one lit at all times. Seeing the wick needs trimming, Davina finds the sharp instrument used and cuts it back, the wax low and seeping out across the flat surface.

Taking a switch of wood from a vase beside the chest, Davina lights six candles, one for each loss in the past months. Her father, Castor, Sirien, her unborn child, Americ, and now Eira. So many losses, brokenness, and far too much damage to repair. Kneeling before the flickering candles, Davina clenches at her chest, an emptiness so raw she can barely stand it.

"I swear it, Americ, our son will live and rule and bring your kingdom glory. I swear it in payment for the love you gave me, the child we have bore, and the sacrifices you made. I will avenge you and make everything right till my dying breath." Davina's voice echoes through the space.

"Caution."

Chills wreak havoc on Davina's body at the sound of the voice.

Leaping to her feet, she stammers back at the sight of a woman in the shadows behind the chest of candles, light flickering across her white face. The black around her eyes reminds her of the night of the siege, but the woman is unfamiliar. Her white pallor, silver hair braided and wound in leather ties in places and loose in others. But it was her eyes that unsettled Davina, the silver eyes, ones without sight yet still seemed to see her.

"Be cautious in your anger, for you will lose yourself. And remember, it was not only the young king Sirien saw fall," the woman's voice hisses, sending Davina's heart pounding passionately.

The fave moves forward, leaning into the candles, her eyes never moving from Davina. Blowing them out in one swift breath, the room falls dark. Terrified, Davina flings herself backward, tripping as she runs to the door. Swinging wide, they open in a thundering crash, allowing the moon's silvery light to flood the space. Glancing back, Davina finds no sign of the woman. Her chest throbs and body shakes, breaths ragged, sending her head spinning, and the last thing she hears before crashing to the ground are the guard's feet rushing her way.

* * *

The tips of the mountains pierce the heavens as Amalie, Ascher, Yrin, and Adyra ascend them. The first range is one of the three tribes surrounding the Veil of Illusion, a deep canyon between them. Looking down into the misty cavern, Amalie can't help but feel on top of the world. The trip had been troublesome—not used to such rocky terrain, time extended by days to the border. Drawing her eyes from the crevice in the earth, Amalie moves up the short line of friends to the front, standing at Ascher's side.

"We are home." Amalie gapes as she looks out over the hills of trees, rocks and snow, filling her with a deep satisfaction.

Seeing Ascher, she bursts out laughing. Ice spikes throughout his beard and eyebrows. Looking at her oddly, she reaches out and pats away the little crystals from his hair. Her fingers are stiff and numb from the cold, yet she can feel them tingle at their proximity. Touch had been foreign to them since Eira, and as if reading her mind, Ascher wraps his arms around her, folding her beneath his heavy cloak.

"Can you still love me?" he whispers, touching his forehead to hers.

"I never stopped," she expresses, burying her face into the bear hide draped across his shoulders.

Feeling happy for the first time in months, Amalie knows her decision to join the Aulik was the right one, and no matter what it had cost, she was home.

Stau Haulo im Sempt. Steady Heart and Soul.

ACKNOWLEDGMENTS

First and foremost, I would like to thank my husband for the support and unyielding love given to me throughout this process. I would also like to thank my family for all of their love and support. A special shout-out to Stephen Howard who inspired me to do this, coaching me along the way, and for being an amazing friend.

To all the individuals who supported me during my pre-sale campaign, making the publishing of this book even possible, I also wanted to offer my sincerest thank you to every individual.

Michelle Boudreau, Lucas Emery, Tarrah Moothart, Amy Pond, Joann Wellman, Breanna Zeigler, Katie Smithson, Monica Street, Tiffani Heitz, Jennifer Cikanek, Sheri Nesbit, Sherryce Emery, Megan Curry, Nancy Haggard, Charlotte Bowers, Marissa Smithhart, Lena Williams, Rebecca Hobbs, Jenifer Whitford, Charlene Payton, Andrew Leggett, Jane Thayer, Francise Perry, Sandra Emery, Eva Hysell, Steve Perry, Vicqui Hook, Emily Prevo, Jacqui Perry, Mike Hobbs, Linda Hobbs, Christopher Knox, Alex Raza, Amber Payton, Bruna Hollen, Eric Koester, Jackie Thein, Michael Zeigler, Kaylie Zeigler, Kim Carroll, Ashley Martin, and the community of Baker City, OR.